WALLS OF SILENCE

A bone-chilling
Romantic Thriller

SUSAN N SWANN

Author of *Angels in the Fog*

Published by New Voices Books/New Voices
Copyright © 2024 by Susan N. Swann

Cover design by Shelbi Graham
Interior Design by Will Robertson

ISBN: 979-8-218-97345-2, paperback
ISBN: 979-8-218-97346-9, digital edition

Visit the author at: http://authorsusanNswann.com

*This book is dedicated to the women
who kept going inspite of it all.
You know who you are.*

WALLS OF SILENCE

CONTENTS

PART ONE
BROKEN

CHAPTER ONE

*A*nnie seemed to have the perfect life in Paradise Hills' nicest neighborhood, surrounded by her closest friends. She sat alone, gazing through white window shutters, watching a dark Texas sky turn to a brilliant red. Her vision blurred as tears welled behind her eyelids, muscles weak. She crossed her arms and held onto her shoulders. *At least you're getting out of here for a few days.* Annie dressed, pulling on blue Levi's and brown boots. Then she pulled open the bedroom sliding glass door, stepped onto the deck, and tiptoed down the back steps. The door clicked shut behind her.

When she reached the driveway, her husband Frank was waiting. "Oh, hi," she said, skin flushing. "I didn't know you were out here."

"You can't leave without telling me." He growled under his breath, then turned, and waved a friendly hello to a next-door neighbor. In a voice loud enough for her to hear, said, "I put a cinnamon raisin bagel in this bag for you, Annie. Should still be warm."

"You're a lucky lady to have such a thoughtful husband," Teresa called.

Annie's neighbors had no idea what it was like living with Frank Graves, and she wasn't going to tell them. *In a small town like this, we keep embarrassing problems to ourselves, or the gossip buzzes like bees.* She put on her happy face, smiling over at Teresa, saying, "You're up early this morning."

"I don't want to miss the only legal watering day of the week."

"It's been a tinder-dry summer, that's for sure." Annie nodded.

"Are you off to your ranch?"

"Yes, we're moving cows to the lower meadow."

"I know how much you love being out there." She grinned.

She has no idea. When I'm at the ranch, it's my whole world. It's as if there's nowhere else.

"Say," Teresa said, breaking into Annie's thoughts, "why don't we have lunch one day next week?"

"I'll call you." Annie waved and slid behind the wheel of her cobalt-blue convertible, folding down the white top.

"See you tomorrow, sweetheart," Frank said, leaning hairy arms on her car door.

"See you then."

"When will you be home?" *The question he always asks but doesn't answer when I ask him.*

"I'll call when I leave the ranch."

"You do that," he said, tone deepening. *He insists on knowing where I am, and who I'm with, all the time. It drives me crazy!*

She patted the burner phone in her pocket, then shifted her car into drive, hands gripping the steering wheel. As she drove down the tree-lined subdivision, a local paper boy threw the *Paradise Hills Tribune* onto front porches, whistling as he went.

Reaching the main highway, she gunned the motor. The wind whipped through her hair as she drove past field after field of wild spring bluebonnets, inhaling their warm fragrance, and savoring each deep breath of freedom. Then she stopped at the Longhorn Café and Convenience store, ordered breakfast burritos, and carried the food to an open booth beside the window. Eating slowly, she relished every bite. Annie flung Frank's cold bagel into the trash.

Several miles later she passed oak and maple trees dotting rolling hills, and her eyes brightened. She soon reached the guard gate to the Kingman family ranch. A ranch hand raised the silver bar and tipped his brown cowboy hat. "Mornin,' Miss Annie," he grinned. "You're out early today."

"Yes, I am," she smiled, "happy to be here." She drove for miles along the Pedernales River before arriving at the main house. A tan fence surrounded the large, yellow brick and stone house with soft green curtains framing the picture window. She parked the car and sauntered inside. *I love my childhood home. This is where I grew up and learned the country way.*

Annie walked into the front parlor; the walls hand stamped with images of golden warbler frozen in happy song above the wainscoting. She reached over and traced the outline of one of the tiny birds with her fingertip, remembering. Then walked outside and wandered down the lane to the show barn, passing the corrals and bunkhouse. The sun dappled through branches of oak and pecan trees, continuing its rise in a cloudless sky.

When she made her way inside the barn, her large Palomino turned his head and whinnied. "Hi, baby," she cooed, throwing her arms around his neck as he swished his tail. She reached into her backpack, giving him bits of an apple, then slipped the bridle over his ears. Cinching the saddle around his belly, led him from the barn. "Steady, boy," she murmured.

Hy Hatch rode up, tan Stetson cocked atop thick, graying hair. He sported a long-sleeved shirt covered with a green, button-down vest. Two guns were strapped around his waist. "You ready, Miss Annie?"

"I sure am." Annie settled astride her horse as a flock of black bellied ducks flew whistling overhead.

"Your daddy's itchin' to get started. He's a man in a hurry today."

"He usually is."

"You're right," he grinned. "Good to have you."

"I love being here—especially with the finest ranch hand manager in the state of Texas."

"Thank you, kindly. Thirty-four years I been on the place."

"Before I was born and sounds about right."

"Remember me teachin' you to ride and rope?" Pride filled Hy's voice as they cantered to the upper grasses. "You were 'bout ten."

"Best teacher ever."

He smiled and rubbed his leg.

"That leg bothering you again?"

"Just a mite. I swear the last two weeks has been like tryin' to bag flies what with me and the cattle drovers workin' day and night to wrangle them cattle. They won't take kindly to that long walk down the hill."

"Take care of your leg," Annie said over the sound of 2,000 bellowing Herefords.

"Don't worry 'bout me, Miss Annie." Two cows strayed from the herd, and he rode after them rope snapping, mouthing the sound through his teeth he used to get their attention, *'chtch, chtch, chtch.'*

She watched him go. *Hy's a man who honors the golden rule of cowboys; never go back on your word.* —She twisted her wedding ring.

Ruby, the family's Black Tri Australian Shepard, ran up barking and wagging her tail. "Let's go girl," Annie whistled happily. Her horse lunged and did a little crow hop as Daddy trotted up on his black quarter horse. "Easy boy, It's okay."

"Hello, Darlin," Pete Kingman said, leaning over and kissing his daughter on the cheek. "Thanks for coming."

"I wouldn't miss it."

"Was Frank okay with you bein' on the drive today?" he asked as they rode.

"Yes," she said, hands clenched.

He looked at her sideways. "Everything all right with you two?"

"Let's say we don't have what you and Mama had; never a cross word."

"We argued, but not in front of you kids." He paused, then asked, "Do you and Frank get cross?"

"Sometimes. I think he sees me as a trophy he likes to show off to people in town."

"I'm guessin' he's proud of you, Annie."

She steadied her nerves. *Here goes.* "I think I made a mistake marrying Frank."

As he turned to her, his face seemed to grow longer, a look of disappointment in his brown eyes. "You took a vow when you married him; it's only been two years." Then he quizzed her. "He hasn't hit you, has he? If he has, I'll have that boy's hide!"

"No, Daddy. He's never hit me."

"Honey," he said in a gentler voice, "there hasn't been a divorce in the Kingman family in generations. Find a way to work it out, that's what we do." He galloped away after the herd.

She stared into nowhere, stomach rock hard, tears slipping down her face. She pulled her horse to a halt, gripping the reins. *You're not going to disappoint Daddy. Or damage tradition with a divorce.* Annie closed her eyes. *So, keep your head down and move forward.* A stray calf made a break for the corral. "Oh, no you don't, little critter," she said, nudging her horse in the flanks, riding hard after the calf.

Several hot and dusty hours later the drovers reached the lower meadow, aflame with acres and acres of Indian Paint brush. After the cattle settled in, Annie rode alone to the ranch, her thoughts turning to Frank. *So many things I didn't know about him before we married.*

How could I have been so blind?

When night fell, she walked back into the barn and wiped the sweat from her horse's flanks. She breathed in the smell of freshly stacked hay and watched the full moon's rays fall through slats in the barn door. *The ranch has been in our family for a hundred years, and that's where it's going to stay. Frank thinks Caroline and I should sell it after Daddy dies. Ha! This place is our Great-great grandfather Kingman's legacy. He was a trailblazer.*

Annie threw a blanket on her horse, exhausted and sat on a bale of hay. He gently nuzzled her back. She stood and kissed the white star on his forehead, wiping her wet face on a shirt sleeve. Walking back to the house, the night air felt cool on her skin, a full moon shining in a star-studded sky. She stood and just stared, breathing in the moment.

After Annie reached the house, she took a long hot shower and climbed in between freshly starched sheets. Then fell into a sound sleep.

CHAPTER TWO

*I*t was after ten the next morning when the family housekeeper woke her with a hot cup of cocoa and warm banana muffins. She took a bite; they melted in her mouth. "Thank you, Gabriela."

"You always been my *Chiquita*, Miss Annie. I try to take good care of you and your daddy."

"We're lucky to have you as a trusted part of the family."

Gabriela blushed and raised her double chin, whitish hair bunching around brown eyes. "*Gracias*, Miss Annie."

"I guess I better get up and go home."

"*Despacio*, take it slow and stay with us awhile with us, *por favor*. We miss you."

"I'd like to, but—

Gabriela interrupted. "Mr. Frank can wait," she frowned.

Annie knew Gabriela didn't like Frank. She seemed to be one of the few people who could see through his shenanigans. *She's been such a blessing since Mama passed.* Annie looked at the date on her phone. Almost fifteen years ago, 2003.

A deep sense of gloom crept across the ranch the day Mama died. The little sign she'd hung next to the front door with the words, "Love Blooms Here" sat tipped off to the side, as if it didn't matter anymore. Our home, once a place for smoky barbecues and fun weekend parties, sat so still. I listened as the breeze blowing off the clear waters of the Pedernales River whispered, 'Life will never be the same again.' Tears filled Annie's eyes as she recalled the time…

Inside the house, twelve-year-old Annie sat on an unmade bed staring blankly out the window, barely registering the shrill sounds of the blue scrub jay squawking outside. Her short hair fell limply around her face, round eyes blinking back tears from black lashes. A light dusting of freckles sprinkled across the bridge of her small nose, courtesy of the hot Texas sun.

She smoothed the folds of her crisp, black dress, bare feet hanging off the side of the bed. She squirmed and tugged at the cuffs and collars, hating the dress. Aunt Louise, Daddy's sister, had brought it with her from Houston yesterday." What's wrong with my orange sun dress?" Annie asked. "Mama made it."

"Wrong color," was her aunt's curt reply.

"How can orange be wrong? Orange is my favorite."

She shook her head and walked away.

Footsteps sounded in the hallway, and Annie's sister Caroline appeared in the doorway. She wore a shimmery black dress and heels, auburn hair draping down her back. "Annie, are you ready?" She glanced in the mirror, dabbing at lipstick.

Annie blanched. "I don't wanna see mama like that."

"I know, honey." Caroline put her arm around her sister's shoulder. They'd watched their mama waste away to nothing as cancer ate her organs from the inside out.

"I already miss her so much."

"Me too"

Mama's body was laid out in the front parlor so mourners could come by and pay their last respects. Everyone else took their departed to the Payne funeral home. Not the Kingmans. The Kingmans always had their own way of doing things.

Annie's daddy and older brother Ben stood beside the open casket. As folks filed past, they whispered their condolences in hushed tones.

"Susie Kingman was a real lady."

"We're all gonna miss her."

"May she rest in peace."

Just as Annie was feeling some level of comfort, one lady whispered, "It was a blessing she could go, don't ya' know."

Annie refused to believe that. She'd prayed night and morning for months that her mama would heal. That would have been a blessing. Dying wasn't.

Down the hill sat the Kingman family cemetery, where Annie's mama would be buried later that day. She'd selected the poetic lines that now graced her tombstone. From the poet Wordsworth:

> Though nothing can bring back the hour
> Of splendor in the grass, of glory in the flower,
> We will grieve not, rather find
> Strength in what remains behind.

What do those words even mean? How can I go on without my mama? This is the saddest day of my life.

Pastor Mark offered the eulogy, saying, "Susie was a dear, dear friend to all of us here. She was a person who believed in helping others, and we all benefitted from her kindness. Pete, the two of you shared a beautiful love story. Sometimes things were hard for you, but you kept going. Please know you're not alone. Love is the gift we will all share with you." He finished with the words, "In life and in death, we are the Lord's."

The mourners moved outside to tables set on the wide expanse of lawn facing the river. The ladies of Songbird Community Church brought the usual fare: fresh biscuits, roasted corn, beef brisket, charro beans, and pecan pie for dessert.

When the evening shadows fell, Daddy asked Annie to sing. She rose from the chair where she sat between Ben and Caroline, and in a clear voice sang "Amazing Grace." Her mama's favorite. "'Tis grace hath brought me safe thus far," she glided over the familiar words. "And grace will lead me home." Her voice broke on the word 'home,' and she sat down. Caroline and Ben hugged her close. Daddy stood and thanked everyone for coming, and the mourners straggled away.

Before closing the lid on Mama for good, he turned to his children and said, "Time to kiss her good-bye." Caroline bent over and kissed her on the cheek, and so did Ben. Annie had slapped her hands over her ears, refusing to hear. She'd already touched Mama's stone-cold hand. It felt cold, almost rubbery, like a dog toy. This wasn't her mama anymore.

"No, Daddy," she said, pulling away. "I'm scared."

"Nothin' to be afraid of," he said, urging her over to the casket. She pecked Mama's cheek, then dashed out through the screen door, clattering down porch steps.

"Annie!" he called. She ran, arms pumping and didn't stop until she reached the side pasture. She threw herself face down in the spring bluebonnets, feeling their smooth, soft tops crush under her weight. She rolled and rolled until that hateful black dress with the crisp white collar was muddy and torn. She made sure she'd never have to wear it again. *Aunt Louise will be so mad. Too bad for her.*

Three weeks later, Annie stood in the kitchen with her aunt who was partial to wearing big dresses with large flower patterns. Annie pulled rolls she'd made from the oven. Smells good, honey," Louise said. "I'm sorry I got one of my sick headaches and couldn't help."

Annie knew the polite thing would be to say, *It's okay.* But she didn't. She didn't say anything. *My aunt has sick headaches every day. She spends more time lying down than she does standing up. She's supposed to be here to help but doesn't even pull her own weight.*

The tea kettle was whistling on the stove. "I'll get that," Louise said getting up, just as Daddy walked into the room.

"Thank you," he said to her. "I don't know what we'd do around here without you."

Louise smiled.

Annie grimaced and wanted to say, "Seriously, Daddy! You think she does anything to help?" Instead, she stirred the soup vigorously.

"What's eatin' you?" he asked.

She threw the spoon, splashing soup on the stainless-steel stove. "I lost my mama, Ben doesn't 'do housework,' Caroline's gone to college, and I'm left to take care of things around here. And you ask what's eating me?"

"That's enough, Annie," he said, turning and storming out of the house. It wasn't dark yet, so she figured he'd saddle up and go for a ride. That's mostly what he did since Mama passed.

"All this commotion has given me another sick headache," Louise said moaning, leaving the kitchen and lumbering up creaky wooden stairs to a guest bedroom she'd taken as her own.

Annie sat down; sorry she'd shouted at Daddy. He was so sad all the time now.

She heard a knock at the door. Who could that be? It wasn't as if the Kingmans had close neighbors. It took fifteen minutes to drive from the front gate to the front door, and they didn't get many drop-ins out this far.

She didn't want to answer. She wanted to be left alone. But the knocking persisted. She peered around the frosted glass in the heavy oak door to see who it might be but couldn't tell. She creaked the door open.

It was Pastor Mark's wife Cindy, mama's best friend. "Hi Annie," she wrapped her arms around Annie's neck. Annie melted in her arms. Cindy whispered in her ear, "I love you."

Annie sobbed in her arms.

Cindy wiped away tears, saying, "I brought my lemon pie."

"Thank you. I'm so glad you're here."

"Where is everyone tonight?"

"Aunt Louise has another sick headache, and Daddy's out riding."

"I see," Cindy said walking into the kitchen. "That soup smells delicious. Did you make it?"

"Yes," Annie mumbled softly.

"Your mama would be proud of you."

"I don't think so."

"Why not?"

"I shouted at Daddy. I know he's disappointed in me."

"It's okay, honey," Cindy said holding her close. "He loves you, and so do I. God loves you too. Never forget that." Cindy fished another tissue out of her purse.

Annie wiped her nose. "If God loves me, how come he let my mama die?"

"Sometimes people we love get hurt or even die. And that's so very hard." She gently stroked Annie's hair. "Our faith in God and love for each other helps us get through. Does that make sense?"

Annie nodded. She'd always believed there was a heaven. *That's where Mama is now.*

"Just remember, you're not alone. Ready for pie? I brought Bluebell vanilla bean ice cream too."

Her face lit up. "You know I love Bluebell ice cream, and vanilla's my favorite!"

An hour later, Daddy came in from his ride.

"Annie," Cindy said. "Why don't you give me some time to talk with your daddy."

"Okay. Thanks again for the pie and ice cream."

"You're welcome. We'll do it again soon, I promise."

Annie left the kitchen and closed the door behind her. She never knew what Cindy said to her daddy that day. But the next week, Aunt Louise packed her bags and flew back to Houston. That's when he hired Gabriela…

A bird chirping outside the window brought Annie back. She pulled off the covers and dressed. In no hurry to leave, she spent the day at the ranch making cookies with Gabriela.

By the time she reached Paradise Hills, it was after nine pm. The streets were dark, a silver moon trapped behind clouds. Annie leaned against the wheel of her car in the stillness, taking deep breaths. Then pulling into the circular driveway of her white-stone suburban home, looked up. A small light glowed in the master bedroom window. Parking in the garage, she edged into the house and eased up a flight of carpet stairs. No Frank. *He must still be out.*

She sat in a mauve overstuffed chair in the corner, removed shoes, and rubbed lotion into her sore feet. Hearing something, her eyes widened. *What's that? Sounds like…scratching? An animal inside?* A definite noise. She paused, listening. *It must be my imagination.*

The robe she wanted to change into hung in the walk-in closet. A light shone from the bottom of the door. *That's strange.* She opened the door; Frank leaped at her.

She screamed, face ashen, knees shaking.

"Why so jumpy?" He laughed.

"Why'd you scare me?" She shook.

"Just having a little fun, that's all." He rolled his eyes. "Where's your sense of humor?"

"It's not funny, Frank. My heart's still pounding."

He grabbed her arm. "If I say it's funny, it's funny. Now come here. I've been waiting up for you."

She froze under his touch and didn't dare resist, as he forced himself. She fell emotionally to her knees. Stop! She wanted to shout. She'd tried that before; it only made him angrier. Annie disappeared in her head, trying to think about being anywhere but with him.

Fifteen minutes later, she stood in the bathroom splashing cold water on her sore chest while Frank snored. She stared in the mirror at her pale skin and jumbled brown-blonde hair. *My marriage is a nightmare.* Annie sobbed silently. *He's breaking me…*

CHAPTER THREE

*F*rank sat at the kitchen table nursing a bowl of cold cereal. Annie had no idea he was seeing someone else. Nor did her rich, arrogant, cowboy of a father. He chuckled under his breath.

Frank had informed his lover up front he couldn't afford to be caught with another woman.

"No problem," Kelly said the first night they were together, a year ago. Nobody needs to know but us."

"Are you worried about your husband?"

"Such a bore. He wouldn't know a fun time if it bit him in the rear end."

Frank laughed. "What'd you expect from a financial analyst?"

"I expected security, and that's what I got. But I'm starving for affection, so I figured you might be open to a little fun."

Turned out he was. Her husband had no idea how good he had it.

They'd been careful; he'd seen to that. Frank was running for mayor of Paradise Hills and couldn't afford a scandal. Besides, being elected mayor was merely a steppingstone on his path to the Texas State House of Representatives. He tingled all over just thinking about it.

Frank knew he'd win the upcoming Special July Election. The only one running against him was that piss-ant Merv Martin. He and Merv had gotten into a little altercation a week ago over at the city offices. They'd exchanged words before, but this time their disagreements got physical. Merv had hauled off and hit him in the face, so Frank hit him right back in the nose. What else was he supposed to do?

One of the secretaries tried to stop the fight, and she wound up getting slammed against the wall, falling to the floor. But it turned out she was all right. Both he and Merv went to the courthouse where they signed non-prosecution agreements, and then they shook hands.

Annie was fit to be tied when she'd seen Frank's eye. "You should see the other guy," he told her, laughing. "Wasn't my fault, Merv started it."

She sounded exasperated when she said, "So, you had to finish it."

"That's right, I did."

Frank looked forward to the game of politics, which would be better than practicing law. Hadn't been his idea to go to law school, his father made him do it. So, Frank graduated from the University of Texas law school in Austin—with a lot of help from his friends.

Now he had the best of both worlds: an inexhaustible lover and a wife whose family held a decades-long social standing in the Hill Country. The 'holier than thou Kingman family' money would come in handy when he needed it. Which might be soon.

Frank made a pot of tea and carried it up to Annie. *Time to play the thoughtful husband.* "You awake," he asked looking through the door.

"Yes," she said, hands by her side.

"Brought you some tea."

"Thanks, just leave it over on the dresser," she said, rubbing her eyes.

He sat next to her. "You've got an appointment for a haircut today, right?"

"At ten."

"I better come with you. Last time Sarah cut it too short."

She looked surprised. "My friends' husbands don't go with them to the salon."

"Guess they're not as lucky as you are, and besides, it'll be fun. We can get lunch when you're finished."

"Frank, how I wear my hair is my decision."

"You're about to become the mayor's wife, the first lady of Paradise Hills, so the way you look matters to everyone."

"Really, Frank? The length of my hair is important to your constituents?"

"You know you look more feminine with your hair longer, sweetie."

Annie took a deep breath.

"Say, why don't you wear that champagne-colored sweater I bought you? It goes so well with your hazel eyes."

When Annie came out, she wore a black and white sweater. "Where's the other one?" Frank asked.

"It needs to be washed." *Uh huh.*

"Let's see if Kelly and Jim could join us for lunch. You'd like that, right?"

"Sure." *No way I'm going to lunch with you today.*

"You haven't put on a few pounds, have you? That sweater looks a little tight on your bottom."

Annie glared at him. "No Frank, my weight hasn't changed a pound in at least ten years."

"That's my girl. I'll give Jim a call, while you grab your jacket. See you in the car."

"Hang on a minute, looks like I missed a text from Sarah. —It says here her son got sick at school, and she had to go pick him up. I'll need to reschedule the haircut."

"Well, that's disappointing."

"Yes, it is."

"Here, let me see your phone."

"Why?"

"I want to read the text."

"It's already been deleted; you know I don't save them."

His hands balled into fists. "Let's go downtown anyway. We need to see and be seen."

"My head hurts. As soon as I change my clothes, I'll be in the study reading." She walked away.

Frank seethed then left the house and drove to his law office, clouds dripping with rain. He knew what he needed to pump him up. The porn shut up in the walls of his office safe never failed to do the trick. No one, but no one, would ever know about that. He always locked the door to his office when he ran the DVDs on his computer, using headphones to drown out the delightful sounds.

Pastor Mark had given a dumb sermon a few months ago on the 'evils' of pornography, describing its 'exponential growth' in our society. He even claimed that porn was 'maiming the lives of the citizens of our country.' The believers believed him. Frank didn't. After the sermon, Mark handed out a pamphlet that stated, "Research shows porn users are more dominating and harassing. Their attitudes can even lead to violence against women." *Such bull.* Frank had never punched Annie, not once. He sped up the car, ready to pull those naughty little secrets out of his safe.

CHAPTER FOUR

*K*ent Winder slid his key into the familiar lock and opened the door to an empty house. His footsteps echoed across polished wood floors as he wandered past the large rectangular mirror in the entry way he'd left for the new owners. The only reflection he saw in the mirror was his. Everything and everyone else were gone. He jammed his hands into his pockets, noticed the dark circles under his eyes, and kept walking.

He moved to the back of the house and into the great room. Out the large bank of windows, the June gloom of a San Clemente afternoon threatened rain, its mood filling the house and working its fingers into his emptiness. His chest felt hollow. Standing alone, he wished he could remember the good times. But he couldn't.

The movers had packed his belongings yesterday, then loaded them into a long truck, along with his black BMW. He'd stood on the lawn, supervising. "You're responsible for any scratches," he told the movers who were hauling his stuff to Texas.

"Don't worry," the guy grunted. "This isn't our first rodeo."

Kent walked out of the empty house and climbed into the nondescript rental car waiting for him out front. He drove down the hill, parked the car and walked across the green lawn, crossing down toward the sand. The long wooden pier stretching out into the ocean was a California classic. The water appeared calm today; the fog began to lift as the sky faded to blue. Green palm trees waved in a gentle breeze, as a seagull glided over the water.

He wandered down past the shops and headed over to Fisherman's Restaurant, the familiar blue awning flapping gently in the breeze. He walked inside and took a seat out by the water, watching waves crash against pier pylons. Then ordered fried calamari to start and a cup of his favorite chowder with sourdough bread. His cell phone buzzed. Text message from his sister Karla: *You, ok?* He texted back: *Will call you later. Don't worry.*

A few hours later, Kent sat on a plane flying from Orange County to San Antonio. The insurance company he worked for was opening a Texas office, and they'd asked him to oversee. He gazed out the window as the plane rose through the evening clouds, then a flight attendant touched his arm. "Mr. Winder" she blurted, "Please fasten your seat belt."

When the plane neared San Antonio, Kent looked down and caught sight of the Tower of Americas. He'd visited the iconic structure when he'd flown in to check out the new offices and meet his admin. He wanted to bring his nephew Carter here to see the 3-D theatre. He jolted in his seat as the plane bounced on the runway. Then he deplaned and made his way to baggage claim. The plan was to stay a few nights in a hotel while he looked for a place to live.

The next morning, he put on a casual suit and drove around the Hill Country. He pulled his car off the main highway to take a closer look at a Texas longhorn. The bull was mottled brown and white with horns that had a triple twist at the end, wide ears twitching.

An old man came limping up the small lane, straw hat slouched over his head, wearing a pair of bib overalls. "New here?" he asked.

"Is it that obvious?"

He smiled, looking at his suit.

"Right. Name's Kent Winder," he said, offering his hand.

"Howdy, Kent. Jack Reno," he said, shaking his in return. "What brings you out this way?"

"I'm looking for a place to live."

"Where you from?"

"San Clemente, California."

"You're a long way from home boy. Why the Hill Country?"

"I like the peace and quiet, and I need a place with a reasonable commute to San Antonio."

"You'll work in San Antone?"

"Yes."

"After livin' in a city, it could be a mite difficult livin' in the country, don't you think?"

"Maybe," he said, muscles tightening.

"It so happens my place is for rent, son." Jack planted his cane in the dirt. "You're only ten miles outside Paradise Hills, a safe and quiet little community with friendly folks. It's a true western town, but close to the big city of San Antone."

Kent remembered seeing a large billboard on the side of the road with the image of a cowboy sitting in a large rocking chair. The words read: Rest awhile in Paradise… Jewel of the Texas Hill Country. "Where are you going?" He asked Jack.

"Houston. My kids live there, and ever since my wife passed, they've been pesterin' me to move. Maybe it's time," he said with a half-hearted shrug. "But I'm sure not gonna' sell the place."

"I don't want to buy. How much are you asking?

"Got five acres and the house. 1800 square feet, three bedrooms, one bath. Care to take a look?"

Inside Kent saw a cozy house with a large rock fireplace, great room, two bedrooms and a small office. Outside, the yard was fully fenced with several live oaks for shade.

"You'll 'preciate them trees in the fall," Jack said. "Leaves turn bright red."

The covered front porch had a couple of brown rockers. "Could you leave the rockers?"

"Got no use for em' in Houston," Jack said, running his rough hand along the arm of one of the chairs. "There's a barn and workshop out back that has a turn-out pen and two stalls. You ride?"

"Not since I was a kid, but I might take it up again."

"We got city water here."

"How much are you asking?"

"1400 a month, thousand-dollar deposit, cash on the barrelhead."

"Sounds fine, I'll take it. When can I move in?"

"I'll be out in two weeks, but I'll be needin' the cash Monday, if you want the place, along with this here application filled out," Jack said, fishing one out of a desk drawer in the kitchen.

"No problem, I'll bring both by after work."

Then they shook on it.

"What's the address of your place?"

"This here's the Bar S Ranch, son, on Hoots Holler Lane."

It was so not California. "See you Monday." Kent had made a snap decision to rent the place, and that wasn't like him. His sister liked to remind him, "You overthink everything." Not this time. Somehow the mini ranch felt right. It was only about thirty miles from his office, a shorter commute than the one he'd made from San Clemente to Los Angeles.

Kent drove until he reached the city limits of Paradise Hills. In the downtown area, he discovered a wide main street with quaint shops and businesses lining both sides. He walked up the street and located a small library. Books, he'd be needing some of those. He opened the double doors and walked inside.

"Hello," said a woman with glasses hanging from a small, silver chain around her neck. Her short white hair had a slightly bluish tinge, and her smiling blue eyes were generous. "May I help you?

"I'm just browsing."

"Take your time."

He selected a couple of spy novels from the dusty shelves and returned them to the counter.

"Do you have a library card?"

"No, I don't, but I'd like to get one."

"Do you live here?" she asked with a puzzled smile.

"I will in a few weeks."

"Oh? Where?"

"The Reno place on Hoots Holler Lane. You know it?"

"Yes, is Jack selling?"

"Only renting."

"Well good for you, it's a nice place. My name's Dorothy Snow."

"Hi, Dorothy, Kent Winder. Say, do you know anything about an old, tall, white church, timber-frame construction? I passed it on my way here. Songbird Community, the sign read."

"That's my church, built over one hundred years ago by German settlers. Are you a church goer?"

"I haven't been for a while."

"Come join us, everyone's welcome at Songbird Community."

"I might just do that."

"Here's your new library card, and I hope to see you Sunday."

When Kent got back in the car, his cellphone buzzed. Another text message from Karla: *You, ok?* He texted back: *Will call you later, don't worry.*

He'd miss waking up mornings in San Clemente, looking out the back window watching the tide roll in the distance. But life as he'd once loved it was long gone.

CHAPTER FIVE

*A*nnie opened the dishwasher as Frank walked into the kitchen. "I had to reload the dishwasher again last night." He barked. "The plates were all jumbled up."

She looked at him and said nothing.

"I can't believe you still don't know how to properly load dishwashers or fold towels." Frank rolled his eyes again. "Remember, there's a place for everything, and everything in its place."

Having him redo what she'd done drove her nuts. Yesterday, she'd intentionally jumbled the dishes and mis-folded the towels. *Might as well con him into doing some housework.* Annie had turned her aggression into passive aggression. *It isn't safe to get mad, so I got even. Point, Annie. It's juvenile, but it helps.*

"I'm driving to Austin today," he announced.

"Okay, see you tonight." She waved as he walked out the door. Then slammed it behind him.

The rest of the day belonged to her. Cindy was coming for lunch, and Annie wanted to talk. They tried to get together at least once a month, usually at a restaurant, rarely at Annie's house. Today was different; she wanted more privacy. She glanced at the clock. Time to get going.

A few hours later, Annie looked over at the table. She'd inserted tapered-orange candles into two pewter candle holders that bookended a small bouquet of flowers. Moving back into the kitchen, she picked up a large silver spoon and carefully stirred the brown gravy.

The tea kettle whistled on the stove as the doorbell rang.

"Hi Annie," Cindy said with a hug.

Annie returned the hug. "Please come in."

"What a lovely table." Cindy said, peeking into the dining room.

"Thank you." Annie struck two matches and lit the candles before bringing in the food.

They clasped hands, and Cindy said grace. As they ate, she said, "These mashed potatoes are so well seasoned; they're melting in my mouth. And the roast beef? Just right."

"Thank you," Annie said.

After dessert, it didn't take long to put the food away. "Oh, wait," Annie said when Cindy started to store the honey. "Frank likes it to go in that cupboard over there."

"Frank?" Cindy raised her eyebrows.

"He has a certain way of doing things. You should see his closets, everything's color coded and arranged seasonally by clothing type. He tries to make my closets look the same, but I won't have it." The muscles in her face tightened. She didn't usually say this much about him to anyone, even Cindy.

Cindy was choosing her words when she said, "He sounds…particular."

Annie changed the subject. "Would you like tea?"

"I'd love a cup, Thanks."

"Let's take it in the family room."

They settled on the couch, and Annie said, "A few weeks ago, I asked Daddy about his and Mama's marriage."

"Oh, what were you wondering?"

"I grew up thinking they never disagreed, but he told me they had. Just never in front of us."

"It sounds like that surprised you."

"It did."

"So, you believed that in good marriages couples always agree?"

"The only marriage I ever saw up close was theirs, and they seemed to be made for each other. Is it that way for you and Pastor Mark?" She tilted her head to the side, curious.

"Heavens no," Cindy grinned. "We disagree about lots of things. But we try to keep it respectful. No one gets along all the time."

Annie looked away.

"Is there something you'd like to tell me?"

She wanted to tell Cindy about the abuse. She really did. But it was too shameful. "It's not something I'm ready to talk about. Not right now."

"I understand," Cindy said. "I'm here for you, whenever."

"I'd like to ask you a question, though."

"You can ask me anything, you know that."

"You and Mark…couldn't have kids…" She paused.

"We wanted children so much. It was heart breaking when we couldn't conceive." The wrinkles around Cindy's eyes sagged.

"How did you manage it?"

"Some days, not well. It was hard on our marriage. We had rough patches, but we tried not to blame each other."

"Frank and I are having trouble getting pregnant, and he thinks it's me." She looked down.

"It doesn't matter who it is, and it might be both of you."

Her stomach fluttered. *Frank will never believe he could possibly be the problem.*

"Have you tried fertility treatments?" Cindy asked, tenderness in her voice.

"Not yet. Did you and Mark try in vitro?"

"I wish we could have, but it wasn't really a thing back then," she sighed.

"Did you consider adopting?"

"Many times, but it never worked for us. That doesn't mean it wouldn't work for you if you wanted to go that way. We have a few couples in our congregation whose children are adopted."

"I don't think I know who they are."

"No reason you would; their families are like everyone else's. Know this, Annie: Most women can have babies, but not everyone can be a mother."

Annie put her hand to her heart. *I've never thought about it that way.* Her voice filled with emotion. "Thanks for being here for me and knowing what I need."

Cindy hugged her. "Are you okay? I'm still a little worried."

"I'm better since we talked. I love you, Cindy."

"I love you more," she smiled. "Guess I should get going."

"Until next time."

"Call me anytime, about anything." She left, and Annie finished drinking her tea. *I really, really want a baby. But with Frank? I don't think so. Maybe it's a good thing we can't get pregnant.*

CHAPTER SIX

*K*ent sat alone in a wooden pew at Songbird Community Church, staring at the pointed arch windows and doors. He liked the dark wood floors, and the rustic black piano sitting in the corner. He whispered a prayer just as a woman dressed in a peach-colored dress and white heels, rose from the choir seats. He read her name in the program: Annie Kingman Graves.

His breath caught in his throat as she sang, "Amazing Grace." She caressed each note in a way that left him mesmerized. No one moved; not even the babies stirred.

After Annie finished the song, he still carried her voice in his head. Her husband Frank sat up a row. Kent hadn't met him but knew who he was. He was running for mayor, and his picture was plastered everywhere. Kent glanced at Graves, who seemed distracted, twisting the band of his gold Rolex. He was on the short side compared to Kent, who stood at 6'5. Graves' closely cut blue suit was custom made, his cowboy boots a black, polished leather.

When the service ended, Kent stood to leave, just as Graves turned and introduced himself.

"Hey, name's Frank. Nice to meet you," he said, standing, legs spread wide, arms hanging loosely by his sides.

"Kent Winder, nice to meet you, too." He stiffened. *Who does this guy think he is?*

"You're new here," he boomed.

"Moved in a few months ago."

"Where from?"

"San Clemente."

"A California man?"

"That's right."

"What brings you to these parts?"

"Job."

"What do you do?"

"I oversee insurance claims adjustments. You?"

"Law and commercial real estate, here's my card."

"Thanks." Kent forced a smile, sensing that Frank didn't care about getting one of his cards in return.

"I'm also runnin' for mayor, you a votin' man?"

"Haven't registered yet."

"Well, I'd advise you to get that way, we're all patriots here," he said, tilting his head to the side.

Annie approached them just in time. Kent couldn't take another five minutes with this insufferable idiot.

"Hello," she said, extending her hand. "I'm Annie. I've seen you here before, but we haven't met."

"Name's Kent," was all he could manage. "You sing like an angel." When he shook her hand, her eyes smiled, then so did his. Frank ignored them both, busy scanning the congregation for potential voters.

"That's nice to hear," Annie said.

Frank pulled her to him, escorting her down the aisle, pressing the flesh as he went. She never moved an inch from his side. He gripped her arm as he might a briefcase.

"Hello, again," Kent heard someone say. It was Dorothy.

"Hi yourself." He smiled.

"I have something for you," she said, fishing around in her outsized brown handbag, removing a small picture book of birds, native to the Hill Country. "I thought you might like this," she said. "No rush to return it, I'll renew it at the library until you bring it back."

"Thanks for thinking of me."

"You're welcome. Were you here for Annie's song?"

"I was. She has an incredible voice."

"It's lovely, always has been. The first time I heard her sing that song was at her mama's funeral."

"Is her father alive?"

"Pete Kingman is very much alive, in some ways. He keeps to himself out there on that big ranch of his, rarely comes to town and never to church since his wife passed."

Pastor Mark walked back into the chapel. "Are you two still here?" he asked, looking surprised.

Kent knew parishioners didn't stick around long after the morning service ended. "I've taken up too much of Dorothy's time," he said.

"Not at all," she said.

"Since you're here, why don't you both have lunch with Cindy and me."

"My stars," Dorothy said, checking her watch. "Where has the time gone? Betty and Buster will be starving to death, got to get going. Thanks, anyway." She grabbed her jacket, rushing away.

"Betty and Buster?"

"Her cats." Mark smiled.

Kent grinned. "Got it. I should get going too," he said, uncomfortable at an invitation he thought might be offered out of obligation.

"Cats?" Mark asked, smiling again.

Kent laughed. "No, I'm allergic to cats."

"Then stay. Cindy always makes plenty of food, and we've been meaning to have you over. Today's as good as any, unless you have other plans."

"Well, no…" he said, rubbing the back of his neck.

"That settles it. Please follow me, the parsonage is just behind the church. They entered the kitchen as Cindy pulled pie from the oven. "Smells good, honey. Kent here's agreed to join us for lunch."

"Hi, Kent, welcome," she said, seeming not the least bit surprised her husband had invited him. She blew away a wisp of curly blonde hair that had dropped into her face. "We're having chili, rolls, and green salad with my pecan pie for dessert. I hope that sounds good."

"It sounds and smells great, thank you." Kent pulled up a chair to a large round table covered with a flowered tablecloth, set with everyday silverware.

The couple sat on either side of him, and they all joined hands. Cindy offered grace and then dished the chili. "You may not know, Kent, that chili is the state dish of Texas," Mark said.

He dug into the hot chili. "I didn't know that. This is so good," Kent said, mouth swimming in perfectly spiced cubed beef steak, chunks of plum tomatoes, onion, and corn.

"Cindy's chili won first place at last year's cook off at the county fair."

"I'm not surprised, it's the best I've tasted."

"I hope the jalapeños aren't too hot?" She asked.

"I love jalapeños, just right."

"Did you enjoy today's services?" Mark asked, passing him the green salad.

"A lot. Your sermon on hope was just what I needed. Thank you, Pastor."

Kent had a pleasant meal with good company until Cindy said, "Tell us about you. Mark and I've been doing all the talking."

"No worries," he answered, checking his watch. "I should go. Got some work to catch up on." Kent asked if he could help with the dishes.

"Nope," Mark replied, "that's my job."

"Okay, well, Thanks for dinner."

"You didn't get dessert," Cindy said. "Here, take some pecan pie with you." Kent accepted a couple of generous slices she'd wrapped in foil. He'd never seen whole pecans that large.

He walked to his car, slid inside, removed his boots, and reached into the back seat for his running shoes. Ah, that's better, he thought, pulling them on. He wasn't accustomed to cowboy boots, just an effort to fit in with the locals.

Kent stopped by the market, and on his way in, spotted Frank standing beside a sidewalk booth. The outside was decorated with red, white, and blue bunting, and inside the folding table was edged with lights and littered with bumper stickers that read, "Elect Frank Graves." Stacks of yard signs contained Frank's grinning mug. You'd think he was running for president instead of the mayor of a small town. Kent tried not to look his way. Too late.

"Come on over, Kent," Frank called, so he did.

Annie sat at the table passing out political literature. Kent smiled at her and then tried to stay interested, listening to Frank's silly shtick.

"Hey, cowboy," she smiled, looking Kent up and down, ending with his shoes.

He felt himself coloring. He must look ridiculous in his running shoes, paired with the new western shirt. Then he smiled.

"Would you like a lollipop?" she teased.

"No thanks, they look great, though."

She laughed, then they both laughed. Frank turned to ask what was so funny.

"Nothing important." Annie said.

"Seems like she's always thinkin' somethin' or the other's funny," Frank said, "even when it's not."

Kent's low opinion of Frank dropped a few more notches as Annie busied herself with flyers on the table and said nothing. He took a deep breath and wondered how a class act like Annie came to marry such a narcissistic jerk.

CHAPTER SEVEN

*A*nnie desperately needed a break from Frank and the campaign. She wanted a day where she could be with lots of people she didn't know and just shop. El Mercado in downtown San Antonio might do the trick.

She drove to the city, found a place to park off Commerce Street, and walked over to the plaza. It was alive with music and mariachis. She smiled, the tightness in her chest disappearing. She wandered among shops with colorful Mexican blankets on sale, passing restaurants and art galleries.

Then, she saw him. *Is that Kent?* Annie walked over. "Hi." She smiled.

He turned around, looking surprised. "Hi yourself," he beamed. "How are you?"

"Good, I'm good. I can't believe you're here." She spoke in a soft tone.

"I'm taking a long lunch, hoping to find a piece of local art."

"You've come to the right place. El Mercado is the largest Mexican marketplace outside Mexico."

"Sounds perfect," he said.

"Do you work in San Antonio?"

"Yes, at Sound Solutions for Life."

"Insurance Company at the City View Building, right?"

"Right. What about you? What are you up to today?"

"I'm going to shop till I drop," she grinned.

He laughed.

"Have you been to El Mercado before?"

"No. It's my first time."

"I'd be happy to show you around."

"I'd appreciate that," he said in a voice like velvet.

Annie blushed. "Let's go to Market Square first and see Botica Guadalupana."

"Sounds interesting," he said as they walked.

"It's the oldest pharmacy in the city. The building dates to the early 1800's, when it was a mercantile store. Later, it was a theatre. It's cool."

"Thanks for being my tour guide."

"You're welcome," she sighed happily. "If you're up for it, we can stop by MiTierra Café and Bakery and see the pharmacy another day."

"My admin recommended that place, said they have really good food."

"The tortillas are made in house, and the food is excellent. MiTierra is the oldest and best-known Tex-Mex restaurant around."

"I'm impressed. Say, why don't we have lunch together? I'll buy."

She hesitated.

"I don't bite, I promise."

She smiled. "Okay, but we may have to wait up to an hour, since the place is so popular. Have you got that much time?"

"I'll make time."

They put their names on the wait list, then Annie took Kent to the mural in the backroom dining area. "I like art, and since you do too, you'll love this."

"It's huge and so colorful," Kent said, admiration in his voice. "How long has it been here?"

"A Mexican artist named Jesus Diaz Garza started painting it about twenty-five years ago to honor the laborers and farmers who sold their wares at El Mercado. So, a long time."

Kent examined the painting more closely. "It seems to be appropriately titled, 'American Dream,' but there are more people shown here than farmers and laborers. Who are they?"

"The mural has grown to include three generations of the Cortez family, who own MiTierra. It also features more than one hundred influential Latinos in our area."

"Impressive," Kent said as they wandered down the long mural.

"San Antonio is a place rich with history, art, and culture."

"I'm starting to realize that. —Look over there. Who's that guy coming in with paint and brushes."

She craned her neck. "It's Ytuarte, the current artist working on the mural."

"He's here? Why paint at such a busy time?" Kent asked surprised.

"There's no quiet time in this restaurant, which opened in 1943, and hasn't been closed one day since. He paints while the patrons eat, and they love it."

"I don't think I've ever watched a real artist at work."

"Let's stand over there where we can see better. I love watching him."

As they lingered, Kent smiled and said, "Ytuarte is beyond good."

"I think so too, and he's not someone you get to see every day."

"I'm glad you brought me here."

She could feel her pulse in her throat.

Moments later, their table was ready. When the waiter came, Annie ordered the Ladies Special and Kent the Chalupa Compuesta.

"Tell me about you," Kent said as they dined. "How long have you lived in Paradise Hills?"

"All my life, but on our ranch outside the city. My family's been in the Texas Hill Country for generations. You come from California, right?

"Born and raised in San Clemente." He took another bite of chalupa. "This is amazing."

"I've never been, but I've seen pictures of the pier."

"The pier is my favorite." His smile started slowly and spread across his face.

"Do you miss California?"

"There are things I miss."

She nodded, listening. "Do you still have family there?"

"My older sister Karla, her son Carter, and my grandpa. How about you? Do you have siblings?"

"My sister Caroline's a lawyer in Dallas." She didn't want to mention Ben. Too sad.

"Do you see her much?"

"Not as often as I'd like, but we catch up every week."

"I call Karla every week too. Older sisters. You can't live with them; you can't live without them."

They both laughed, understanding.

While they waited for the check Annie said in a soft tone, "I liked our conversation today."

"Me too," he said, body still. "A lot. I'm sorry I have to get back to work."

Annie had lost all awareness of anything but him. "Why don't we have some pan dulce from the bakery on our way out."

"What's that?"

"Mexican sweet bread."

"I'm full of chalupa, but it sounds too good to pass up."

"The breads are delicious, you won't be sorry," she said as they wandered into the bakery.

"How about we split one?" he asked, turning toward her.

"Perfect." She said moving closer. "You good with chocolate and cream."

"How could we go wrong with that?"

Annie cut the warm bun in two and handed him the larger piece. "What do you think?"

"Words fail. So good," he said chewing.

She reached up and brushed crumbs from his chin. "You don't want to go back to the office with stuff on your face."

He laughed. "You're right, I don't," he murmured.

When they left the bakery, Annie thanked him for lunch.

"Best time I've had since moving here."

"I had fun too." She skimmed her fingertips along her jawline.

Then the rain started to pour, so they ducked under a nearby awning. "Do you have an umbrella?" He asked. By now, the rain was coming down in sheets.

"In the car. A lot of good it will do me there."

"I've got one in my man bag, here, take mine."

"You'll get soaked."

"True. How about I walk you to your car instead?"

"That would be nice, thank you," she said gazing into his arctic-blue eyes. *Why am I so drawn to him? I never felt this way about Frank.*

"Ready?" On three. One, two, go." He held the umbrella over Annie's head, taking her under his arm. They bolted for her car, dodging puddles, laughing. When they reached the car, Kent opened the door, and she stepped inside.

Annie tapped on the window. "Thanks again," she said.

"My pleasure," he tapped back.

Annie watched him go. He turned and waved at her with that boyish grin and black, curly hair. He looked like a movie star. Her heartbeat quickened. *I've never believed in love at first sight. Until now. I wish I were free to be with him. But I'm not.*

CHAPTER EIGHT

*F*rank sat alone behind the hand-carved pecan desk in his law office, squeaky ceiling fan whirling overhead. The solid-gold gavel his daddy had given him—when he finally passed the bar on the third try—sat on his credenza, along with a bronze sculpture of Justitia, the blindfolded lady justice. Justice was blind. Yeah, right, not in his world she wasn't.

He heard Joe Coykendall coming up the steps. Frank stood and opened the front door, the sounds of light traffic outside. Joe was a private detective, good at what he did: background checks, infidelity, you name it, anything of a confidential nature. He'd helped Frank discredit several witnesses. But today, his visit was more personal.

"Come in," Frank said, shaking his hand. "What ya got?"

Joe tossed paperwork on the desk. "Not much…yet, but this is my first report."

"Sit down and tell me what you found."

"Okay, here's the low down. Winder grew up in California." –Best thing about the place are the bars, as far as I'm concerned. Anyway, he has a sister Karla, divorced and single, and an 8-year-old nephew. His dad owned and operated a local clothing store before he and his wife died in a car crash years ago. Middle class, religious family."

"Sounds pretty boring so far."

"Winder graduated from San Clemente High and then went to USC, which is where he met Sally."

"Who's Sally?"

"His wife."

"So, he's divorced. Couldn't keep it together, huh? Too bad for him. What was the wife like?"

"A real looker, but they're not divorced. She's dead. They were married two years with no kids, then lost a baby to a late-term miscarriage. The wife died in the hospital two years ago."

"Tough luck. But why move here?"

He shrugged. "I don't know yet, but I'll find out."

"Fair enough, anything else?"

"Well, according to my notes, Winder graduated with a degree in business. Worked as a VP of data analytics for an insurance company in Los Angeles when he and the missus lived out in San Clemente. Drove past the old neighborhood, a nice area. That's about it, so far."

"Well, keep on it, I don't trust him. Why leave L.A. for this one-horse town?"

"Will do, boss," Joe said. "See ya later."

Frank closed the office and walked in the direction of Rojas Elementary, passing the Texas Ranger Museum and the local swimming pool. One of the reporters from Paradise Press online was scheduled to meet him in front of the Peach Street Brewery. He wanted to do a short video interview that he promised to post before the polls closed.

Too bad his daddy hadn't lived to see this day. Maybe for once he would have been proud of him, but probably not. Frank hated the man. He'd locked him in a tiny basement closet for hours when Frank was a child and didn't behave. He was still claustrophobic in small, dark spaces.

When he turned the corner, the reporter was waiting for him. "Over here," he motioned, starting the video.

"Howdy," Frank smiled into the camera, pointing to his campaign button 'Graves believes in Texas.'"

"I guess we know your choice for Mayor in this election." Mike smiled. "Let me ask you this, where do you stand on prop 6?"

"I'm for it, we've got to increase the county water supply. I don't know anyone who would be against it—unless it was Merv Martin," he laughed.

Mike laughed, too. "Where's your lovely wife today? She's supporting you, right?"

"Of course. I expect she'll be along directly."

"Do you have any final thoughts you'd like to share with the voters?"

"I will work hard to make Paradise Hills an even better place for all the good folks who live here," he said, smiling again into the camera. "Vote Frank Graves," he said flashing 'V signs' with both hands.

"Thank you, and good luck."

"I guess I'd better get over to the elementary school, find Annie, and cast that ballot. See you around." Off he swaggered.

A few blocks later, Frank reached Rojas Elementary. The sign out front of the polling place read: Vote. Aqui. Here. Polls open 7 am to 7 pm. It was now going on five, and Annie was supposed to meet him, if she was on time, which she rarely was.

Voters were lined up outside. He shook a few hands and then got in line to wait his turn. *Where is that woman? She knows how important this day is to me.*

Then he saw her walking toward him in black high heels, wearing black trousers with a matching jacket, and a shimmery teal shell underneath. Annie waved at friends and sidled up in line beside him. "Where've you been?" he asked under his breath. "This is a big day for me."

"I went to pick up your suits from the cleaners."

"Why now? Couldn't you have done that this morning?"

"I had other things to do this morning."

"Like what?"

"Does it matter?"

"Yes, it does."

"Ok. I went to breakfast with Kelly if you need to know."

He smiled. She had no idea about their affair. "Today. You went to breakfast today?"

"Yes, Frank, now hush. You're making a scene."

"You're right, we'll talk about this later."

"I'm worn out from talking about it now."

He glared at her. "Let's vote and then head back to campaign headquarters. Plenty to eat there, and the votes should be mostly counted by nine."

When they reached the little frame store front Frank called campaign headquarters, a crowd of people waited inside. They whistled and clapped as he walked in. A three-piece band played country music in the corner, and round tables were scattered around the room, filled with a variety of hot and cold appetizers. It was all for him—course he'd paid for it.

He noticed that Winder was there with Dustin. They both waved, and he waved back. Frank turned to Annie and said, "You do know Winder is all hat and no cattle, right?" She smiled one of her maddening half smiles and walked away to talk to Cindy.

A few hours later, most of the votes were in and counted. The Paradise Hills Tribune declared Frank the winner. He wasn't surprised he'd won, and neither was anyone else. He walked to the front of the room to give his acceptance speech, and people clapped, calling his name. Once all eyes were on him, he approached the microphone. Reaching down, he took Annie's hand and said, "Come on up here with me, sweetheart." Then to his constituents, "Join me now as we look to a better future together. I want to thank you for your confidence in me and for granting me the opportunity to serve the good people of Paradise Hills. I won't let you down." His night to shine, and he loved every minute.

Long after the celebration ended, Frank and Annie were back at the house, and he was still higher than a kite, talking about his win all the way through brushing and flossing his teeth. Annie was sitting up in bed and reading when he walked out of the bathroom. "Let's call it a night," he said. He took her book away and climbed on. *She isn't Kelly, who's hip, hot and sexy. But she'll do for now.*

CHAPTER NINE

*T*he next morning, Annie left the house while Frank was still in the shower. She drove to the ranch, parked by the barn, and saddled her horse. The two of them rode for miles, watching the sky burn orange. She closed her eyes and took another deep breath. Leaving Frank would be impossible now that he'd been elected mayor, running on a platform of family values. *How ironic. An abusive politician sounding off about family values.* But Annie had watched political wives on the national stage and learned that even bright and accomplished women stood by their men, no matter what. Her mind raced, needing a new focus.

You have a bachelor's degree in social work you've never used. What about helping kids? Her horse whinnied and shook his head up and down. "What do you think, buddy?" He turned his head. Was that a smile? What about helping kids using horse therapy? Annie had passed a new billboard on the drive to the ranch advertising an Equine Therapy

Center, close to Paradise Hills. A wide grin broke across her face. *It's meant to be.* "Come on, boy," she whistled, as they galloped for the house on a dead run.

When Annie walked into the kitchen, Gabriela was brewing tea. "Miss Annie, you're here."

"Good morning, Gabriela, may I have some of that orange tea?" Just what she needed to boost her energy level.

"Sit down, sit down, have you had breakfast?"

"No, I came out early for a ride. I wasn't very hungry."

Gabriela had a quizzical look on her face but said nothing. "I'll get eggs and toast cooking, and I've got strawberry and fig jam."

Annie smiled, "That sounds delicious. Thank you. I'll be in the office on the computer. Please call me when it's ready."

"I bring it to you," she said with a hug, then shooed her out of the kitchen. "Get going, get going. You got work to do."

Annie cherished Gabriela. "You're the best," she hugged her. "Thank you." After she fired up the computer and began researching, she found a site called BerkshireHorseWorks, just outside of Massachusetts, where "people tackle their mental-health issues by getting up close and personal with thousand-pound hairy beasts with whiskers." Annie laughed. *I love the descriptive words.*

She read on and found that horses in that part of the country had nuzzled children into recovery after the

Sandy Hook school massacre. She had no idea. There were the usual online critics who scoffed that there was little evidence indicating that equine therapy worked, but it was so popular that there were more than seven hundred programs world-wide.

Annie had grown up with horses and knew in her bones how attentive they were to their riders' emotional states. And horses couldn't be bullied. Since they were so big, their riders had to build relationships with them. *Life's all about relationships, so why wouldn't horses help? Yes, that's what I'll do, makes so much sense. And while I'm not licensed, I could probably work under someone who is.*

She gobbled her breakfast, picked up the phone, and scheduled an interview for that afternoon. Now, she had to tell Frank what she was up to. He would no doubt resist her new idea—unless it was in his best interest. A grin spread across her face. *Of course.* Annie called his office.

"So, where'd you go again this morning before I even got up?" He sounded grumpy.

"I went for a ride and got an idea I think you'll like."

He snorted. "Go on."

"I was thinking about you being the new mayor and wondering how I could help support you as the mayor's wife."

"Really?"

"Yes, maybe I could do some of my own work to build on your family values platform." It still stunned her that an abusive male touted family values, but she reminded herself again that it wasn't unusual.

"Hmmm, might be a good idea. What'd you have in mind?"

"Children's mental health."

"Folks love anything that helps kids."

"Yes, they do. I could volunteer at the Equine Therapy Center."

"Do you think they'd take you on?"

"We'll find out. I'm going there this afternoon. So, what do you think, Mr. Mayor?"

"It's great to hear you call me that." He laughed, sounding pleased. "We could get good publicity out of this," he said. "So, go ahead."

If there's something in it for him, it's all good.

"Thanks. Frank. I'll let you know how it goes."

That afternoon, she met Mary Lowe, Marriage, and Family Therapist, specializing in Equine therapy. Annie took to her right off the bat.

"Welcome," Mary said. "I understand you're interested in equine therapy."

"Hi. Annie Kingman. Yes, I am."

"You're a Kingman."

Annie nodded. Everyone knew her family, which might come in handy today.

"So, you grew up with horses," Mary said.

"Ever since I was a kid."

"Tell me about your formal education."

"Bachelor's degree in social work from UT. No masters," she said, rushing her words.

"That's not a problem, I can train you under my license. We're looking for people."

"Sounds good."

"Insurance companies don't like paying for treatment, so you wouldn't make much."

"How about a dollar a year?"

"Seriously?"

"I'm not doing this for the money. I want to help children."

Mary looked pleased. "We work with adolescents ages 14-19 with depression and anxiety issues. Do you know anything about teenagers?"

"I teach a class Sundays at my church to kids ages 15-16. I love listening to their ideas, asking them questions, and watching their minds work. It's a fun age."

"You could be a good fit here. How many hours can you work each week?"

"How about twenty?"

"That works for me. Can you start after Labor Day?"

"Absolutely, yes I can."

"Okay." Mary rose and shook Annie's hand. "I look forward to working with you."

"Thanks, me too, see you in September."

Annie's step was light as she walked out the door. So now she was a working girl. Instead of making her anxious, the day's tension drained from her shoulders.

On the way home, Annie stopped at Paesano's and picked up a limoncello cheesecake. She wanted to thank Kent for his kindness that day in the rain. She'd thought about their conversation so many times. Checking the online church directory, she found his address and cell phone number. She called.

"Hi Kent, it's Annie."

"What a nice surprise. How are you?"

"I have a little 'thank you' something for you, are you home yet?"

"I just walked in the door. Do you know where I live?"

"Hoots Holler Lane, right?"

"That's the place, see you in a few."

When Annie arrived, Kent was waiting outside, his kind eyes smiling. He'd grown a little scruff on his face, which looked good on him. Annie's breath caught in her throat.

"Welcome, come on in. May I help you with that box?"

"It's for you. Limoncello cheesecake from Paesano's. Do you like cheesecake?"

"You're unbelievable. It's my favorite."

"Mine too," she smiled.

"Do you have time for a slice?"

Annie checked her watch. Frank was working late again. "I'd like that."

Kent offered her a chair at the kitchen table and pulled a few plates from the cupboard.

"Your place looks good; different from when the Reno family lived here."

"It's comfortable, and I like it. Thanks again for bringing cheesecake."

"I owed you one for rescuing me in the rain." Her lips parted.

He laughed. "That was the least I could do after you showed me around El Mercado. We have a love for art in common." His eyes were glossy.

"We do, and I like that. Did you get that painting?"

"Not yet. Would you have time to help me look again? I could use another opinion."

"Sure, but let's do it before I start my new job."

"You got a job?" he asked surprised, moving his chair closer.

"Yes, part time at the Equine Therapy Center in Stone Oak."

"I've seen that billboard. I don't know much about horse therapy, but my guess is you'd be good at any kind of therapy."

"Why would you say that?" she asked, surprised.

"You're considerate and empathetic; an unbeatable combination," he said, offering words of support.

"Thank you, Kent. That's kind." Her voice cracked with emotion. He'd made it about her, not about him. He looked at her with penetrating eyes, as if what she said mattered. *I've never felt anything like it.*

CHAPTER TEN

*I*t was a blistering August day in the Hill Country when Kent's new friends from church, Dustin and Gina Johnson, and their seven-year-old son Sam, invited him to the County Fair and Rodeo. He'd never been to a county fair, and he thought it might be fun. Sam was participating in the mutton bustin' event, whatever that meant.

When they came to the fairgrounds, Kent spotted a large lighted sign over the entry way that read, "Grab life by the horns." The recorded sounds of Willie Nelson twanged, 'Mama don't let your babies grow up to be cowboys.' The smell of fried funnel cakes and hot kettle corn pierced the air.

There were several places to buy food just inside the entrance, and some of the local churches were holding fundraisers, selling barbecue with fixings. Pastor Mark stood in a grease splattered white apron, cooking brisket.

"Lunch is on me," Kent said to the Johnson family as they walked over to the booth.

"Oh, no, we couldn't," Gina said. "There are three of us and only one of you."

He laughed. "That's okay, this is pay-back for having me over for dinner one night and ice cream another." When Dustin seemed about to protest, Kent said, "I insist."

Mark loaded their plates with beef brisket, coleslaw, and roasted corn on the cob. Cindy added hot peach cobbler for good measure. They washed lunch down with ice-cold Cokes from The Thirsty Horse. Kent felt so relaxed.

After lunch, they walked over to the ticket booth, bought Big Carnival wrist bands, and rode the Ferris wheel, the Tilt-a-Whirl, and the Scrambler. Then, Sam tugged on his mother's sleeve. "I got to get ready."

"Okay," she said, taking his hand.

"What happens if you win?" Kent asked.

"Then I get a trophy…tall as me!"

"Pretty cool. How did you get ready for the event?"

"I rode around on my big dog—and a couple of times on my daddy."

Kent laughed. "So how do you stay on the sheep?"

"I have to hold on really tight up by its neck, squeeze my legs together, and not fall off."

"That's right," Dustin smiled. "Sam's ready, and he'll do great."

"I bet he will," Kent said.

"Last year I stayed on for five seconds, and this year I want to beat my record!"

"Good call, Son," Dustin said. "You're almost eight, so this will be your last year to compete."

Sam looked determined.

"The kids participating in the event have to be between the ages of five and seven," Dustin said, turning to Kent. "They ride with helmets on, so it's pretty safe. They must weigh less than 60 pounds, so the sheep don't feel much weight on their backs."

"How do they get the sheep to run?"

"Sheep are herded animals, and once they're let out of the shoot, they make a beeline for the small flock on the other end of the arena, trying to knock the kids off their backs. It's a hoot to watch."

Kent and Gina took their seats in the grandstands, and Dustin stayed with Sam. The first contestant didn't last two seconds, going head over heels, tumbling into the dirt. The next kid made it almost four seconds. Sam was rider number three.

"Go, Sam!!" Kent shouted, cupping his hands around his mouth.

"You can do it, Son!!" Gina hollered.

One of the adult handlers held the sheep still in the small metal chute and another placed Sam in riding position atop a sheep. Then, they opened the chute, and out came a big, woolly rocket with Sam clinging to its back. The announcer boomed into the microphone, "Here comes rider number 3 from Paradise Hills, Sam Johnson. Good luck, Sam."

He bounced all over the place, trying to hang on, as the sheep weaved back and forth, attempting to knock him off. He slid a little to the side, but his legs stayed wrapped tightly around the sheep's torso. He lasted a full six seconds, making it almost to the flock of sheep at the end, before tumbling off. A second rodeo clown grabbed him before he went onto the rail. Win or lose, Sam beat last year's record. He got up, and with a grin that covered his whole face, gave his mom the thumbs up sign.

"Quite a boy you have there," Kent said over the noise of the crowd.

"Isn't he great!?"

The winners wouldn't be announced until the next night, so they didn't know if Sam had won. "Should we go find Dustin and Sam?" Kent asked.

"No, they'll find us. The Queen's Coronation starts in twenty minutes. You won't want to miss that. The rodeo queen represents the rodeo association, the city of Paradise Hills, and the ranchers."

No one had told him there'd be queens. *Sheep, goats, cotton candy, BBQ, and now queens?*

"Annie's this year's chairperson of the coronation committee, and she'll be riding out in a minute to open the ceremonies. She was crowned herself when she was in high school."

Kent did not want to miss watching Annie open the ceremonies.

By now, Dustin and Sam were back in the stands. "Way to go, buckaroo," Gina said, giving him a hug. "Sure do love you."

"Aw, mom, not in public."

"Hey, here's Annie now," Gina said, pointing down at the dusty ring.

Kent watched as Annie rode, hair pulled back in a ponytail, showing off silver earrings. She wore a blue shirt with white chaps that fell below her boots, a stunning cowgirl. Annie was the most multifaceted woman he'd ever met. Taking a deep breath, he turned to Dustin. "What's the deal with Frank?" He asked.

"He's a dumb ole cuss who likes to put on airs. Don't mind him."

"How did someone like Annie end up married to someone like him?"

"Beats me. I've wondered that myself."

When the coronation finished, and the new queen of the rodeo crowned, Kent stood and thanked his friends. He'd driven separately so he could leave whenever he wanted. This might be a good time.

"Aren't you staying for the dance?" Gina asked.

"There's a dance?"

"Gruene Hall over in New Braunfels. George Strait tonight."

"THE George Strait?"

Dustin laughed, "You bet. Gruene Dance Hall is the oldest dance hall in Texas. Strait, Willie Nelson, Leon Russell, they all love coming here. And we got you a ticket."

"Wow. That's awesome. Thanks. But what about Sam?" he asked glancing at the boy who was fast asleep in his mom's lap.

"Gina's mom is meetin' us at the dance hall, and I just sent her a text. She'll take him home and put him to bed. The rest of us are goin' dancin!"

By the time they reached the hall, a large crowd had gathered outside. Men in black caps, black shorts and black and yellow shirts with the word Sheriff stenciled on their shirts did crowd control. Inside, signed pictures of famous people who had sung in the dance hall lined the walls.

Kent loved the bar made of old wood with a mirror on the back wall. Above the bar the sign read: 'In God we trust. All others pay cash.'

"Let's grab a seat over here," Dustin said. Kent and Gina followed him to a table, occupied by another couple. "Kent, meet Jim Williams. Jim, Kent Winder."

"Nice to meet you," Jim said offering a firm handshake. "Where you from?"

"Southern California."

"How do you like Texas?"

"It's great. Really like it."

"Good answer," he laughed. "I'm pretty new here myself."

"Where'd you move from?"

"New Jersey. That's where I grew up, and both our boys were born there."

"How old are they now?"

"Five and eight."

"I have a nephew who's eight. Is your boy in cub scouts?"

"He is in fact. And I'm the cub head."

"Nice. You sound like a good dad."

"I'd like to think so."

A woman with red hair, blue eyes, and dressed to the nines, walked up to them. "Kent, this is my wife Kelly," Jim said.

"Hey, Kent, you can sit here next to me."

"Yes, ma'am, my pleasure."

As he sat down, he felt a light, cool touch on his back, then he heard Annie say, "Hey y'all, mind if I join you?" She'd traded her chaps and boots for a dress and heels. His throat grew thick.

"Right here by me, honey," Gina said from across the table, patting the bench beside her. "Where's Frank?" She asked.

"He's over at the Peach Street Brewery talkin' business with his buds."

The foot stomping and clapping commenced, and out came George Strait. Kent turned in his seat, and there he was, big as life, the King of Country himself from Poteet,

Texas. He started off with, "All My Exes Live in Texas." The crowd loved it, and so did Kent. Dancers began filling the floor to the sounds of Strait singing. Kent looked at Annie and said, "Guess neither one of us has a dance partner tonight. May I have this dance?" he asked, offering his hand.

Annie paused, then said, "Sure, why not."

When he took her in his arms, Strait sang the words, "But if I'm ever goin' mend this broken heart, you look like a real good place to start." He gazed into her eyes, and she rested her head on his shoulder. He pulled her close, then hesitated. *She's married, she's married. What are you doing?* But he found himself lost in the lights and music, the scent of fresh lemon in her hair, a light glisten on her bare shoulders. The two of them were sealed in a soft embrace, moving together across the floor, wrapped in each other's arms. Heat radiated through his chest.

When the song ended, they walked back to the table. Strait was saying, "I'm a religious person. This next song is for my daughter Jennifer, who died. I honestly believe we will see each other in heaven someday." Then he sang, "You'll be There." When he reached the words, "I'll see you on the other side," Kent saw tears in Annie's eyes.

"Excuse me." She stood and walked across the dance floor.

He followed her outside, wanting to help. "Are you okay?" he asked.

"Not really."

"Feel like talking?"

"Not really."

"Okay, why don't we take a walk?"

The night air felt humid. Neither said much of anything for several minutes until she ended the silence. "That song reminds me of my older brother Ben. He died five years ago."

"That must have really hurt."

"It did, so much."

"Do you mind telling me how he died?"

"Ben was a horse racer. He was nearing the finish line in a big race, when his horse swerved off into the inside rail. He fell and cracked his head. Daddy rushed to him, and the paramedics came, but it was too late. He died right there on the track. His passing broke all our hearts."

"I'm so sorry, Annie." He looked down. "I get how it feels to lose family."

"You do? What happened to you?"

"My mom and dad died when I was fourteen, leaving me and my sister Karla alone. We lived with our grandparents after that."

Annie touched her heart, then his hand, listening.

"They died in a horrible car accident."

"You were just a child. That's devastating."

"It was." *I'm not going to tell her about Sally. I'd break down.*

She looked at him, and they walked on in silence. Then Annie said. "I don't really know you that well, but I feel like I do. Our conversation has been so real."

"The best kind, and rare for me. I'm mostly a private person,"

"Me too. We're talking like we've known each other for years, not months."

"It's true." His eyes smiled. *Intimate conversations with her come easy. Why is that?* He felt breathless.

"We'd better get back inside," Annie said. Near the dance hall, they saw Frank pacing up and down. "This isn't good. He's going to be angry. Frank has a temper."

"I'll talk to him. Explain things."

"No, stay out of this, please. Be my friend and let me handle it. You don't know Frank."

"Where ya' been, darlin'?" Frank asked, a deep frown creasing his forehead.

"Hi, honey, I didn't mean to worry you. It got hot inside. Kent here walked me outside."

"Well, that's right nice of you." Frank glared. "I can take care of my wife from here."

"Bye, Kent," Annie said, "Thanks for helping a lady out."

He walked back into the dance hall. Concerned, he took a chair just inside the door, listening to their conversation through the screen door.

"You know I don't like it when you wander off, little girl," Frank sputtered. "I was expectin' to find you here when I came over from the brewery, not off walkin' with some stranger from California. It doesn't look right, you alone with him."

"It was so hot in there. Next time, I'll bring a fan."

He grabbed her elbow. "Let's go dance. The whole town's in there tonight, and we need to make an appearance."

When Kent heard them coming, he went back to the table, and sat beside Gina.

"Where'd you and Annie go?" she asked.

"I took her out for some air. We ran into Frank on our way back. There they are, coming in now."

"Was Frank upset?"

"He was, yes. What do you know about him and his temper?"

"I know he can get pretty riled up. Annie doesn't like talking about it."

Before he had a chance to ask more questions, Kelly stood and announced, "Here comes our new mayor, Frank Graves! If he isn't one of the most accomplished men around, I don't know who is."

Jim glared at her as Frank led Annie onto the dance floor, taking her in his arms and moving her around the room, while smiling at the other couples.

"Hello, Mr. Mayor," one of the men called.

"Ya won big!" said another.

"Congratulations," said a couple as they danced past.

Annie looked pale; smile forced.

Kent stood. "Thanks for a wonderful day and for buying me tickets for George Strait. It was cool to see him up close and in person."

Dustin got up and shook his hand. "Thanks for coming. See you in church tomorrow?"

"You bet."

Kent walked outside and sat alone on an empty bench. He was so drawn to Annie, it somehow felt like they were meant to be. But she was married. One thing he knew for sure; he'd never be the kind of scumbag who slept with another man's wife.

CHAPTER ELEVEN

Songbird Community was planning an annual Labor Day picnic at Canyon Lake, and Pastor Mark had asked Annie to help. He'd assigned her a committee, mostly women—except for Kent and Dustin. They were meeting in one of the open classrooms at church when Annie said, "I found a lake island retreat on Canyon Lake that's big enough to hold us. It has a stellar view of the lake, a large, covered pavilion with a flagstone patio, and a big fire pit for roasting s'mores."

Dustin spoke up. "Sounds great. How about games for the kids?"

"We'll assign people to bring volleyball equipment to use when we're not out boating or wake boarding. And we'll have a splash pad for the little guys, along with some face painting."

"Sounds fun."

Kent said, "You mentioned wake boarding."

"I did."

"How many boats will we have?"

"We're still calling people about bringing boats, but several."

"Are you a wake boarder, Kent?" Dustin asked, slapping him on the back.

"All my life. Next to surfing and basketball, it's my favorite."

"This will be a fun day for you, Kent," Annie smiled.

The day of the picnic, Annie and Kelly drove together to one of the boat ramps at Crane's Hill Marina, and Frank followed in his black SUV, pulling a 12-passenger family fun boat. It was filled with water skis, wake boards, and brisket.

"I love this place," Kelly said, as they got out of the car. "You were so lucky growing up here."

"My daddy took me fishing on the lake when I was five and told me, 'Anything I know how to do on this ranch, I'm going to teach you.'" Annie smiled at the memory.

Kelly stared at her feet and took a deep breath.

"Are you okay?" Annie asked, putting her arm around her friend, hoping she hadn't upset her. South Texas was very different from South Jersey, where Kelly had grown up. When she and her family moved to the Hill Country five years ago, the two of them hit it off immediately.

Kelly was a nurse at Central Baptist hospital. Blunt and outspoken, she always said what was on the tip of her tongue. Annie tended to couch her words more carefully. Maybe Kelly was upset that Jim wasn't here?

"I'm sorry Jim had to work today and couldn't join us."

Kelly looked flustered, "Hey, look!" she said. "White-tailed deer."

"What's all the excitement, ladies?" Kent asked, walking up behind them.

"Kelly spotted a deer."

"Nice."

"If you're lucky, Kent, you might get to see a roadrunner."

"I've never seen one."

"My Grandpa Kingman carved local birds, and he's got a good one of a road runner in motion. Remind me to show you sometime."

"I'll do that. What can I do to help?"

"You might give Frank a hand with the gear."

"You got it."

An hour later, Annie and Frank climbed into their boat, along with Dustin, Kent, and Kelly. The day was clear and hot, no wind. Annie was first up for wake boarding. She slid easily into the cool water, and Frank floated the wake board in after her. "Ready for the tow rope, Frank," she said. Keeping her arms straight and knees bent, she let the boat pull her up out of the water. "Hit it," she called. Frank threw the throttle forward and then cut it back after she was up. Annie switched her feet, coming into slalom position, crisscrossed behind the boat, and jumped the wake easily.

"Nice," Kent said aloud.

She took a few laps around the lake, then Frank gradually slowed the boat, and Annie sank into the water. "Well done, sweetheart," he said, hooking up the ladder to the side of the boat.

"Thanks," she said, pulling herself into the boat. He tossed her a large, dry towel and kissed her wet cheek. "That's my girl."

Kelly looked away.

"I'm impressed," Kent said.

"You sound surprised," she laughed. "California isn't the only state that takes its wake boarding seriously. In Texas, we go big, or we go home."

"I can see that," Kent said. He was up next. As he slid into the water, Annie floated the wake board in after him.

"You ready?" Frank asked.

"I was born ready," Kent grinned.

"We'll see about that, Winder." Frank tossed out the tow rope. "I'll try to go easy on you."

"Don't do me any favors," Kent said, getting into position. "Hit it!" he yelled.

Frank jammed the throttle forward, but didn't throttle back after Kent was up, forcing him to let go of the rope. He face-planted, hard.

Frank laughed.

Annie poked Frank in the arm and took control of the wheel. "What are you doing?" she asked, getting up in his face. "That wasn't fair!"

Frank shrugged. "He told me not to do him any favors."

Annie swung the boat around and pulled up next to Kent. "Sorry about that," she said. "We had a little user error in the boat here."

Frank glared at her, angry.

"No harm done," Kent said, sputtering and gasping for air, shaking water out of his black hair.

Annie couldn't help but watch muscles ripple across his chest. When she smiled at him, his eyes shone back at her. *What's happening here?* Light seemed to radiate from his skin.

"Let's go again," Kent said. "I'll give you the thumbs up when we're at the right speed." When he was in position, Annie pushed the throttle forward and then pulled it back, just enough. He gave her the thumbs up, lifted the front of his board, pushed off with his back foot, and did a back flip. Kent took the tow rope in one hand and waved from the water.

"He's good," Kelly said.

"I'd say he's a showoff," Frank growled. "Let's get him in the boat and go back to shore. I've got some brisket to barbecue."

As Kent climbed back in, wiping the water from his chiseled face, Annie said, "Let's hear it for the man from California."

He grinned and bowed. "Thank you."

Frank busied himself stowing the gear, flinging the rope into the back of the boat.

A few hours later, Kent sat alone on a log with a plate of peach pie, looking over the water. Annie came up behind him. "What are you looking at?"

"Check out that sky." The dark trees in the distance faced a ribbon of silver water, white clouds dissolved against a vanishing blue sky, and the sun glowed orange on the horizon. "This is a great place," he said.

She sat down beside him. "One of my favorite events on the lake is the Fiesta Regatta in April. There's sailboat racing, a piñata party for the kids, and then a big fajita dinner for the whole family. You'd love it."

"Sign me up for next April," he said grinning, sliding closer.

"Thanks for your help today." Annie smiled.

"No problem, I had fun,"

When he looked at her like that, her heart stopped.

She blushed. "Let's go get some of those s'mores."

"Right behind you."

Annie's thoughts fixated on Kent. *There are so many things I like about him: he's handsome, smart, and kind. So different from Frank. No denying there's something between us. And we both know it.* That night, she got into bed and fell on a pillow with a smile on her face. Kent filled her dreams.

The next morning, she woke up and stretched. She listened to the wind rustling through the trees, and birds tweeting in the sky. Then she dressed, walked into the kitchen for a cup of tea, and found Frank going through her purse. Her eyes widened, and she sucked in a quick breath. "What are you doing?"

"Looking for a pen, don't be so sensitive."

"Don't touch my things." Her back stiffened. She wasn't going to let it go.

He picked up her handbag and waggled it in front of her. "Technically, this is mine."

"What? Are you serious, give it to me," Annie said, the blood rushing through her arms.

He shook his head. "Everything in this house is mine, including this bag. I bought and paid for it."

"This is crazy, and that bag is not yours. It doesn't matter who paid for it."

He grabbed her arm hard.

She yelped, chin trembling.

"Let me be clear. EVERYTHING in this house belongs to me."

"I'm out of here."

He blocked the kitchen doorway, leering. "Where do you think you're going, Missy?"

"Get out of my way, Frank."

"Make me."

"What's your problem today?"

"You know, come to think about it, I could be a wee bit consternated over your behavior at the lake yesterday." He cracked his knuckles.

"What are you talking about?"

"Could be the way you socked me in the arm when Winder fell. Like that." He punched her in the arm.

"Ow! That hurt. I barely tapped you."

"I always give at least as good as I get. You should know that by now." He glared at her.

She flinched.

"And then there was that little comment about user error." His tone deepened, and he shook his head.

She rubbed her arm. "Why'd you dump Kent in the water?"

"Because I could, don't question me. And don't ever embarrass me in front of our friends. You got that!?"

"Don't shout at me!"

"Or you'll do what? Leave me?"

"I might just do that," she said, braver than she felt. She reminded herself that whatever she said or did, Frank always had the physical upper hand. *I need to be careful.*

"Right." His laughter had an edge to it. "Why, what would people think?"

Her cheeks burned, eyes wet with tears, knees weak.

"Oh, the shame of it," he chortled. "Your daddy doesn't care about you."

"You're wrong, he does care about me."

"More than he cares about the family legacy? I don't think so."

Silence.

His tone suddenly shifted. "Forgive me for getting riled up?"

He hurts me and now I'm supposed to forgive him? Not the first time.

"You know how many times the Bible says we're commanded to forgive each other? Seventy times seven."

She stared at her hands. Annie had always thought of herself as forgiving. *But abuse is never, ever right. He's trying to manipulate me again, still, always!*

"Now, here's your purse, let's let bygones be bygones."

She couldn't believe it.

"What are you up to today?" he asked in a curious voice.

She took a deep breath. "I'm having brunch with the girls."

"Where?"

"Le Peep in Stone Oak."

"You ladies enjoy yourselves." He walked to the cabinet, reached for a cup, and slammed the door, making the dishes rattle. The door slipped off its hinges.

She jumped at the noise.

He glared at her and said, "Guess I'll have to fix that door. See you later."

Annie picked up her keys, walked out and drove fast. When the car next to her honked, she jumped. *Deep breaths. Deep breaths. Slow down.* She'd been looking forward to a relaxing lunch with friends. Now it would feel better to go hide somewhere.

She pulled up to the restaurant and walked inside. She smelled bacon and tacos cooking, and pancakes sizzling on the griddle. Looking around the room for a table, she spotted a little girl wearing a pink shirt, drawing pictures in a gray notebook. When they made eye contact, the little girl waved and smiled, and Annie waved back. She liked coming here. It was a nice little bistro.

When her friends arrived, she put on her public face. Air kiss, air kiss, hug, hug. Then, they sat down.

"Let's share some almond breakfast starters," Gina said, and they all agreed.

"I'll have salmon and eggs," Annie said when the server came.

Teresa ordered the 'Hen House, and Becky got one too.

"Too bad Kelly couldn't join us," Becky said, and they all nodded.

"She had to work a shift at the hospital today," Annie said.

"How's everyone doing?" Teresa asked, brightly.

"Oh, fine, fine," they all said.

"I don't believe I told you how much I enjoyed Frank's post-election party," Teresa said putting a dollop of sour cream on her avocados.

"I'm glad you did, it really was quite a night," Annie said, gripping her hands under the table.

"You must be proud of him, being elected mayor and all."

"Of course." She swallowed.

"What's he up to today? City business?'

"He may be fixing one of our kitchen cupboard doors that unexpectedly came off its hinges this morning," she said, willing her expression to be unreadable.

Becky sighed. "I wish my Wayne were handy like that, he can't fix a thing. I'm always having to call a handyman."

"Brian's handy," Teresa said, but he's lazy as a possum. "So, I still have to call a handyman." She and Becky laughed.

Where's Dusty today?" Sarah asked Gina.

"I have no idea. We don't keep tabs on each other."

Annie couldn't imagine what it would be like to have a marriage where her husband didn't keep tabs on her. She toyed again with the idea of leaving Frank. *Maybe one day, I'll just up and leave. Walk out the door, and never look back. Poof, I'll be gone. Yeah, right.*

Sarah was nattering on about purchasing a new car. "Of course, we're not going to buy it from Baker Motors. We don't buy cars from the local dealer. We don't need the whole town knowing what we paid and how much we put on credit."

Becky spoke up. "Say, did you hear the latest about Constance?"

"No," Sarah said, whispering. "What's going on?"

"Seems her boss dropped her home from work. When Julie drove by, they were standing in the driveway, making eyes at each other."

"Whoa. How'd you find out? Did Julie tell you?"

"No, she called Peggy, who called Mary, who called Marilyn, who called me."

And the tongues wag on and on. There's nothing like the Paradise Hills rumor mill.

Teresa had the decency to change the subject. "This might be a fun question. Who's the luckiest woman at this table?"

"Where did you come up with that?" Becky asked.

"It's a little ol' game I saw on the Internet," Teresa said. "Come on, it'll be fun."

Annie decided to go first and get it over with. "I think Gina is."

"Now you have to say why you believe that's true."

"I've known Dusty most of my life. He's a generous husband and dad. Sam is adorable and so is little Greg. I'd say she's a lucky woman."

Gina blushed. "Thanks, Annie."

"And she's modest," Annie said, smiling at her friend.

"I think you are the luckiest," Becky said, nodding at Annie.

"Now, why?" Teresa asked.

"Her family has lived here for generations, she has deep tap roots, and everyone knows and respects her family," she said to Teresa. Then, she turned to Annie. "You have standing in the community, a wealthy father, and a husband who gives you anything you want. I'd say that's pretty darn lucky."

"I agree with you, Becky," Teresa said. "For all the same reasons, and now, you're the mayor's wife, too, Annie. You're one lucky lady."

Annie forced a smile. *They have no idea what my life is really like. I hate keeping the abuse secret. But I don't want to be an outsider with the people I need most. I don't want to deal with whispers and stares about being abused.*

An hour later, Annie was on her way home. If she came up with a safe way to leave Frank, her friends would think she was the crazy one. *That would hardly become a Kingman.*

Being a Kingman had always been a challenge. Her teachers expected her to get excellent grades. People at Songbird Community expected her to be a staunch church goer with no doubts. Even the kids she grew up with looked at her differently. Some thought she was uppity because of who her family was. *Perfect Annie, I have to be perfect Annie. —But not when I'm with Kent. He doesn't stereotype who I am, or who I'm supposed to be. He sees the real me.* Her lips parted, nerves tingling. *Now stop. You're married.*

CHAPTER TWELVE

*I*t was an unseasonably frigid morning in late October, the kind of Saturday that would have been good for Kent to stay indoors with the rest of John le Carre's, *A Perfect Spy*. He'd gotten up at seven instead to go for a run. He needed something to clear his head, although even five miles couldn't do that. As he pulled on his shoes, his phone buzzed with a text message from Dustin.

"Going to see a man about a horse. Come with."

"Getting ready for a run."

"Will wait, pick you up at 8:30."

"Sounds good."

Dustin pulled up out-front, right-on time. "Hey, man. It's friggin cold out," he said, as Kent climbed into the cab of his black Ford pickup.

"Feels good to me." Kent wiped the sweat from his face with a towel from his gym bag. "Are you thinking of buying a horse?"

"Yep, promised Sam that I'd get him one for Christmas."

"Which ranch you looking at?"

"Kingman, they got the best quarter horses."

Kent had been wanting to see the Kingman ranch, meet the secretive Pete Kingman. See where Annie grew up.

Ten miles later, they were on Ranch Road 2, driving along the Pedernales River. Kent spotted a few deer grazing in the field off the road. When they reached the gates to the ranch, Dave waved them through. "It'll be a few more miles before we get to the main house," Dustin said driving on. "Hey, check out the blackbuck antelope over there."

The only antelope Kent had ever seen were in a zoo. This one lay sprawled in the grass, hooves tucked under him. Dustin slowed the truck, so Kent could take a better look. The antelope turned its curvy-horned head in his direction. White on the top half of its body and black on the bottom, its black face had a white ring around each eye. Graceful looking animal.

As they drove on, Kent spotted a few wild turkeys and hundreds of white-faced Herefords.

"This place is huge," he said, "how many acres?"

"About 50,000. It's been in the Kingman family for generations. Besides raising cattle and selling horses, they keep bees and sell honey. It's quite the operation."

"I've never seen a place like this," Kent said as they passed the show barn.

"There's Pete," Dustin said, pulling his truck into the yard. "Mornin,' Pete," he said, climbing out of the truck. "This here's Kent Winder from California."

"Kent," Pete said, extending his hand. "You're a long way from home, boy."

"Yes, sir," he replied returning Pete's firm grip. "Like they say, I wasn't born in Texas, but I got here as fast as I could."

"Hadn't heard that one," he laughed, "but I like it."

"What kind of horse you have in mind, Dusty?" Pete asked, leading the way into the barn.

Kent turned and mouthed the word 'Dusty'?

He smiled at Kent and walked into the barn behind Pete.

"Lookin' for a quarter horse. Somethin' good for Sam to learn on."

"Good choice. Got a nice gelding over here that might be right. Hy, bring Palumbo around."

"Sure thing, Boss."

"Aren't quarter horses really fast?" Kent asked, surprised.

"Yep, but docile and quiet by nature, and a bit lazy. Also, intelligent. There's the odd one that's not good with kids, but not sweet old Palumbo here," Pete said, patting the neck of a bay horse.

"Looks like he might have some potential to be a show horse." Dustin looked over the well-muscled animal, noting the black hind socks.

"Good eye," Annie said, walking into the barn. "Hi, Dusty, hey Kent," she said.

"You already know this guy?" Pete asked.

"From church. "If you came sometimes, you might meet some of the new people," she said, linking her arm through her daddy's. No comment.

"Let's take Palumbo for a ride, Dusty," Pete said. "See what you think. I'll saddle up Diablo and ride along. Annie, maybe you could keep an eye on Kent here for an hour or so?"

"I think I can handle that. We'll take a walk up to the main house, and I'll see if I can rustle up some pancakes."

"Save some for Dusty and me." Pete pulled out a tan leather saddle that had a black seat with blue-crossed pistols and a hand tooled floral skirt. "I got a western youth saddle here that might work for Sam," he said digging through the tack room.

As Dusty and Pete saddled up, Kent and Annie started for the house. It was quiet on the dirt road, only the two of them for miles around. He watched their breaths mingle together in the frigid air.

"I hope you like cinnamon roll pancakes topped with bananas," she said, wrapping her white woolen scarf more tightly around her neck, rolling her matching cap over her ears.

"I can't say I've tried them but sounds good."

They walked a few minutes without talking. Then turning to her, he said, "Can I ask you a question?"

"Go ahead." She said, curious.

"You and Frank…"

"Yes…What about us?"

"How'd you end up together?" He leaned in, listening.

"We met at the University of Texas, Austin. Frank was in law school, and I was a senior, finishing my bachelor's degree. I saw him one night at a dance. He was confident and outgoing. He seemed kind. He didn't even hold my hand at first."

He raised his eyebrows, interested.

"We dated on and off for six months, and then one weekend, we drove out to the ranch. Frank didn't fit in with ranch life and horses, so I broke it off."

"Not the end of the story. Are you okay talking about it?"

"Yes, not sure why. I don't usually say what's on my mind."

"Me neither. Not to most people." His fingers touched her hand, and she smiled.

"He chased me like wolves were running after him. He wouldn't stop calling. Then his aunt called, demanding to know why I was breaking her nephew's heart. She told me he couldn't eat or sleep."

"What a guilt trip."

"I see that now," she sighed. "It got worse when Frank came by. He wept so hard, I had to hand him tissues. I felt sorry for him."

Talk about manipulative. He'll do whatever it takes to win. Even bawl like a baby.

"He told me again that he loved me and begged me to give him another chance. So, I did."

"Was that the only reason you went back to him?"

She paused. "My friends reminded me he had a bright future."

They continued walking, she talked, and Kent listened. "When Frank asked me to marry him and promised me a good life, I felt…well, secure. So, I said yes. But I know now I wasn't listening to my heart." Annie stared into the distance. *The red flags didn't start waving until after we married. When I told him no, he wouldn't stop.*

Kent broke into her thoughts, "Are you sorry you married him?"

In a hushed voice she said, "Yes. But that's between you and me."

"You can trust me," he said.

"I want to believe that. Were you ever married?"

"Once, about two years ago."

"What happened?"

He swallowed hard. "Sally had a late-term miscarriage, and we lost our baby. Then she died too, the result of severe blood loss and complications from lack of oxygen. I lost them both. I felt like such a failure." A pained stare filled his eyes.

"Oh, Kent," she said voice rising. "I wish I could say something to make you feel better."

"It's okay." His body stiffened. "I've asked myself over and over what I could have done to save her." A single tear dripped from his eye.

Annie touched his cheek and wiped the tear, whispering, "It's not your fault."

He hung his head. "I buried myself in work. Day and night that's all I did." The color drained from his face, and he choked out the next words. "Everywhere I looked, I saw her and the baby.

I left California and moved here when the chance came up at work. I had to get away." He'd never said this much about Sally and their baby to anyone but his sister. "I thought moving here might free me from being so sad."

Annie stopped walking and looked at him with tenderness. "You don't have to do this alone, you know. I'm your friend. I'll be here for you."

"Thanks," he said. "I like the way you just let me talk. No suggestions. No observations. Just empathy. It helps a lot."

She touched his arm and smiled. "You're welcome."

When they reached the house, Annie said, "Please come in, and let's get breakfast started."

Kent found a warm and welcoming stone and wood home with at least two fireplaces and a couple of floor-to-ceiling bookcases. There was a table for playing dominos set up and ready, very homey.

"Come help me with those pancakes," she said, walking him into the kitchen, tying a blue and white frilly apron around his waist.

"I look ridiculous." He laughed.

"Does it matter?"

"I guess not, what do you want me to do?"

"Please remix the batter I've got stored here in the fridge," she said, showing him the large electric mixer and handing him the batter. "I'll fry the pancakes, then we'll layer them with cinnamon sugar, and add a cream cheese glaze on top."

"Sounds like a heart attack waiting to happen."

"Don't you go making fun of my pancakes." Annie grinned.

"I wouldn't dream of it." He took a small pinch of flour and flipped it on her apron.

"Why, Kent Winder, if you aren't the worst tease." She dumped a spoonful of sugar on his head.

"I'll get you for that." He chased her around the kitchen, shaking the sugar from his hair. When he caught her, he wasn't sure what to do. Kent looked into her eyes, saw her sweet, full mouth, and stepped back.

"Is it getting hot in here?" Annie whispered.

Kent leaned forward and kissed her softly on the lips. He felt something shoot straight through him. Then he pulled back.

"Even better than I imagined it would be," she said.

"It feels good to be close to you," he breathed, stroking her hair.

"You need to let me go…because I don't want you to."

"You're right," he said, pulling away. "I'm so sorry. I'll step outside and cool off." He grabbed his coat and headed for the porch. A few minutes later, Annie walked over and sat beside him on the glider.

"I know you're married, and that means something," he said.

"Yes, it does."

"We can't let our feelings take us where we shouldn't go."

"No, we can't. And I don't want to lose our friendship."

"Same here."

"You care what I think, who I am, and how I feel."

"I do, Annie."

"I feel the same about you."

He could feel his own heart beating. This wouldn't be easy. "Have you ever considered leaving Frank?"

"If I could find a way to manage my daddy's disappointment and the social fallout in Paradise Hills, I'd be gone in a flash." She touched his face. "Now, I'm freezing out here. Let's go back inside."

An hour later later, Dusty walked in through the front door, blowing on his hands, trying to warm them. "Hey," Annie said, turning from the griddle. "Where's my daddy?"

"He'll be along directly. He stopped by Susie's grave, said to go ahead without him."

"Then, he'll be awhile," she said. "Sit down and let me get you some pancakes."

PETE

Pete climbed down from Diablo, letting the reins drop over his neck. "Steady there, old boy," he said, rubbing his horse's black nose. Then leaving him to graze on the short grasses, he walked across the family cemetery to Susie's grave. He sat down next to her headstone on a large piece of weathered limestone, picking up a rock he'd carved especially for their visits. Then tugged his wool-lined jacket tighter against the frigid wind.

Pete liked the family cemetery. Some folks might find it odd to spend time with the dead, but not him. Besides his wife and son Ben, he was surrounded by his parents, grandparents, and great grandparents, who had all long since passed. One day he'd be here, too, so he might as well get comfortable with the surroundings.

He remembered the day he met his wife Susie at the Tarleton Horse Park outside Atlanta. He was looking for a quarter horse to stud when he saw her jumping a beautiful brown thoroughbred on a cross rail course. She sat high in her saddle and had the right amount of energy to ease her horse over the jumps. So graceful. For him, it was love at first sight, but for her, it took longer. Her parents hated it when she married him and moved to Texas.

He wanted nothing to do with other women after she died, even though he was only forty-eight at the time. The women at Songbird Community tried to set him up a time or two, but he'd have none of it. He told them to quit pestering him about dating; no one could ever replace her.

He knew folks at church called him a recluse and some of them gossiped that he was no longer a believer because he never came to church. But his girls, Mark, and Susie herself knew better. They were the only ones who counted as far as he was concerned.

Now he was pushing sixty-eight. Inside, he didn't feel that old, but outside his knees creaked and cracked whenever he stood up, and lately his left hip had been bothering him some. His grandfather had been right when he said, "Getting old is for the birds."

"Hi, darlin," he said softly to Susie's grave. "Annie's on the place today, up at the house makin' your special pancake recipe. Dusty come out looking for a horse for young Sam and brought some feller with him from California. The whole dern state of Texas is crawlin' with em.' Times are sure changin' and not for the better, as far as I can tell," he grumbled.

"Frank is still a pompous idiot, so nothin' much has changed there. Got himself elected mayor last month, so I expect he'll be cockier than ever." He sighed. "I wish Annie had never married him. But it is what it is." He shook his head.

"Caroline's in Dallas, still not married, and I don't see her as much as I'd like. She's a big shot lawyer and manages her own firm. You'd be right proud of her. She doesn't seem to lack friends but claims she hasn't located the right feller yet. Both our girls like to think you and I had the perfect marriage. I keep telling 'em we didn't. Caroline's chasin' after a mirage, looking for something she will never find. She's so independent, I don't know what kind of man it'll take to tame her. She might have listened to you, darlin, but she won't listen to me.

"Annie might be more practical about marriage, but I don't think she's happy." He paused and thought about what that meant for her. "Don't you worry, I'll be here for her, if she ever really needs me, you know that," he said in a controlled tone of voice.

"I'm growing old, my love, old and tired of the back-breaking work of runnin' a ranch." He noticed the new tremor in his left hand was making it shake again. He grabbed his left hand with his right and made it stop.

"Sure, I've got Hy and the boys helpin' me, but Hy's gettin' on too. Thinkin' I might have to replace him with someone a mite younger. That'd break both my heart and his." Pete pulled at his ear and went quiet. If only Ben had lived, he could take over the ranch. It isn't a job for a woman.

"Well, guess I better get on back up to the house. Annie keeps me locked up in a cage pretty tight when she's out here. Never stops worryin'. Bye for now, old girl," he said, kissing the palm of his worn hand, then pressing it against the headstone.

When he reached the house, he saw Annie watching out the window for him, like Susie used to do. She looked so much like her mama. Annie met him at the door and took his coat. "Come into the kitchen, Daddy, there's fresh pancakes waiting for you in the warmer."

He smiled, squeezed his daughter's hand, and sat down to eat delicious pancakes.

CHAPTER THIRTEEN

*A*nnie left the ranch around noon, relaxed and happy. She tried not to think about the kiss with Kent. How could a simple kiss make her feel more alive than she had in years? –But it did. It was so gentle and tender, not forced. Frank was waiting in the living room.

"I expected you'd be home earlier," he growled. Then cussed at her again.

"I don't always know the exact time I'll be home. That's ridiculous."

"I didn't even know where you were. Did you turn your location off?"

"I don't know what to tell you, Frank. Maybe it's the app." She crossed her fingers behind her back.

"If you'd checked your cell phone, you'd see I messaged you, over and over." He snapped at her.

She changed the subject. "You were out running when I got up."

"What does that have to do with you bein' here for me when I get home?" he asked, nostrils flaring. "I wanted to take you to breakfast and now it's too late."

"I ate breakfast at the ranch."

"Course, you did, you take better care of your daddy, than you do me. The sweat was visible on his skin. "What'd you cook?"

"Mama's special pancakes."

"The cinnamon ones with cream cheese glaze?"

"Those are the ones, with bananas."

"Did you think to bring me any?"

"Sorry, we ate them all."

"You and your daddy ate a whole batch of pancakes?"

"It wasn't just us. Dusty was there looking at a horse for Sam, and he brought Kent Winder with him. They both acted like they were starving, the way they gobbled down those pancakes."

"I told you to stay away from Winder," he yelled, face red.

"He's in our congregation, and friends with our friends. I will run into him sometimes."

Frank looked closely at her.

"Don't order me around." She said, tired of playing games.

"Don't go down that rabbit trail, girlie girl. I'm your husband, and I will tell you what to do. As my wife, you should be obedient."

"Obedient? I'm not a child." It was so absurd, she laughed. Bad idea.

"Don't you laugh at me. Ever." He shook with rage.

Annie knew Frank hated people laughing at him. It made him crazy. Growing up, his nickname had been Fat Frank, and plenty of kids had laughed at him. Some folks in Seguin still called him Fat Frank behind his back, even though he hadn't been heavy since middle school. People could be so cruel.

"I didn't mean to laugh at you, honey," she tried to soothe him. "Come on now, come on over here and give me a hug."

"Like hell you ain't laughin' at me."

"I'm going to change my clothes," she said, turning to walk away.

"No, you're not," he shouted. "I'm not done with you."

"Too bad! Because I'm done with you." *That felt good.* As she started for the door, he jumped in front of her, blocking her path.

"Get out of my way," she ordered.

"Not a chance. Now sit DOWN!" he bellowed, grabbing her shoulders, and throwing her on the loveseat.

She landed backside down on the cushions, legs flying up. Annie had never seen him this angry. "Please let me go," she said softly.

"When I'm good and ready, and not a minute before. You pay attention to me."

Fear seized her heart. When she tried to get away, he raised his hand and slapped her hard across the face. She touched her hot cheek, then froze in place, unable to move. She was shocked. "You've never hit me."

"You've got to stop agitatin' me like that. You understand?"

"So, it's my fault?"

"It was just a little slap, not a punch." He shrugged.

Not wanting to suffer through another fire storm, Annie sat silent.

He took a deep breath and calmed down. "You're my wife, and I want us to work together. We work as a team; long as you remember I'm the captain of our little team." He said, eyebrows raised.

This is getting out of control. Time to start thinking about my own protection.

Frank opened his wallet and counted out five 100-dollar bills. It wasn't unusual for him to be carrying that kind of cash, but handing it over to her? Not so much. He typically kept her on a tight budget, often pleading poverty whenever Annie wanted something new for the house. He was the one who managed all the finances.

"Here," he said. "Go buy yourself a new dress and matching shoes."

Does he think he can pay me off?

"No need to talk about this any further," he said.

"So, that's it?"

"What do you want from me? I gave you money." He shrugged, turned, and walked out of the room.

Her cheek burned where he'd slapped her and left a mark. Her lips and skin trembled, and she shut her eyes. *I need to get out of here, now.* She left the $500 behind, grabbed her leather jacket and purse from the mahogany table in the entryway, and walked out of the house. She slid into her car, driving aimlessly.

She turned toward the ranch, then stopped. If her daddy saw that Frank had hit her, he'd have his hide. She couldn't go to him, not yet. She could call Caroline, but she'd call the police. Annie imagined sirens screaming through the neighborhood and red lights flashing across the house. *Nope. People will talk. Maybe I can call Gina? She's probably busy with her kids. I thought I could get through this by myself. But I can't.*

On its own, her car approached the short, dirt lane that led to the small Bar S Ranch, Kent's place. When she pulled up, Kent peered out from his kitchen window, then pushed open the screen door, letting it slam behind him. He walked down the back steps and looked happy to see her. Until she rolled down the window. His smile turned to shock as he saw her tear-stained face with a fading red handprint on her cheek.

"What the…." he said. "Who did this to you?! Was it Frank?

"Yes." She used her hair to hide her face.

He opened the door and helped her inside, putting his arm around her. "You got bruised and more than a little. How about I call the cops?"

"No, please. Not that." She crumpled onto the sofa, muttering, "How could I let this happen?"

"Are you kidding me? You're not responsible. He is. He's the abuser." Kent took her into his family room, sat down, and left a spot for her to sit beside him. She fell into his arms, tears wetting his neck and face. He held her close.

She couldn't meet his eyes, feeling nauseous.

"Please stay here with me for awhile," he said.

Her throat was thick, and she wished she could just fade away. But she soon relaxed in his arms and closed her eyes.

An hour passed; Annie had fallen asleep. Kent wanted to help. She was hurt and needed him to be there for her. *What kind of miserable excuse for a man hits a woman? What to do about Frank?* He couldn't let him get away with it. Kent played various scenarios in his head while she dozed fitfully, curled up next to him.

A few minutes later, she woke with a start.

"It's okay," he said. You're safe, you're with me."

She buried her face deeper in his neck and let out a deep, shuddering sigh. "Thank you, Kent. I know I'm safe with you," she whispered.

"I'd like to punch that husband of yours."

"No, stay away from him, please. I don't know what he might do to you, or to me."

"But if he hit you once, chances are it will happen again. Next time, it might be worse."

She stood and straightened her clothes, still feeling light-headed. "You won't tell anyone, right?"

"Not if you insist."

"I do, please."

"Since you won't let me do something, how about talking to your dad?"

"Not yet, but I will." She stewed, wondering if she really would.

"What about calling the abuse hotline?"

"I don't think we have one of those in Paradise Hills, and even if we do, what would people think? Like I told you, this is a small town where everyone talks about everything."

"I can't let him do this to you again."

She turned away, avoiding eye contact. "Now you're scaring me."

"I'm sorry. I didn't mean to."

"I don't want him to hurt you too. I should go. Thanks for being here for me today."

He held her hand. "Thanks for trusting me enough to tell me what happened."

"It means a lot to have someone I trust. I'll look for a way to handle this." They hugged. "See you later." She walked out the door to her car.

He watched her through the window, hands in his pockets. She needed someone to help her no matter what she said. He wished she hadn't gone home to Frank. It was the very last place he wanted her to go.

PART TWO
CUTTING A DEAL

CHAPTER FOURTEEN

"**H**urry up, Annie," Frank cupped his hand and called to her. "We have to be downtown by 4:00." It was the first Friday after Thanksgiving, and the annual Paradise Hills Holiday Lights Spectacular was today. All the businesses in town and most of the homes were participating, vying for the best set of lighted Christmas decorations in their category.

Annie walked in from the kitchen.

"There's my girl," Frank said.

"Ready when you are."

"Good, let's go, let's go."

Frank looked forward to this festive event. It was especially important this year. "You look gorgeous," he said, approving. "Just right for the mayor's wife." As the mayor, Frank was proud to be offering opening remarks and initiating the crowd countdown.

"Will you zip me up, please?"

"You bet," he said, touching her shoulder. "Did I tell you Don Little's coming today?"

"Don's coming? Has he been to our Paradise Hills Holiday Spectacular before?"

"Nope, first time. He's coming to support my eventual run for the House."

"You haven't been mayor five months yet, Frank."

"Got to be thinking ahead." Frank lamented the fact that Annie understood so little when it came to politics.

"Just so we're clear, if you win, I'm not moving to Austin."

"No one asked you to. I'll get paid a per diem when the legislature is in session, which I'll use for a hotel, if we run late into the night." *Of course, we'll move to Austin but that's a battle for another day.* "Since we get so many constituents from out of town, Don will assist me with the glad handing.

"The glad handing?"

Frank smiled smugly and said, "Glad handing means we use every free minute to shake hands warmly with our loyal supporters—emphasis on the word 'warmly,' whether we like them or don't. I can tell you no one's better at it than my friend Don."

"I know what glad-handing means, Frank, and I find the whole thing disingenuous."

"Politics is a game, Darlin, and everyone plays it. You'll just have to trust me on that one."

Annie collected her gloves from the table.

By the time they reached town, the clouds had cleared, and the day was cool. "Perfect day for an outdoor venue," Frank said. "Let's start at the co-op, since they won the prize for best lights last year."

When they walked through the door, Frank strolled up to the owner. "Wayne, good to see you."

"Hey, Mr. Mayor," he said shaking his hand. "And Mrs. Mayor."

"Hi, Wayne, how are you? And how's Becky?" Annie asked.

"She's in back, so I'll let her tell you herself," Wayne said walking around the corner. "Becky, Frank and Annie are here."

"Hey, Annie," Becky said, closing the books and walking out of the office. "Nice red plaid coat, and is that a new necklace?"

"Thanks, yes, it is."

"It matches your eyes. Are you all set to introduce Mr. and Mrs. Claus?"

"Oh, yes. I love watching the kids' eyes light up when Santa pops onto the stage."

"Me too. And how are you, Frank?" Becky asked.

"Looking forward to the festivities. Is it possible you have even more lights strung up outside than last year?"

"We do," Wayne said. "Ted's Mercantile is hoping to take this year's prize away from us."

"Well, you can't let that happen," Frank said, smiling and shaking Wayne's hand again. "I hate to drop in and run, but we'll see you at the park."

"We'll be there with bells on—literally," Wayne said laughing.

Frank laughed and clapped him on the back.

The power couple's next stop was Ted's Mercantile. When they walked in, Frank said, "Hmm, Smells like peppermint in here, Ted."

"Hey, Mr. Mayor, welcome. You too, Annie."

Frank and Ted shook hands. "Can I offer you some hot apple cider?" Ted asked.

"We'd love some, wouldn't we Annie?" Frank asked, not waiting for a reply.

Annie took a sip of hot cider. "I can taste the cinnamon spice; this is so good. Thank you."

"Impressive array of lights you have outside," Frank said.

"My plan is to take the lighting prize away from Wayne's co-op."

"I'm pulling for you," Frank said, draining his cup of cider and taking Annie's half empty cup from her. While he'd expressed the same support for Wayne, he could care less who won the prize. "We should get over to the park, see you there at 5:30?"

"Wouldn't miss it."

A block off Main Street, the City Park was stuffed with trees just waiting to be lit. The Paradise High School band had set up next to the cupola, and they were playing a variety of holiday tunes. "Band sounds good," Annie said. "Let's go over and say hi to the kids in my Sunday School class."

"They're too young to vote, Annie, it's a waste of my time."

"I'm going to see them."

"You say hi, and in the meantime, I'll stop by the Paradise Hills Garden display. Meet you there," he said walking off.

When Frank reached the display, their neighbor Teresa, who was president of the Ladies Garden Club, was working with her crew setting out hand-crafted ornaments, gifts, and decorations. "Hey, Mr. Mayor," she said as Frank approached.

"Hey, yourself. The display looks great."

"The ladies have worked extra hard all year long making these ornaments."

"And it shows. Thank you for using the proceeds from your sales to support our holiday celebration."

"As always, it's our pleasure. We look forward every year to the Spectacular."

Annie walked up. "Teresa, the ornaments are lovely, such vibrant purple and blue colors, along with the red and green."

"Thanks, Annie, I'm hoping you'll join us as a member of the Garden Club in the upcoming year."

"You're going to, right Darlin?" Frank asked, pulling her next to him.

"That's the plan."

"Annie, I see Don's arrived," Frank said. "Why don't you stay here and chat with Teresa, and I'll go let him know where we are."

Frank stepped across the lawn to meet Don.

"Hey, man, good to see you," Don said, offering his hand. "This is quite the operation."

"Yes, it is," Frank said, returning his grip. "Paradise Hills will not be outdone at Christmas."

"You're telling me. When I drove through downtown, it looked like the whole block of old oaks were strung with thousands of lights.

"There're more than two million lights if you include the courthouse. They're brilliant against the night sky when they're all turned on, which they will be, at 6:30 pm on the nose."

"That sounds expensive."

"All the money comes from donations."

"Don't forget to mention that tonight, for the out-of-towners, when you give your speech."

"Good call will do. Annie's waiting for us over there," Frank said, nodding in the direction of the Garden Club display. "Let's go collect her."

Everyone gathered at the cupola, waiting for the lighting. A local choir was singing, 'Joy to the World.'

He walked to the microphone, said a few words, and then introduced Don Little. "I've invited my friend and distinguished member of the Texas State Legislature to help us celebrate today," Frank said. Don stood and waved amid the sounds of hearty applause from the crowd.

"And now, the moment you've all been waiting for," Frank said, "The ceremonial lighting. Ready for the count down?" The crowd counted down with him. "5, 4, 3, 2, 1," and then switches all over town and in the park were thrown, just as the town hall clock struck 6:30 pm. The whole town lit up like magic, the lights blinding.

"Truly spectacular," Don breathed, as the band played, 'We wish you a Merry Christmas.' Annie introduced Mr. and Mrs. Claus, and Frank and Don walked through the mob and shook hands. Then Frank suggested grabbing a bite to eat at the Chuckwagon. "Are you good with chili cheese fries, corn on the cob and brisket?" He asked Don.

"Why not, have you got funnel cakes?"

"Of course."

After they ate, they all boarded a horse-drawn carriage, and passed through colored lights woven through tree branches and wrapped around trunks. The Courthouse was edged in white lights, beginning at the top of the dome, spilling into light lattices down the sides. The whole town twinkled.

"Do you have time to ride over and see Songbird Community Church's Nativity before you go?" Frank asked. "Their pageant is almost forty years old, and it's a big attraction on the Hill Country Regional Christmas Lighting Trail."

Don checked his watch. "I might need to pass on that one. I should get back to Austin, but you go on ahead. It's been great seeing you both."

"We appreciate you coming."

"Frank's a lucky man, Annie," he said turning to her. "You're the perfect wife for a politician; well-connected, well-spoken, supportive—and beautiful, if you don't mind me adding."

"Thanks," Frank said speaking on her behalf. "I know how fortunate I am to have this woman by my side." He slid his arm around her shoulder.

After Don left, Annie pulled away. "You know, Frank, it's just like Don said. You need me to get elected to the House next November."

"Don't let it go to your head," he snorted, mood shifting.

"Oh, but I am."

"What ARE you talking about?"

"We both know what you need from me. Now let's talk about what I need from you."

Frank laughed. "Ours is not a quid pro quo relationship."

"Remind me again what that means in legal terms."

"'Quid pro quo' means that something is given or received in exchange for something else. Under the law, it's often viewed as a bribe."

"That's exactly what I'm talking about, Frank. I'm offering you a bribe. And here it is: You treat me the way I deserve to be treated. With respect. No following my every move, no abuse in bed, no shouting. And never, EVER will you hit me again."

He started to say something, and she put her hand up. "I'm not finished. This is what I'm offering in return. You treat me the way I told you, and I'll be the involved, dutiful wife supporting your next election. I'll smile, shake hands, and be by your side. You know you need me and the Kingman name to win."

The air grew sticky and still. "All right," he said in disbelief, taking a step back. "You give me what I want, and you'll get what you want. Bribe accepted." They shook on it. *She doesn't know this offer holds only until after I win the election.*

CHAPTER FIFTEEN

*I*t was Christmas Eve, and Annie was oh, so happy to be at the ranch. She sighed. *Yes, I'll have to spend tomorrow with Frank. But Christmas Eve is reserved for my family. The one time he joined us, he complained we overdid the 'night before Christmas.' Glad he isn't here to ruin the mood…*

Caroline had flown in from Dallas, and Pastor Mark and Cindy would arrive soon. They'd joined the family to celebrate Christmas Eve for as long as Annie and Caroline could remember.

Gabriela had knitted six new Christmas stockings, red with white lace at the top and arranged them neatly along the mantle. A tall green pine, glowing with lights, stood in the corner of the room. Underneath the tree lay one small present for each of them to open after dinner.

Caroline and Annie had cooked the traditional Christmas Eve dinner that their daddy loved. He walked into the kitchen as they finished, his mouth watering at the roast turkey with dressing, mashed potatoes with giblet gravy, and sweet potato casserole.

Mark offered the blessing. "Lord, thank you for this food. We are grateful to be together tonight. Amen." Then they ate, relishing every bite. "

"Please pass the string beans and venison sausage," Caroline said.

"Here you go, sis," Annie said, mouth full of food.

"Thanks." Then whispering to Annie, said, "I really miss Ben," Caroline took care that Daddy wouldn't hear. He made a big effort every year for his daughters to be happy at Christmas.

After dinner, they moved into the parlor, taking their places to listen to Cindy read Charles Dickens' *A Christmas Carol.* By reading selected passages, she'd managed to time her oration over the past few years to just over an hour. Cindy smiled and began with the words: "Marley was dead." They listened to the tale with rapt attention as if they'd never heard it before.

After reading both the beginning and thick middle of the story, with the appropriate level of drama and wild hand gestures, Cindy reached the ending:

"Scrooge was better than his word. He did it all, and infinitely more; and to Tiny Tim, who did not die, he was a second father. He became as good a friend, as good a master, and as good a man, as the good old city knew, or any other good old city, town, or borough, in the good old world. Some people laughed to see the alteration in

him, but he let them laugh, and little heeded them; for he was wise enough to know that nothing ever happened on this globe, for good, at which some people did not have their fill of laughter in the outset; and knowing that such as these would be blind anyway, he thought it quite as well that they should wrinkle up their eyes in grins, as have the malady in less attractive forms. His own heart laughed: and that was quite enough for him. And it was always said of him, that he knew how to keep Christmas well, if any man alive possessed the knowledge. May that be truly said of us, and all of us! And so, as Tiny Tim observed...”

Cindy paused and looked at Annie, “God bless us, everyone!” Annie said. Then they all clapped for Cindy. Annie had always loved the story of Scrooge’s redemption. She knew more than one person in their congregation who had turned their lives around. *Is it possible that Frank could change someday?* She wondered. Then shook her head. *I doubt even three ghosts could make him believe he needs to change.*

“Please go to the piano, Caroline,” Daddy said. “Let’s sing your mama’s favorite carol of the season.” She sat down, they gathered around, and held hands, singing, ‘I’ll be Home for Christmas.’ *I can feel her here with us.*

Then Pastor Mark read from the Book of Luke. “And there were in the same country, shepherds abiding in the field, keeping watch over their flock by night. And lo, the angel of the Lord came upon them, and the glory of the Lord shone round about them. And suddenly there was with the angel a multitude of the heavenly host, praising God, saying glory to God on the highest, and on earth, peace, good will toward men." Mark closed his Bible.

Cindy held her husband's hand and said, "May we all find the peace the season brings. Thank you, Kingman family, for making us part of your family. As the Muppets like to say," she grinned, "Wherever we find love it feels like Christmas. My heart is grateful for each of you."

Pastor Mark said. "We miss those who are not with us. But we'll see them again one day."

Annie said, "We love the love Ben and Mama left behind for us."

"That's beautiful," Cindy said. "May they sleep in heavenly peace."

Daddy put his head down for a moment. Then looked up and said, "Time to open a present." Annie took his hand, and they sat next to the tree. The others joined them.

The gift opening tradition began with the youngest, Annie, and would wind up the line to Daddy, the oldest at 68. But not by much. Annie's eyes sparkled when she found a beautiful teal sweater inside her gaily wrapped package. Caroline was next, happy with a new pair of tan winter boots. Then it was Gabriela's turn.

"A very merry Christmas, Gabriela," Annie said, walking across the room, giving her a hug. "And thank you for the lovely Christmas stockings. They are a treasure."

"You're welcome. *Feliz Navidad.*" Gabriela said, opening the box to discover a fluffy new pink and white blanket.

"*Feliz Navidad.*" They all chorused.

Then Cindy and Mark opened their gift and found a white-marble nativity scene that Caroline had made from a mold. "This is lovely," Cindy said. Thank you."

"Best gift ever," Mark said.

Daddy opened his gift. Divinity filled with pecans. It was his favorite, and he immediately chewed a candy or two. Then took a deep breath. Annie looked closely at him, detecting a look of exhaustion in his eyes. Mark and Cindy must have noticed it too. They stood up and said, "It's time for us to say good night. Thank you for another wonderful Christmas Eve."

"Guess I better go too," Annie said, hugging everyone. She walked outside, slid into her car, and drove slowly home to Frank.

CHAPTER SIXTEEN

*K*ent had never owned a gun. He'd never wanted to. He didn't really want anyone else to own one either, at least not automatic weapons. That was before he moved to Texas. Now, life was complicated, and he saw things differently. He noticed that most Texans owned guns. Even demure little church ladies had concealed weapons permits and packed heat in their handbags. He decided it was time to buy a gun. When in Rome, he thought. *What a way to ring in the New Year.*

He wasn't sure what kind of gun to get, but he knew his Uncle Byron had carried a Colt 1911 in the Vietnam War. Yep, that's the weapon he wanted. He did a little research and found that the compact ones were popular concealed weapons with their slim width and powerful .45 cartridges.

The only gun he'd ever shot was a .22, but he could learn. There was no shortage of shooting ranges around, and Dustin had told him that there was a guy at Songbird

Community who taught a concealed weapons class. Kent called him and signed up, then looked around for a gun shop in San Antonio. After work, he stopped by one near to the Alamo, which seemed fitting somehow.

A small buzzer rang as he pushed open the door. He'd never seen so many guns in one place. The man behind the counter looked up. He had short black hair, a black short-cropped beard to match, and he wore black cowboy boots with painted red roses winding across the toes and up the sides.

"What can I do for you?" He squinted at Kent, who was still dressed in a suit and tie.

"I'm looking for a Colt 1911, you got any?"

"Yup, you ever owned one?"

"Nope."

"Gold standard in semi-automatic handguns, excellent choice. Ever fired one?"

"Does it matter?"

"Not particularly, so how much you want to spend?"

"For the right gun, I might go as high as $1300."

"Got just the thing here. Factory/semi-custom and the best personal defensive firearm ever made," he said, handing him the gun.

"What's so special about this one?"

"Stainless steel with a cured finish, which is more expensive but won't corrode. Single stack holds eight rounds, and the beavertail grip lets you hold the gun deeper into the web of your hand. Prevents hammer bite."

He'd never heard of hammer bite, but he could guess. He turned the gun over in his hand, inspecting it. "Does it have night sights?"

"Yup, and a safety on both sides."

"How much?"

"1200 dollars. Has a custom high-quality magazine and comes with a lifetime warranty."

"I'll need an inside shoulder holster, too."

"Got one right here, along with a box of .45 cartridges," he said. "You'll need those."

"I'll take 2 boxes to start," Kent said, pulling out his wallet.

Five minutes later, he walked out of the store a new handgun owner, just like that.

A week later, he had his concealed weapons permit, and then he completed the obligatory first-time finger-printing process. The next Saturday, he practiced target shooting at a range in Austin, far enough away that he wouldn't run into anyone who knew him.

He decided he was ready to try the Lone Star Range and Gun Club, a few miles outside Paradise Hills. Dustin told him several of the men from church belonged to the club. It was tradition to spend the first Saturday of every month clay shooting, skeet shooting, or firearms target practicing. He counted on running into Frank today.

As he neared the club, he saw a large sign over the front door that read: "Established in 1982 to provide

Firearms Training so that YOU can exercise YOUR 2nd Ammendment Rights. Kent noticed that the word amendment had been misspelled. He smiled, walked up the ramp and through the wooden door, sporting his new brown, right-handed shooting vest and his polycarbonate shooting glasses.

When he made his way inside, he spotted Frank over in the showroom. He walked up to him and said hello.

"Howdy," Frank said, looking surprised. "What's a California boy like you doin' here?"

"Same as you, target practice."

"You're punchin' way above your weight here, Winder. I tell you what, why don't we see if you know how to use that shiny new gun," he said, tightening his jaw. "Let's go shoot some targets."

"Right behind you."

"I reckon you don't have a lick of sense, do you, boy?" He turned on him. "That why you couldn't save your own wife?"

Kent's face blazed in anger. "You don't know what the hell you're talking about. Who told you about Sally?"

"Who do you think?"

"Annie?"

"You said it, not me, pardner."

"Leave Sally out of it." He said, face red.

"Easy there. Looks like I hit a sore spot."

"Watch yourself, douche bag." *Why would Annie share anything about my personal life with Frank?*

"Nobody talks to me like that, peckerwood." Frank reached over and shoved Kent, who shoved him right back. Frank threw a punch in his face, and Kent ducked to the side.

"Is that the only way you know how to settle things? Hitting people in the face?" Then Kent grabbed him by his vest, pulled him close, and said, "If you ever hit her again, I'll kill you myself with my bare hands."

Frank pulled away and looked surprised. "Her, who's her? I'd never hit a woman."

"Oh, really?"

"If you ever repeat that little falsehood, I'll sue you for slander."

"Bring it on."

"Whoa there, gents." Dustin walked up and stepped between the two of them. "I tell you what, let's take it outside?"

"You take HIM outside," Frank yelled. "I'm going to go shoot myself some pigeons." Then turning to Kent, he said, "I'm warning you to stay out of my business. You have no idea who you're messin' with." Then he tipped his cowboy hat to Kent and Dustin, "Good-bye, ladies," he said, walking away.

"What was that about?" Dustin asked.

"It's personal."

He shrugged. "I see you decided to become a gun owner. Somehow doesn't fit you."

"When in Texas."

"You got yourself some expensive hardware there. Is that a Colt 1911?"

"Yes."

"Want to get in some target practice?"

"Not right now, think I'll head home. Catch up with you later."

"Okay, buddy, and when it comes to Frank, my advice is to keep your saddle oiled and your gun greased."

It was raining hard when Kent got home and spotted a few water moccasins slithering through a puddle out by his back fence. He hated snakes. He went inside, lit a fire, pulled on thick wool socks, and heated a big pot of chili. Today did not go as planned.

As he was dug into his chili, he heard someone knocking on his front door. Now what? When he peered through his curtains, he saw Annie. He opened the door.

She walked inside. "Why did you tell Frank I told you about the slap? He's so mad."

Kent froze. "I'm sorry he's mad. But I hope he'll think twice about hitting you. I threatened him."

"So, you bought yourself a gun?"

"I did, yes, Colt 1911."

"Why a handgun?"

"To protect you from Frank. I wanted to make sure he knew he couldn't hit you. When I confronted him, he denied it."

"So, he told me—right before shaking his fist at me."

"I didn't mean to put you in danger. Let's go after him, legally, please. I'm trying to help."

"I know," she said, reaching up and touching his face. "And I appreciate that, I really do. But I told you I'd take care of it. And I did."

"Are you sure?"

"Yes."

"How?"

"I offered Frank a bargain. If he wants my help with his campaign, he must treat me right. I'm lucky to have leverage. Most women don't."

Kent nodded. "Smart move. Listen, I crossed a boundary, and I'm sorry. I'll do better next time. But promise you'll still be careful?"

"I will," she said, kissing his cheek.

"Something else. Why did you tell him about Sally? I thought that was between us."

Annie looked surprised. "I promise I didn't tell him anything about her. Hmmm. Did you tell anyone else around here?"

"No one. Only you."

"I'm afraid there is one other possibility. He might be having you investigated."

"What? He'd do that?"

"He has his own PI, Joe Coykendall. Frank uses him for court cases, and yes, he'd do that."

"Really?

"I'm sorry I got you mixed up in this, Kent. It's getting out of hand, and now you've been hurt. That's the last thing I wanted." She looked down. "Let's forget you and I ever, almost, happened."

"Too late for that. I'm in this for the long haul, as they say in Texas." He reached over and stroked her hair.

Pressing her hand to his cheek, she said, "It's like we're breathing the same air."

"I'm just sorry you're married."

"Not half as sorry as I am." She drew her finger across his lips.

"Maybe someday."

"Someday," she repeated. "I'll leave him. —Now, I hate running off, especially with that nice fire going in the fireplace. But I should go." She opened the door and disappeared into the night.

Kent put his loaded pistol on the closet shelf and reheated his chili. He could still smell the scent of her perfume on his shirt. He sat on the couch. *What if she never leaves Frank? What if I lose her too?* He closed his eyes.—*Don't do this to yourself. It's not going to happen. She'll leave him.*

CHAPTER SEVENTEEN

*F*rank searched the closet for his cufflinks. "Annie," he called from the bedroom. No answer, so he stepped into the hall. "Annie, can you hear me?"

"I can now, what do you need?"

"I can't find my albino squirrel cufflinks, where'd you put them?"

Annie walked up the stairs. "I didn't put them anywhere," she said. "Are you going to Austin again today?"

"Yes, and I need those cufflinks on me."

"I know, I know, they're your good luck charm, along with half the students who went to the University of Texas at Austin. –If you see an albino squirrel on your way to an exam, you're guaranteed an A."

"Exactly," he smiled. "It's too bad you're not coming with me, since you're my other good luck charm." He winked.

"Here are the cufflinks, right where you left them last, on the top of your dresser."

"That can't be, you know I always put my stuff away."

"Not when you come home drunk."

"Which doesn't happen often," he growled. Then he cussed again.

"Are you meeting with a client today?"

"No, Don Little," he said, tying his tie.

"Ah, yes. Don."

"As you know, he's my connection to the State House of Representatives, and an old frat buddy."

"Well, tell him hi again from me."

"I will."

"Here, let me put those on for you."

"Thanks, they're solid sterling silver, you know."

"Yes, I do," she sighed. "You're all set, so just keep calm and look for the albino squirrel."

He laughed. "See you tonight, and don't wait up for me."

Frank got in his car and headed for I-35, anxious to reach Austin. He loved the city and wanted to spend more time there. Oh, how he hated the forgettable town of Paradise Hills. He wanted Annie to be part of a 'white glove society,' not ride horses.

Once he was elected to the House, there were no term limits. Course the pay sucked at $7,200 a year plus a per diem, and the legislature was in session less than six months. Frank still couldn't believe a state the size of Texas still had a legislature that didn't meet annually; such a throwback to the 1800's. But despite the low pay, the pension benefits were sweet. He smiled. *Anyway, politics isn't about the money, it's about power. Don Little's the guy who can help me realize my dreams.*

Frank drove through downtown Austin to South Congress Avenue. He and Don were meeting for lunch at the Magnolia Café, where they used to eat regularly when they attended UT. Frank appreciated the constantly changing menus, and the place was funky and fun. Austin had a lively and ever evolving downtown and wasn't just a town full of hicks out in the Hill Country.

When he walked into the café, Don was waiting. "Got us a table."

Frank followed Don outside, picking up a menu.

"What are you going to have?"

"Pork dumplings."

"You?"

"Steak and eggs for me," Don said, putting his menu down. "Say, how about our Longhorns going to the Sugar Bowl and winning! Could not believe it. Bout time, right?"

"Sure was. Heard a guy on the local news say, "We sure put some sugar on them horns.""

Don laughed. "I like it. How did you like the seats I got you to the game."

"Are you kidding? They were awesome. Annie and I loved that game. I'll never forget January 1, 2019."

"It was a big moment for the old alma mater. I was sitting with the frat brothers, so it was just us guys, which is how I like my football."

Frank bumped fists with Don, and they repeated in unison, "On this day, you will conquer."

"Speaking of the brothers, did you hear the latest on our former congressman?"

"No, what's the word?"

"Federal jury in Houston found him guilty of tax fraud. He used hundreds of thousands of dollars in campaign monies for his own personal use. Solicited more than $1 million in donations, based on false pretenses, so says the U.S. Attorney's office."

"That's bad, felony charges, right?"

"Twenty of them, to be exact, including money laundering and tax fraud."

"Tax fraud?" Frank asked, learning forward, his voice low.

"Yep. He's looking at up to twenty years in prison. Two of his staffers ratted him out and pleaded guilty."

Frank let out a low whistle. "That's tough, man."

"For sure, either don't do it, or don't get caught, I always say."

Frank nodded. "You got that right. Tax evasion too?" he asked, hands clammy.

"Kept some of his income unreported and off the books, couple million, I hear."

"Wow, who does that stuff?" Frank asked, thinking about gambling winnings he hadn't reported to the IRS. The tendons in his neck stood out and pulsed.

"Not you and me, buddy, that's for sure. We need to get you elected to the Legislature when your term as mayor is up, so we can convince the House to meet every year, and not every other year."

Frank licked his lips and took a gulp of water, beads of sweat on his forehead. "Right, right, nothing I want more."

"You okay, man?"

"Yeah, yeah, of course, can't wait to spend more time here in the city."

"Country life getting you down?" He laughed.

"You know it."

"After you get elected, you'll either have to take on a partner in your law firm or open a new firm here in Austin."

"Or do both."

"That's the ticket, think big."

"Annie sends her love."

"Send some right back from me," Don said, taking the last big bite of rare steak, juicy blood rolling off his chin.

"I don't think I told you she's been helping kids, doing horse therapy."

"That's brilliant, your idea."

"No, hers, but I gave my approval."

"Good call. That'll impress your constituents."

"Absolutely."

"Well, I should get back to work, so let's get our bill. Waiter," he snapped his fingers.

After they left the café, Frank checked his watch. He wasn't meeting Kelly until later, so he decided to take a drive out to Lady Bird Lake and relive a few good memories of all night keggers. He drove through the East Riverside neighborhood and parked where he could get a view of both the lake and the downtown skyline.

This was the place Frank wanted to raise his family after he was elected to the House. Now if Annie would just get pregnant. What's her deal? He wondered. Whatever it was, they needed to get her fixed and pronto. Frank wanted a male heir or two.

CHAPTER EIGHTEEN

*I*t was a mild day in February with a cold bite in the air when Annie left the house for Stone Oak. After five months of working at the Equine Therapy Center, today would be her first day alone with a client. She walked into the building and blew on her hands to warm them.

Mary was waiting at the front desk. "Good morning. Thanks for being early."

"Of course."

"Big day."

"Yes, it is." Annie's stomach fluttered.

"How are you feeling?"

"I'm excited, and nervous."

Mary hugged her. "Perfectly normal."

Annie relaxed and smiled.

"Let's go into my office and chat for a bit, and I'll give you a little background on the boy you'll be riding with today."

"Okay."

Mary pulled a file from her cabinet. "Tony's been with us a month now. Nice kid. Sixteen years old and locked up as tight as a drum. Lost his mother in a sailing accident when he was twelve."

Annie winced. "Must have been so hard for him."

"Chad's been working with Tony with not much progress."

"He has more experience than I do, so why me?"

She paused. "You lost your mom at an early age too."

"I'll give it a go," she said, in a flat voice. Her body felt cold.

Mary placed her hand on Annie's. "Thank you. We'll talk when you get back. Chad should be outside helping Tony saddle both horses."

"Hey, Annie," Chad said when she reached the corral. "Meet Tony."

Tony shuffled over to say hello. He was tall, thin, and his hair was all tangled up.

"Hi Tony, nice to meet you."

"Yeah, Thanks." His chin trembled.

"You ready to ride?"

"Sure, why not," he shrugged.

The two of them rode for a while and talked mostly about his school. Annie told him a joke the kids in church had shared with her. Tony laughed and relaxed a little.

A little later his voice broke. "Chad probably told you my mom died."

"I do know that, yes, and I'm so sorry. It's tough to lose your mom; mine died too when I was twelve."

Tony pulled his horse to a halt and looked at her. "She did. What happened?"

"Cancer took her."

He looked down at his hands. "Least it wasn't your fault." He looked away from her.

"Let's dismount and let the horses graze. We'll park ourselves on that rock."

As they sat, tears ran down Tony's cheeks. "I watched my mom drown."

Annie put her arm around his shoulder and listened.

"It was only the two of us that day. She was teaching me how to sail, when we hit a gust of wind that came out of nowhere. I tried to luff the sails, but the boat capsized. My mom got hit in the head with the mast." Tony wailed. "Docs couldn't save her," "I'm such an idiot," he said, hitting himself in the head with his fist, cheeks red.

"Tony," Annie touched his arm, "I know you loved your mom and I get your guilt. But it was an accident."

"I was sailing the boat, so it's my fault." He stuttered, biting his lip.

"It could have happened to anyone, even an experienced sailor."

He wiped tears on his shirt sleeve and shuddered.

"I won't say you'll stop feeling bad about what happened Tony. But please know it's not your fault."

He hung his head, muttering to himself, a haunted look on his face.

"If your mom were still here, what do you think she'd want for you?" Annie asked in a soft voice.

He brooded for a few minutes, then looked up. "She'd want me to have friends, go to school, and go to church.

"I think you're right about that. Please know that God cares about you too, and so do I."

Tony threw his arms around her, and Annie held him while he cried. He pulled back a few minutes later, embarrassed.

He was doing better by the time they rode back to the center. Annie debriefed with Mary, who was pleased with Tony's progress. "You did well today, Thank you."

Annie had loved making a difference in Tony's life and wanted to continue practicing horse therapy. As she rode away, she tilted her head to the side. *But my deep-down dream is to run the ranch. I grew up working in agriculture, and being a cowgirl is in my blood. Daddy doesn't think running the ranch is 'women's work.' But those old ways and those old days are gone. When he can't do it anymore, I want to take over. It's a big, big responsibility, and I'm not ready yet. But one day, I will be. She set her jaw.*

CHAPTER NINETEEN

Kent looked out the window of his office on the tenth floor and watched cars whizz down the freeway. The clock in his office chimed ten. Lynne Leavitt was flying in today from California to review what they thought might be a suspicious death. His admin knocked on the door and let him know she was waiting in the conference room.

"Hey, Lynne," Kent said, offering his hand, as he walked through the glass doors. She had her long reddish hair tied up in a bun, piercing blue eyes smiling under shaped, brown brows. She wore her usual black pantsuit and white blouse with a large collar.

"It's been a while." She said, shaking his hand.

"Yes, it has, my friend." Lynne was direct, opinionated, and one of the best independent insurance investigators in the country. Seeing her in San Antonio was out of context for Kent. He was more accustomed to late night business dinners with her in LA. They'd gone to college together, and she now owned her own agency. Her work included financial crimes investigation and violent crime investigations.

"Let's meet in my office, more private there," Kent said. "This way."

Lynne followed him down the hall. "Nice corner office," she said when they arrived.

"Thanks, I like it. Can I get you something to drink?"

"Diet Coke, if you got it."

"Fridge is well stocked, so let me check. One left, and it's yours." Kent handed her the can along with a cup of ice.

"How do you like Texas? Big change from California."

"It is, and that's what I like about it; seemed like a place where I could get grounded. I rented a little ranch house on a few acres out in the Hill Country."

"It's a little hard picturing you living the country life, but good to know you're doing well."

"Getting there, and you?"

"Couldn't be better, at least, work wise. I've been busy. I don't have much time for a personal life right now, but maybe someday. You ready to review the new case?"

"Yes, let's start from the beginning."

Lynne opened her briefcase and pulled out a sheaf of papers. "Guy's name is Charles Crawley, and this is his version of the story in a nutshell. Several months ago, he and the missus planned a three-week trip to New Zealand to celebrate their tenth anniversary. The day they were leaving for the airport, Crawley was out loading luggage in the car, while she was in the house packing a few last-minutes items in her carry on.

The neighbor saw him, waved, and told him to have a good trip. Crawley thanked him and said he'd touch base when they got back. Then, he walked inside to get the rest of the bags. He claimed he couldn't find his wife, although her bag sat open on the bed. He insisted that he called her name several times with no answer. Then, he alleged that he spotted her sprawled at the bottom of their basement floor and rushed down the steps. He said she was already dead and that her neck appeared broken. The coroner later said that. she died on impact."

"Tragic end for her, and tragic, for him. If it was an accident."

"Exactly. Cops hauled him in for questioning and grilled him for hours. They say he was devastated."

"Have you talked to him?"

"Went by his office this morning before I came here, and his story matches the police report.

"What do you make of him?"

"Not sure. He seemed anxious to get the insurance investigation wrapped up. I want to check to see if there's another woman." Lynne reached over and picked a small piece of lint off her jacket. She was a meticulous dresser.

"Good call to investigate an affair. Any kids?"

"No, she didn't want them. He did. The guy was a devout Catholic and still believed divorce was forbidden."

"That's a tough one, and it may be a potential motive."

"He says he always wanted a big family and was torn in two over not being able to have children, so he was open about that. But he stated emphatically that he loved his wife and would never hurt her. Neighbors saw him as a loving husband and solid church goer."

"How much is the policy?"

"Three million."

"Sizable chunk of change, was it a new policy?"

"Nope, had it seven years."

"But the guy makes you suspicious?"

"Yes, but I was born suspicious," Lynne laughed.

Kent laughed too. "One of the reasons you're good at what you do. Did you visit the scene?"

"Yes, I dropped by the house, and the cops let me in."

"Any evidence she was shoved down the steps?"

"No direct evidence of foul play, at least not yet. Coroner ruled it an accidental death, but Crawley's got friends in high places. He's the VP of a Pharma company and well connected in Texas politically, so it's worth digging deeper."

"I agree, please check it out and let me know."

"I'll do some more snooping around and get back to you."

"How long will it take?"

"Give me ten days, and then I'll call you with an update."

"Sounds good. Do you have time for dinner?"

"I'm in and out this trip, but how about next time I'm in town?"

"Let's do it."

"You seem distracted today, Kent. Everything okay?"

"Been thinking a lot about Sally—it was two years yesterday."

"Sally was a special lady. I can't say I know what you're going through. I do know it can't be easy."

"It's not. But I've made it this far."

"And that's saying something."

"I still ask myself, why didn't I know she was having trouble with the pregnancy?"

"I don't think you ever told me how she died, just that she did after losing a baby."

Kent took a deep breath. "Sally was having headaches, which was normal for her. Blood pressure was running a little high but wasn't out of range. I took her in to the hospital for a checkup, and they said it was eclampsia and admitted her. I spent the night, and the next day, she miscarried the baby. A day later she had a grand mal seizure and lapsed into a coma."

"Geez. I'm so sorry. I can only guess how painful that was."

"She died the next day," he shivered. "Sorry. I didn't mean to go off on a rant."

"It's okay, I asked. Listen, you can't blame yourself for Sally's death when trained medical professionals missed the symptoms."

He nodded, swallowing with difficulty. "Enough about me, what about you?"

"Did I mention my ex remarried a few months ago?"

"Didn't know that."

"Yep, no chance to get back into that relationship, even if I wanted to, which I don't," she added with a shrug.

"You'll find someone else."

"If I do, fine, if I don't, fine. Are you seeing anyone here?"

"Sort of."

"Sounds mysterious."

"It's complicated."

"Cards on the table? Stay out of trouble."

"That's the plan."

"That's always the plan. It's the execution where stuff tends to go wonky," Lynne smiled. "I'll be in touch."

"Thanks, be seeing you."

"Don't get up, I'll let myself out."

Kent waved and got back to his paperwork.

A few hours later, he walked across the parking lot to his car, looking forward to the drive home alone. He believed he was starting to get over Sally, but today his feelings were raw.

They'd shared so many good times together. Walks on the beach holding hands, watching the waves roll across their feet, and squishing through the soft sand. He missed the ocean, the clean salt air, and the peace they felt looking over the blue horizon.

Sally always laughed at his jokes, even when they were stupid, and listened to his troubles at work. He exhaled. *Sally will always be with me. But I'm finally finding some peace.*

CHAPTER TWENTY

*F*rank leaned back in his office chair and gazed out the window at the gathering clouds. A huge storm was brewing. And it wasn't the only one. His financial empire was crumbling around him. Even the trust fund from his daddy's inheritance was running low. He ran his hands through his hair and eyed the bills stacked on his desk, noting that several were past due.

It didn't help that Annie was spending his money like there was no tomorrow. Then, he chuckled to himself, because while she was shopping for silly household items, he was spending money on hotel dates with Kelly. He loved his expensive habit, and he had no intention of kicking it, so something else had to go.

He drummed his fingers on the table. What to do? For starters, he'd tell Annie she'd have to cut back. Of course, she didn't know anything about their finances.

If she knew, she'd tell Pete. Seemed she told her father everything. *Well almost everything. He smiled.* Women: you can't live with them; you can't live without the sex.

To make money matters worse, when he picked up the mail yesterday, he found another letter from the IRS. The federal government took far too much of his hard-earned money, and then, there was the state of Texas. Property taxes were high and continuing to rise. The lawmakers liked to say that Texas had high property taxes, because taxpayers didn't pay state income tax. *Hah.* Compared with the other eight "no income tax states," Texas had the highest property taxes by a big margin.

He picked up the letter from the IRS, which he hadn't opened yet, but he could guess the contents. Last year, he hadn't had the money to pay what the government claimed he owed, so he'd set up payment arrangements. Unfortunately, with his legal business off, he'd fallen behind in making payments. Then there was the little matter of the money he hadn't declared in campaign contributions. He'd need to file an amended return to take care of that.

He slit the letter open. IRS was threatening to put a lien on his bank account in Austin to pay the back taxes. He couldn't let that happen. He needed to get to the bank, and fast.

He ran out to his car and was soon on the road. He'd pull the money out of his accounts and stuff it under his mattress if it came to that.

He arrived at the bank, pushed through the double glass doors, and hurried up to the nearest teller. "I want to close my account; I can get better rates elsewhere."

"Let's talk about that," she smiled. "Please sit down, maybe we can work something out to get you better rates."

"No, I've made up my mind, so take it all out. I want it in cash, just give it to me in thousand-dollar bills."

She fired up her computer and her smile faded. There's no money in your account."

"What?! That's not possible. There must be some mistake."

"There's no mistake. The IRS seized all your money this morning."

"They can't do that!"

"Unfortunately, they can, and they did."

Frank stumbled out of the bank, found his way to his car, and sat dumbfounded. They'd taken all $10,000, and he still owed another $10,000. This was crazy.

When he got home, he picked up the phone and called the IRS, wanting to renew the payment arrangements and get them to put the money back in his account. After waiting an hour on hold, he got a voice on the other end. "IRS. How may I help you?"

"You levied my bank account, and my money's gone."

"I'll need your social security number, please."

He gave it to her and slumped down in his chair.

"You're behind in making payments on your back taxes."

"Right, sorry about that, things have been tight lately. What can I do to renew the payment arrangements and get my money back?"

"That depends. I see you haven't filed your taxes for this year, you filed an extension."

"Yes, I'm still working on pulling the paperwork together. It's complicated."

"Will you owe any taxes for this year?"

"Not sure yet, but maybe." Of course, he owed taxes for this year, but now was not the time.

"I can't make new payment arrangements, until I know how much tax you're going to owe this year."

"I'll get back to you." He hung up the phone; this was serious. He could pull money from the trust fund to replace what he'd lost in his bank accounts, but that wasn't a permanent solution. No, he needed a new source of money, and the sooner the better. Maybe he could ask Pete for a loan?

No, while Pete had never come right out and said it, Frank knew Pete didn't have much use for him. He tolerated him; that was about it.

Frank turned in his chair and watched the darkening sky. Then, it came to him. There was one really big thing Pete could do to help with the money problems.

The next day, Frank drove his black SUV through pouring rain to the ranch. The forecasters had been warning for hours of continued heavy rains and almost certain flooding. He wanted to cross the low-lying bridge over the Pedernales River before the bridge washed out.

Annie had been at the ranch for the past twenty-four hours, helping with the spring calving. Most of the 1200 cows had been dropping their calves all day. He figured Annie, Pete, and the ranch hands would be working feverishly to herd as many of the newer calves as possible into the calving barn to prevent them from getting chilled in the windy, wet weather. He expected they'd already lost several.

Annie had called him earlier and told him there was nothing he could do, so he might as well stay as warm and dry as possible in town. Normally, he would have, but today he had special plans for Pete. What with the calving and the flooding, there would be enough activity and confusion at the ranch to present Frank with what he hoped would be the perfect opportunity.

Next to him sat a bottle of Pete's favorite whiskey. In Frank's pocket was a small vial filled with a tablespoon of tincture of aconite root. Half tablespoon of the stuff was enough to kill a man much larger than Pete. Frank knew that the alcoholic extract of the aconite, when mixed with the whiskey, would go unnoticed. There was a reason aconite was hailed as the perfect poison to hide a murder. Superstitious folks called the plant wolf's bane, devil's helmet, or blue rocket. The Greeks had long ago dubbed aconite the queen of poisons.

When he reached the ranch, the lightning was flashing in huge sheets across the sky, and it was beginning to get dark. The sound of the cracking thunder, high winds, and rushing river created a sound like low-flying jets. He heard wood splitting and watched as one of the large pecan trees on the riverbank broke away and toppled into the river. He jumped out of his SUV, wearing his long black raincoat, and made a break for the calving barn, boots sliding on the soggy ground.

When he walked inside the barn, Annie was yanking a plastic disposable rectal sleeve all the way up her arm, and she and Pete were preparing to pull a calf. They had chains tied to both feet of the calf. "Frank don't stand there with your bare face hangin' out," Pete shouted. "Hand me that big bottle of lube."

He handed the lubricant to Pete, who applied it generously. Then Pete and Annie started pulling the calf out with the chains, applying steady pressure. Frank knew they needed to be careful, or they would kill the calf. He hated this kind of thing. He hated everything about the ranch, except for the revenue it generated from cattle sales, which would soon be his.

As the calf's chest emerged, Annie rotated the calf to prevent hip lock. The wet, slick calf finally delivered. "We've got him. We've got him," she said. "Come here, baby." She sat the calf up on its breastbone and tucked its legs underneath. Then she stimulated its breathing by sticking a rigid piece of straw up its nostril. By now, its mother was on her feet and coming over to lick her baby dry. "We got him!" Annie said.

Frank heard more trees snapping and falling into the river. "Enough with the calves," he shouted. "We've got to get to the house."

"You're right," Pete agreed, pulling on a gray rain slicker, and tossing one to Annie. "Storm's getting much worse, and it's cold as a frosted frog out there. Bring those kerosene lanterns along with you, Annie, in case the power goes out."

They ran for the house through the driving rain, and the river continued to rise. Frank figured it would be up over the bridge by now, so they were cut off. He ran on ahead, stopped by his car, and tucked the bottle of whiskey into an inside pocket of his raincoat. When they all reached the house, they were drenched.

Gabriela handed them large towels and a hand-made quilt. She'd laid a fire in the fireplace, and he could smell thick country bacon and eggs frying on the stove. When he glanced at Pete, all he could think about was the old saying, "the condemned ate a hearty meal." He smiled.

They took their plates filled with hot food over by the fire to ride out the storm. Hy came in from the barn and joined them for dinner, as Pete clicked on the 10:00 news. All the local channels were broadcasting the weather. Twenty-four inches of rain in the past twenty-four hours in Blanco County, which was unheard of.

The Newscaster reported that a family of three from out of town had already lost their lives driving across a road flooded with water, not believing the warning sign: Turn around, don't drown. Their car washed away with all of them in it.

Then the power went out, and the screen went black. Pete took matches, lit four lanterns, gave one to each of them, and told them to get some sleep, saying he would watch the river from the upstairs porch. "I'll make sure it doesn't rise too close to the house or bunkhouse," he said. "If it does, I'll wake you."

"Okay, Daddy," Annie said, kissing him on the cheek."

"It's a good thing we're sitting on higher ground," Frank said.

"Some folks won't be as lucky," Pete replied.

While her daddy watched the river from upstairs, Annie fell into bed, looking exhausted. Frank crawled in next to her and waited until he could count several deep and regular breaths. Then, he slipped out of bed and out into the dark hallway, carrying a flashlight with him. He checked his watch, almost midnight, and still raining hard. He uncorked the bottle of whiskey, poured in the aconite tincture, and replaced the cork. He started up the stairs.

He found Pete seated outside in a chair on the covered porch, watching the lightning flash across the night river. "What are you doing up?" Pete asked.

"Couldn't sleep, so I thought I'd keep you company. Brought you a bottle of Jack Daniel's."

"Thanks, right nice of you. Join me?" he asked, taking a glass from the table beside him.

"In a bit, you go ahead. I'll keep an eye on the river."

Pete downed a couple of shots.

That's right, old man, drain your glass.

"Smooth," Pete said. "Thanks."

"My pleasure." Frank waited.

"Funny," Pete said a minute later. "My mouth feels parched, numb, and tingly. What the…my belly and throat are on fire!" he shouted against the din of the storm.

By now Frank guessed Pete could no longer move his legs.

"What have you done?!" He croaked hoarsely.

"Poison. In a minute or two, you'll lose both your sight and your hearing, and you'll start convulsing." He smiled. "You'll feel like your limbs are being flayed. But you'll be clear headed right up to the end. Right before dying from respiratory failure."

Pete tried to rise from his chair, but his legs wouldn't support him.

"In another five minutes you'll be gone. As far as the rest of the world can tell, it will look like a heart attack."

"You're an evil loser, Frank!"

Frank hissed, "No one calls me a loser, old man, but then, you'll be dead soon." *Killing people is fun.*

"You're makin' a mistake," Pete croaked. "You won't get away with this."

Frank laughed. "Sure, I will. No one found out the last time, so why would this time be any different?"

Pete looked dumbstruck as Frank continued, "I'll use Annie's inheritance to pay off my debts and buy us a big place in Austin. You're doing us both a big favor by dying."

There was stark fear in Pete's now dilating eyes. Frank touched the old man's hand, which was cold and clammy; almost over now.

Pete squeaked out the word, "Annie," and then spoke no more.

Frank pulled on gloves, wiped his prints from the bottle, took one of Pete's oxycodone pain pills from his medicine cabinet, and dropped it in the whiskey, just in case. Then, he left the room, closed the door, and went back to bed. When he slipped in beside Annie, she was snoring softly. The rain was beginning to let up. *Money problems solved.* Frank fell into a deep and satisfied sleep.

CHAPTER TWENTY-ONE

*F*rank's heavy snoring woke Annie. She slipped out of bed and stared out the window at the mess. The water had crested by the corner of the fence, and oak and pecan trees were uprooted on both sides of the river. A few mattresses laid on the lawn that had floated out of people's doors, along with one dinged up white washer lying on its side near the barn. She guessed they'd lost several head of cattle, but at least the house was intact. The power was back, and they were all safe.

Time to check on Daddy. She pulled her blue fleece robe from the open closet, then shutting the door behind her, walked into the kitchen to get him a glass of milk and a day-old muffin. She walked up the stairs to his bedroom and knocked softly. "Daddy?" she whispered. No answer. She knocked again and opened the door a crack. *He isn't in his bedroom, and his bed hasn't been slept in. What? I know. The old sweetheart must have fallen asleep on the porch.*

When she walked out onto the porch, she saw him asleep in a chair. "Daddy?" She walked over and touched his shoulder. His face looked pasty and drawn, eyes wide, mouth gaping open. "Daddy, wake up, please, wake up!" Nothing. He felt cold to the touch. A shudder ripped through her body. *He's dead?!* She screamed and dropped the glass of milk. It shattered, sending splatters of milk everywhere. *No, no, no! It can't be!* She shook him again and called his name again. Then tripped to the stairs and shouted, "Frank, Gabriela!"

They ran out of their rooms and up the stairs. When Gabriela saw Pete, she crossed herself. "*Madre de Dios!*" she wailed, collapsing on the floor.

Frank reached over and closed Pete's eyes and mouth. Then took Annie in his arms and held her close. "I am so sorry, baby," he said, stroking her hair. She clutched him and sobbed. Her heart felt as if it would break in her chest. She could scarcely take a breath. "He was fine last night," she said, voice rising.

"The physical exertion and excitement must have been too much for him," Frank said. "I imagine his heart just gave out."

"No, no, no. It can't be. Why didn't I watch the river and let him go to bed?" She cried. "Why didn't I check on him earlier?! I might have saved his life."

"Don't do this to yourself," Frank said. "You're not to blame for his death. He was an old man, and this kind of talk won't bring him back. It'll only torment you. Let me take you downstairs where you can lie down."

"No," she said pulling away. "I want to be with Daddy."

"I'll get Hy and a couple of the men to come in and carry his body downstairs to the parlor. You can sit with him there."

"First Mama, then Ben, and now Daddy," she wailed. "This is not happening." *What's wrong with my life?!*

Gabriela returned with a cup of hot tea. "Drink this *chiquita*," she said, patting Annie's hand. Hy and his ranch hands climbed the stairs, then lifted Pete's body from the chair and carried him to his bedroom. To a man, they had tears in their eyes. "We're here for you, Miss Annie," Hy said, taking her hand between his wrinkled and weathered ones.

Tears ran down her face. "Thank you, Hy." Annie walked downstairs to grab her cell phone. Service had been restored, and she needed to call Caroline and give her the heart-breaking news. Annie's hands shook, and she almost dropped the phone.

Caroline answered immediately. "I've been trying to get through for hours," she said. "I've been so worried. How are you doing? Everyone okay?"

Annie was relieved to hear her sister's voice. She sounds so close she could be in the next room. She gulped, tears running like a river. "It's Daddy," she paused. "It was too much for his heart."

"What?! "Are you calling from the hospital? How's he doing?"

"There's no easy way to say this. He's ddd…dead," she said, pacing back and forth.

"No, no, that can't be! Are you sure? Has a doctor checked him?"

Frank walked into the room and took the phone. "Here, let me talk to her."

Annie glared at him hands clenched.

"Yes, 'fraid it's true. His heart gave out, couldn't believe it, either. Did you say you can be on the first flight here in the morning? We'll pick you up at the airport. Let us know what time your flight arrives." He hung up handing Annie her phone. Then turned to her, and in a soft voice said, "Why don't you go sit with your daddy in his bedroom." He kissed her cheek and left.

Her body felt cold, and her vision blurred. *He pretends to understand my grief. But he has no idea. Does he even care that my daddy is dead?*

She walked slowly back up the stairs and sat by her daddy's side, and held his hand, crying. "It's too soon, Daddy, it's way too soon," she whispered. Her head shook back and forth. *What will I do without you? I love you.* Then bowed her head. "I'm so sorry you died alone. I should have been there for you." She sat still in the silence for the better part of an hour, eyes red and raw. Then she prayed for strength, walked back to her own room, and tried to regain some control of her emotions.

She sat in a chair in the corner, listening to the sound of chain saws cutting up fallen trees. Then peered out the window. While the sun was shining, the lawn was pock marked with water holes, debris strewn everywhere. The swimming pool overflowed with mud and grass.

She watched as several men loaded wreckage into trucks. Hy supervised. Annie heard him tell the men to haul everything away from the house and burn anything that could be burned.

When she looked at her phone again, she found several new texts from Kent, "Heard from Pastor Mark about your dad, so sorry. Please know I'm here for you. Thinking of you and praying for you and your family."

She texted a message back. 'Please keep the prayers coming. I'm a mess. Caroline's flying in tomorrow.'

The next morning, it was the house phone that rang. Annie picked it up. Gary Payne from the Payne funeral home. "I'm sorry to bother you at a time like this, but I need to ask you a question."

"Go ahead," she murmured.

"The County Medical Examiner's office called about an autopsy. I told them your dad seemed to have died in his chair of a heart attack. They wanted to know whether he had a history of heart problems."

"He had atrial fibrillation," she said, "but we were controlling it with medication. Dr. Kendall told us he'd be fine. He was only sixty-eight."

"Not that old in my book," Gary said. "You might want to order an autopsy, but it's up to you. We take care of all the transportation on our end if you decide to go ahead. Then the medical examiner will call with a verbal report in the next few days."

"Okay, thank you, and please go ahead. Caroline and I will come by tomorrow to talk about the funeral."

Annie looked at the clock, 1:30 pm. She planned to pick up Caroline at the airport by herself. No Frank. It was best to take the SUV. Time to get in the shower.

A few hours later, Annie drove across pastures and over bumpy back roads, spotting a few black vultures hunched over, picking at cattle carcasses. When she reached the bridge over the Pedernales, the water was down, and the road passable. Annie turned on the radio. All the news centered around the flood.

The broadcaster reported that some people had up to five feet of water in their homes, their furniture ruined, and several hundred head of cattle lost. He estimated it would take up to 75 years to regrow some of the old Cyprus trees that had been uprooted along the banks of the river. *Life is a wreck, and my daddy is dead.*

She arrived at the San Antonio airport, parked in short term parking, and walked to baggage claim. When she glanced at the flight board, there were several cancellations due to weather. But Caroline's flight from Dallas was on time. Her plane would land soon.

Annie was anxious to see her sister. *She's the only one who can understand how sad I am.*

When Caroline came down the escalator, Annie noticed a weak smile, breaking across her tear-stained, flushed face. Caroline was dressed in her usual tailored blue pantsuit and black boots, a double-breasted black trench coat around her shoulders. When she reached the bottom of the escalator, they fell into each other's arms, and wept, un-phased by the looks of people passing by.

"Come on," Caroline said a few minutes later. "Let's grab my bag and get out of here."

"How long can you stay?"

"I took five bereavement days and two personal days, so with the weekends, almost eleven days."

"Do you want to stay with Frank and me in Paradise Hills?"

"I want to stay out at the ranch. Gabriella can keep me company. Right now, we need a place to talk. Let's get something to eat."

"Come to think of it, I haven't eaten since last night."

"How about Flora's Kitchen? We could share a plate of chicken fried steak?"

"Over 5,000 served," they chorused, laughing, then crying. *Daddy loved the place.*

"His death just isn't real," Caroline said, clutching herself.

"I know. I've seen him dead, and I still can't believe he's gone."

An hour later, a few miles south of Paradise Hills, they dug into a big plate of chicken-fried comfort food. Flora had been serving what she advertised as "epic portions" to the locals for the past fifteen years.

The sisters didn't talk much at first as they cut through tender meat topped with crunchy breading. Then Caroline began firing questions. *Asking lots of questions and getting answers seems to calm her down. Guess that's why she makes a good attorney.*

"How could he have died of a heart attack? He had a physical last month. So, what happened? Are you sure it was a heart attack?"

"What else could it be?"

"I don't know, but I can't believe it. Something doesn't make sense."

"They're doing an autopsy, so we'll know for sure in a few days. But I don't know what there is to know."

"I imagine you're right," Caroline said, the stress in her voice rising. "It's probably only a formality." She sighed. "I'm tied up in knots over his death. I apologize for hitting you with so many questions all at once. You've been through a lot in the past twenty-four hours." She placed her hand over Annie's, and Annie did the same.

They finished their pie and asked for the check. While they waited for Caroline's credit card to run, Annie's cell rang. She answered, and It was Frank. *Yuck. It's no secret that Caroline has never liked him, and he doesn't like her either.*

"Yes, yes, we'll be leaving soon. In the next half hour or so, I imagine. Yes, you and I can drive home together. I'll leave my car for Caroline at the ranch."

Caroline had a funny look as she listened.

When Annie hung up, she said, "Frank sends his love."

"Uh, huh. Is everything all right… at home?"

"It's fine…fine," she said, not wanting to go into it.

"How about you stay with me tonight at the ranch? Daddy would have wanted us to be together."

"Sounds good," Annie said, shoulders loosening.

When they reached the river, it was still light enough for Caroline to see the extent of the damage. "Watching it on the news doesn't do it justice." Her shocked gaze swept over the dead cattle and birds still lying by the sides of the road.

"I know. It looks like a war zone."

As they pulled up to the house, it was impossible for Annie to believe that her daddy wouldn't be there to greet them. When she came home, she almost always called his cell as she passed the show barn. He'd wait by the front door, watching through the glass. When he saw her car, he'd walk out on the porch, face lighting up. *I'll miss his warm smile and bear hug more than I ever thought possible.* Her shoulders drooped.

Instead, it was Frank who opened the front door. *What a horrible substitute.*

As the sisters walked into the house, Frank said, "Hi, Caroline, and welcome home. I am so sorry about your daddy."

Who's he to say welcome home? It's not his home. No way we're ever selling this place.

"Hello, Frank. Thank you," Caroline said politely. "You know it would help me if Annie stayed here at the ranch tonight."

He paused. "Under the circumstances, sure, that's fine." He pecked Annie on the cheek. "See you tomorrow, Darlin."

"I'm going to stay here through the funeral, Frank," Annie said, looking him right in the eye.

"Do what you want," he said through gritted teeth, then walked out the door.

CHAPTER TWENTY-TWO

*F*rank left the ranch, wishing he'd known earlier he'd be free to spend a few nights without Annie. Maybe he could still arrange to be with Kelly downtown at the Menger Hotel in the King's Ranch suite, his favorite. Too late tonight, but tomorrow night?

He picked up his phone and texted her. 'Meet me downtown tomorrow night at 7, the usual place.' He knew Kelly would find a way to get out of the house and be with him for several hours. She always did.

The next night at 6:00 pm, Frank sat having a drink in the bar, waiting for Kelly. They couldn't afford to be seen together, of course, so he'd left a key for her in a pre-arranged potted plant in a corner of the lobby.

Frank liked spending time in the Menger bar, soaking up the history of the old hotel. He pictured Teddy Roosevelt sitting right here, recruiting the Rough Riders, back in the day when men were men. Robert E. Lee and

Sam Houston had frequented the bar as well, and Frank believed he was rubbing shoulders with political giants of the past. Those had been the wild and woolly days of Texas. He was sorry he'd missed them; sure that he would have been one of the greats.

Of course, not everyone liked the Menger, Kelly included. The hotel had the reputation of being the most haunted hotel in the state of Texas. Frank didn't believe in ghosts, but Kelly did. That's what made being here with her so much fun. He always picked the King's Ranch Suite because Richard King had died in that suite, quite on purpose, it seemed.

According to the story Frank had heard, when King found out he was dying, he booked his favorite room in the hotel, and died right there on the spot. The bed frame in the room was supposed to be the same bed frame he died on, although the hotel claimed that the room had since been remodeled, and the door moved from where it had been. According to the legend, King's ghost still walked through the wall where the original door had been.

Frank had never seen his ghost, and neither had Kelly, but she kept asking Frank to pick a different room, because this one gave her the creeps. But he never did. He laughed and reminded her that there were supposedly at least thirty-one other spirits haunting the Menger, besides King. So why did it matter which room they used?

He finished his drink and made his way up to room 2052 to meet Kelly. She was a nice distraction and didn't pressure him to leave Annie. In fact, she felt guilty about cheating on Annie and Jim.

Kelly and Jim had two kids, and Frank was sure she would never leave her children, nor would he leave Annie. No, what he and Kelly had was bed rocking, good time sex. What a pistol she is, he thought, and if Annie didn't find out, they were in the clear. He had no intention of losing her or her daddy's money.

Annie never would forgive him for poisoning her daddy, if she knew about that, but then she didn't know and would never find out. Part of him was sorry to have killed Pete. Frank had killed large animals his whole life, but the only other person he'd ever killed before was his own father.

If anyone deserved to die, it had been him. What a horrible old man. Constantly criticizing Frank, lording it over him, never having faith in him. And locking him in the basement closet regularly. The man was a terror, and the world was a better place without him in it.

So, several years after his mother ran off with another man to parts unknown, Frank poisoned his father. No one knew of course, except his father, whose death was also ruled inconclusive. Everyone assumed it was a heart attack, just as they had with Pete. His father's death was more than five years ago, and no one suspected.

Frank was a little sorrier to have killed Pete, but the plan had worked perfectly. Pete would have died eventually anyway. His own father had died of a heart attack at 73, so Pete only had a few more good years left in him.

Frank looked at his watch. Time to meet Kelly, he smiled taking the stairs two at a time. Life was good.

CHAPTER TWENTY-THREE

*K*ent was home when his sister called. He had a lot he could tell her, but what was he supposed to say? That he'd fallen in love with another man's wife? Karla wouldn't understand. He didn't understand it himself. *What are you thinking?*

"Hi, Karla," he said, casually.

"Hey, little brother, good to hear your voice. How's your job going?"

"It's good, how's Carter?"

"Doing great. He's right here next to me, waiting not so patiently to talk to his Uncle Kent."

"Please put him on."

"Hi, Uncle Kent." Carter said excitedly.

"Hey, buddy, what's going on?"

"I finished my bear badge in Cub Scouts, and I'm a Webelo now!!"

"No, you're kidding me, a Webelo already?"

"Yep, and I already finished my first activity badge, and my citizen badge when I was at Cub Scout Camp."

"Cool, I'm very proud of you."

"Thanks, mom told me you got your Eagle Scout when you were sixteen, and I want to get mine, just like you."

"That's great, Carter," Kent said. *Leaving Carter behind was the hardest part about moving to Texas.*

"When am I going to get to see you? Mom and I miss you."

"I miss you all, too. Hey, here's an idea. Why don't you come to Texas in August, right before you go back to school? We'll see the Tower of the Americas and the Alamo on the first day. The next day, we'll drive over to Canyon Lake and do some boating and fishing, and even catch ourselves some rainbow trout. Just the two of us, what do you say? Sound good?"

"I say, AWESOME! I could even work on my aqua man activity badge."

"Yes, you could," he laughed. "What do you think, Sis? Can you spare him for a couple of days? My treat, and I'll take care of the arrangements."

"I don't know," she said, teasing, "I might miss him too much."

"MOM! You have to let me go. It would be only us guys," he begged. "Please say yes."

"Okay, yes, you can go."

"Yay!! I got to go tell Jimmy, see you later, Uncle Kent."

"Be back in half hour," Karla called after him, "It's getting dark out there."

"Okay," he promised as the door banged after him.

"Thanks, Kent," she said. "This means so much to him, and to me, too. Are you still coming to California for the July 4th weekend?"

"Still planning on it," he said, hesitating.

"You don't sound sure. Okay, out with it, what's wrong?"

"How can you always tell?"

"I helped raised you, remember?"

"True, and you did such a good job of it."

She laughed. "Your humility is showing again."

He went silent. He didn't want to tell Karla about Annie, not yet. She wouldn't understand how he felt about her, or the fact that she was married. He didn't understand it either. "I'll keep you posted on the 4th, how's Grandpa doing?".

"Not bad for a man who's 94 years old."

"He adapting to the new care center? I haven't talked with him in a few weeks."

"You know Grandpa. He puts up with anything and never complains."

"The man's tough as nails."

"I know, right? He has a reunion coming up with a few of his World War II buddies in L.A."

"I can't believe there are many of those guys still left around."

"I was poking around the Department of Veteran Affairs the other day, and on average, 372 veterans die every day."

"We're losing an amazing generation."

"Makes me sad, Kent."

"Me too. They were people of honor, like our grandpa."

"Hang on a sec, I wrote down a statistic about how many are still alive."

Kent waited.

"Okay, I found it, the Department of Veterans Affairs estimates there are around 450,000 vets left out of the 16 million who served in the war."

"Wow, not that many," Kent said.

"Less than 5 percent."

"Do you think Grandpa is okay?"

"He's in pretty good shape physically, but he misses Grandma every day."

"How's he getting to Los Angeles for the reunion?"

"I'm driving him."

"When is it?"

"I'm not sure yet."

"How about I fly out and ride along with you?"

"He'd love that, Kent. So would I."

"I'll find a way to get there. Just keep me posted on the dates."

"You're a good man and a lot like our grandpa."

Kent could hear the pride in her voice. He didn't feel much like a good man these days.

"I should go next door and get Carter."

"Love you, Sis."

"Love you, too, you care of yourself."

"I will, you too. Talk soon." He hung up guilty; he and Karla never kept secrets from each other. His love for Annie was a big one.

Then he called her. He'd been so worried. This time she answered.

"I've missed you," she said.

"I've missed you too. Did Caroline get in okay?"

"She's here at the ranch with me. We're making plans for the funeral. It's in two days. I want you to meet her."

"I'd like that. And how are you holding up?"

"I'm guess I'm okay, considering."

"Anything I can do to help?"

"Not right now. But will you come to the funeral?" she asked, voice rising.

"I'll be there for you, sitting with Dustin and Gina."

"That means a lot, thank you." She sighed audibly.

"Know that I love you, Annie. Wow. That was sudden."

She paused for a minute, then said, "And I love you, too."

A warm feeling radiated through Kent's body. "There, we've both said it."

"I know, and I'm speechless. —It's not that I don't know how I feel about you. But I might be a little stuck, afraid of making another mistake with a man."

"Making one mistake doesn't mean making another. I would never, ever treat you like Frank does. That's not me."

"You're right, it isn't." She took a deep breath. "You make me feel safe. I'm listening to my heart this time."

"That's good, because you've won mine,"

"Thank you for being here for me today."

"Hey, any day and every day."

"I'll call when I can." She whispered. "We'll figure this out."

"Good night, Annie," he said, hanging up, heart drumming in his chest. Then he clenched his fists. *Frank's a pernicious abuser, and he's hurt Annie physically and emotionally. That's a crime and he should be arrested for it. Annie owes him nothing. Not her mind, not her body, and not her loyalty.* He sat down and took a breath. *She's a smart and tough woman who's trapped by abuse. Even they aren't immune. I've been reading up on it, and I'm sure that even though Frank's agreed to stop the abuse for now, it won't last. She's got to get out. When she does, we can be together, out in the open. Until then, I will be here for her.*

CHAPTER TWENTY-FOUR

*A*nnie woke again in her childhood bedroom, stretching underneath warm covers. It was a drizzly, rainy day outside, and she burrowed in deeper. Then she remembered the funeral was in two days. Wiping her eyes, she looked at the clock. It was after 9 am, and her cell was ringing again.

"Just a minute," she croaked into her phone, then putting it on mute, grabbed the bottle of water on her nightstand, and took a long swig. "Go ahead."

"Shoot, Annie, sorry to wake you, it's Gary again. I'm callin' with the preliminary results of your fathers' autopsy report."

"I should have been up by now. Hang on a minute, please. I'm out at the ranch with Caroline. I'll get her. She'll want to hear this too."

"Caroline," Annie called out. "It's Gary Payne, you up?"

"Yes," she said, walking into the room.

"Ok, Gary, sorry to keep you waiting." Annie put her cell on speaker. "We're both here now."

Caroline asked, "What did you find out? Was it his heart?"

"I'm afraid the results of the autopsy report are inconclusive."

"What exactly does that mean?" Annie asked. "Didn't he die of a heart attack?"

"It means, we're still not sure how he died. We do know there's no evidence of damage to his heart muscle, no valve obstructions, and no necrotic areas."

"That is puzzling," Annie said. "Then how did he die?"

"We don't know. We could order a toxicology report if you want. This is not a suspicious death in the eyes of the law, so it's up to the two of you whether you want to go on from here."

"How long will a toxicology report take?" Annie asked.

"A few weeks, even three. They're backed up down at the county lab right now."

"Pray tell, what may we expect from a toxicology report?" Caroline said, curious.

Caroline sometimes spoke in the dulcet tones of their mama's Atlanta upbringing, while Annie's speech typified the native Hill Country Texan, she was proud to be.

"The toxicology report will look for potential toxins in the blood, urine, or hair, such as prescription medication, alcohol, or any other drugs that might have been used or abused."

Dead silence, then Caroline asked, "Are you suggesting he took his own life?"

"No. I would never think that, and neither would anyone else in this town. I grew up with Pete; I was explaining what a toxicology report would be looking for," he said more cautiously.

"I understand," she said. "Thank you, if we decide not to proceed with a toxicology report, what will the coroner put on the death certificate?"

"He would use the word "probable" or even "presumed" cause of death to specify that he's not completely certain, which would indicate there's not sufficient information to provide a specific cause of death."

"And is that a problem?" Annie asked.

"In this case, no, I'm sure it wouldn't be. A heart attack is the most likely thing, in this instance, given your father's age, his history of a-fib, and his own father's cause of death."

"Then I don't think we need to proceed with the toxicology report," Caroline said. "I'm satisfied, Annie, are you?"

"I think so." She wondered if they might be missing something.

"All right, ladies, no toxicology report. We'll have your father's body ready at the funeral parlor tomorrow. I'll take care of it."

"Thanks, Gary, we'll see you then," Caroline said.

"Bye, Gary." Annie ended the call. "You don't think Daddy could have taken his own life, do you?" Her eyes widened.

"Certainly not, he would never do that. I don't know what's going on down at that lab, but they probably made a mistake. It happens. But one thing I know for sure, we don't want tongues wagging about suicide."

"You're right, Daddy would have hated that."

"Agreed, then it's settled. Come on downstairs, Gabriela's made breakfast."

"You go on ahead, I'll be down as soon as I can make myself presentable."

"Speaking of presentable," Ruben Salazar called this morning."

"Daddy's attorney?"

"Yes. He wanted to come out this afternoon and go over the Will with us."

"If we're going to have a reading of the Will, I expect Frank might want to be here."

"Two things," Caroline said. "First, Daddy's Will is technically none of Frank's business, although once it's filed with the court, it will be a matter of public record. He can see it and read it then unless you choose to show him beforehand. Second, the 'reading of a will' is purely theatrical. These days, there is no legal requirement that a Will be read aloud to anyone."

"Interesting, and how is it that as a corporate attorney you know so much about reading Wills?"

"I Googled it after Ruben called this morning."

"That is so you," she laughed. "What else did you find out from Ruben?"

"Dad named him both the Estate's Attorney and the Executor of the Will. He always trusted him. Herman Nelson was his CPA, and he'll be the accountant for the estate. He'll take charge of paying any debts and taxes. Daddy was not a man to incur debt, so I expect there'll be little of that. You and I are the only two beneficiaries. There's no one to contest the Will."

"Couldn't Ruben have waited until next week to meet with us? This all makes Daddy's death too real."

"Actually, he didn't need to meet with us at all, and he could have mailed us copies of the Will. Daddy wanted him to sit down with us and go over the details, and Ruben has to go out of town for a few weeks tomorrow. I asked him to come by this morning around eleven. Are you all right with that?"

"I'll shower and dress."

Ruben rang the bell at 11:00 on the dot. As he walked through the door, he hugged them both. "I'm sorry so about your dad. He was a great friend to me and my family. I'd do anything for Pete Kingman."

"Thank you," Annie said, hugging him back. He felt like a teddy bear, all round and a little soft, yet distinguished with his pewter gray hair and impeccable black and gray suit.

"You girls are all grown up and beautiful. Your daddy would be so proud." He wiped his eyes with the back of his hand.

Caroline said, "Please sit down."

He snapped open his briefcase and handed them copies of the Will. "Your dad's Will lists all his assets. As you can see right up front, he left you each $500,000 in cash, as well as the ranch, cattle, horses, and equipment worth collectively over $5 million. And a life insurance policy that he upped not long ago from $1 million to $2 million."

Annie looked at Caroline, thinking about the numbers, which were even higher than she expected.

"Pete had no debt, and you are his only heirs, so probate should be a pretty straightforward process. I took the liberty of filing an application for probate with the court. There'll be a two-week waiting period, so by the time I get back to town, we should be ready for the hearing. Simple as that. Why don't you two take a few minutes to read over the Will, and then I can answer any questions."

Caroline read quickly, while Annie checked unfamiliar legal details.

"Looks like Daddy was very definite about us not selling the ranch, and about how his property is to be passed on," Caroline said.

"Yes, he was. He wanted you girls to receive income from the ranch for the rest of your lives, and then after you die, the ranch passes directly to any heirs you have, skipping past husbands and potential husbands, in the event of a divorce."

"Hy's getting too old to run the ranch on his own" Annie said. "Even with the hired hands."

"You can always hire a new ranch hand manager," Reuben suggested.

Annie stepped up. "I'm going to be the one who runs the ranch. With Hy's help." They both stared at her. "Caroline, will you help with the finances?"

Caroline looked surprised, then nodded. "Of course."

"Ruben," Annie said, looking him straight in the eye, you may not know that Daddy gave me a small piece of our property when I was fourteen. 150 acres to be exact. That's how I learned a lot about cattle, besides living on the ranch."

"You have experience, Annie," Ruben said. "In his Will, your dad suggested you conduct a search for a solid ranch hand manager. But there's nothing in there that says you can't take charge. If that's what you want."

"It is," she said in a steady voice.

Caroline said. "I understand how business works, and I'm good with money. You know all about breeding cattle, working with them, and buying and selling them. Together, we can do this."

"You bet we can."

"It'll be fun, working together, you'll see. Our skills complement each other." Her eyes lit up. "I'll call the firm and tell them I'll be working remotely for a while. I can fly in when I need to." She paused and looked at Annie. "I promise to try and not be too bossy."

"Don't make promises you can't keep," Annie laughed. "I'll be happy to have you back home; I've missed you."

"I've missed you too," Caroline smiled.

"Sounds like it's all settled," Ruben said. "It's been my experience that there's nothing strong Texas women can't do, once they set their minds to it. And you two are Pete Kingman's daughters," he smiled proudly. "Herman and I stand ready to help you any way you like."

"Thank you," Annie said. "We'll require assistance from both of you."

The two sisters were still talking and planning when Ruben left, closing the door behind him. Annie barely noticed his departure. *My life has changed for the better in the last hour. I'm on a new path. After the state election, I'll break the news to Frank that I'm leaving him. For good. That's all there is to it. Then I can be with Kent.*

CHAPTER TWENTY-FIVE

*F*rank parked out front of the white-brick, two¬-story Payne Funeral Home, below the sign that read "Serving the families of Paradise Hills since 1905." The old building with its faded blue shutters was all too familiar to him. He walked past the garage that housed the black hearses and took the front steps up to the entrance.

He'd arrived early for Pete's viewing. He needed to speak with Gary alone to see what he knew about the autopsy report. When he walked through the double glass doors, a small bell rang.

Gary walked out to greet him. "Hi Frank, I wasn't expecting you this early. Is Annie with you? We're not ready for her to see Pete."

"No. It's just me, thought I'd come early to make sure everything's in order."

"Give me fifteen minutes, and I'll walk you around and show you what we've done. I think you'll be pleased."

Frank sank into one of the black leather chairs. He'd sat in this same office with his mother after his father died. His mother. He couldn't believe she'd shown up for the funeral when neither he nor his father had seen her in years. Frank demanded that she leave through the side door before the service even started. She had the gall to look hurt and surprised, as she slunk out the door. There was no love lost between Frank and his mother.

She and his father married a few months before he was born, but everyone in town knew he'd been born "too early." This was Texas and that mattered, especially in 1983. His grandfather never let his mother forget she'd tarnished the family reputation. Frank was a symbol of her disgrace, so his grandfather wasn't fond of him either. The mean, old turd was the kind of guy who kicked dogs around.

Then, his mother did it again fifteen years later. Only this time, she skipped town with her new beau, leaving both her husband and Frank behind. He couldn't believe she had the guts to be that bold. He'd known her only as a quiet, submissive woman, who'd never stood up to his father, even when he whipped Frank with a belt. What made her think he'd want to reconnect with her after he killed his father? Of course, she didn't know that part...

Gary walked back into the office. "Ready, Frank," he said. "Sorry to keep you waiting, shall we go to the viewing room?"

As they walked down the hall, Frank asked, "Did you get Pete's autopsy report yet?"

"Yes, and I went over it with Annie and Caroline yesterday."

"And…"

"The results were inconclusive."

"Really? We all thought he died of a heart attack."

"There was no evidence of damage to his heart muscle, no valve obstructions, and no necrotic areas."

"That's odd."

"I asked Caroline and Annie if they wanted to order a toxicology report."

"What did they say?"

"They didn't see the need for it, and as far as the law is concerned, Pete's death is not suspicious.

"Makes sense." The muscles in Frank's shoulders relaxed. He hadn't realized how tense he'd been. There was no need to worry; no one would ever know what really happened to Pete.

Frank and Gary walked into the small viewing room off the chapel where Pete's body was laid out in a gun-gray metal casket with a white lining. The coffin rested in front of two round floor to ceiling windows, the room filled with natural light.

A spray of flowers stood at the foot of the casket, flanked by several arrangements of white flowers in the shapes of hearts and crosses. A large silver bowl bursting with small, inscribed Texas flags sat nearby, serving as a memento for those coming to pay their last respects. It was a Texas themed tribute for a native Texas son.

"You've outdone yourself, Gary."

"Thanks, I added the flags to honor Pete. I don't think you knew he loaned us money to start this business. I don't know where I'd be without his act of kindness."

Frank smiled and rubbed his hand along the side of the highly polished casket. The great man would be rotting in the ground before long. Then he heard Annie's and Caroline's voices.

"You're already here, Frank," Annie said walking in.

"I wanted to make sure everything was just right, before you got here." He pecked her on the cheek.

"It's very dignified, Gary," Caroline said looking around. "Thank you,"

Frank took his place with the rest of the family at the foot of the casket and heard Annie whisper to Caroline, "I hope Daddy's okay that we didn't hold his services at home."

"I don't think the house is large enough for the number of people who will come and pay their last respects," Caroline said. "I'm sure he's fine with what we've done."

She was right about the numbers. In addition to the congregants from Songbird Community Church, the surrounding ranchers, and most of Paradise Hills, folks came from as far away as San Antonio to say good-bye to Pete. He'd belonged to the San Antonio Veterans of Foreign Wars, Post 76, the oldest chapter in Texas, having served in Vietnam.

After the viewing ended, the family and close friends joined the rest of the mourners in the chapel and Pastor Mark delivered the eulogy.

Caroline spoke next to honor her father and was followed by one of the Texas state senators. Pete had earned a good conduct medal for his exemplary behavior in the Vietnam War. He'd never said anything about that to Frank. Frank tried to get him to talk about the war, but like many veterans, he just wanted to put the past behind him.

Then, Annie sang, "God Be with You till We Meet Again." Mourners of all stripes took out their handkerchiefs and dabbed at their eyes. But not Frank, who had no intention of "meeting" Pete, or anyone else, on "the other side." What hogwash. This life was all there was to it, this life was what counted, and Frank meant to make the most of it. Once he had his hands on Annie's money, it would be that much better. He planned to sell the ranch.

When the services ended, he stood with the rest of the pall bearers and loaded Pete's casket into the black hearse. As the cortege left the building, the local sheriff and several veterans honored Pete with a snappy salute. Police officers on motorcycles filled every corner, blinking their lights and standing at attention as Pete's body passed by on its way to the Kingman family cemetery.

After Pete was laid to rest next to Susie, the head of the VA presented an American flag to Annie and Caroline for Pete's exemplary service to his country.

What a lot of fuss, Frank thought, the man is dead. Ashes to ashes and dust to dust, if the Lord won't take him the devil must, he thought, smothering a laugh.

After the grave-side service ended, Frank stood around shaking hands. "Meet and greet" was one of the things he did best. He tried to look appropriately sad when folks offered their condolences on the death of his father-in-law. Good thing he'd taken acting classes in high school.

He overheard Cindy talking with Annie and Caroline. She said, "I love you both, and I understand this is hard. With grace from the Lord, you'll get through." Then she hugged them. "Lean on me. Lean on your friends."

"Bless their hearts," Caroline said looking sideways at Annie.

Right, Frank thought, still listening. *Gotta love those gossipers.*

Cindy said, "I know there are many in our town who pretend to be perfect. If they really had self-confidence, they wouldn't have to pretend. But please know that Paradise Hills is still filled with good people. We at Songbird Community are here for you." She hugged them both. "You're never alone in the house of the Lord. Love is patient. Love is kind."

Frank could see tears glisten in Annie's eyes. *Buck up girl,* he thought. *You'll get over it. So much falderal.* As he was getting ready to leave, he saw Gary Payne standing at the back of the room chatting quietly with his assistant. Frank didn't hear Gary tell him to move Pete's autopsy tissue samples to the back-room refrigerator where they would keep them, just in case.

Frank waved at Gary from across the room and called out, "Thanks for your help today, Gary."

"You're welcome," he said.

Frank swaggered out the door to his car, a gleam in his eye. He felt calm and at ease. They'd never catch him.

CHAPTER TWENTY-SIX

*A*nnie and Caroline sat alone on the same large piece of weathered limestone rock their daddy had hauled in to talk with their mama after she died. The graveyard looked bleak this time of year, no leafy green trees, and no fragrant flowers. They faced their parents' shared headstone, together.

"It's good we decided to wait to inscribe the death date," Annie said. "That makes it so final. I want to hold on to him as long as possible. I can't even stand to get rid of his things."

Caroline squeezed Annie's hand. "I think he would have liked the services."

"I do too, especially the little Texas flags, so thoughtful of Gary. Our daddy's with the Lord now."

Caroline nodded. "I'm sad he never got to retire and just enjoy life."

"Daddy said he wanted to travel, but you know him; home was where his heart was."

"He would have been a good grandpa. Now, he'll never get that chance." Tears smothered Caroline's eyes. "It's just you and me now. We're too young to be left without both parents."

"It grows us up way too fast."

"We were lucky to have parents who loved each other as much as ours did."

"Mostly true. But I think being the product what seemed like a perfect marriage comes with its own set of challenges."

"What do you mean?"

"Our parents were soul mates. Not everyone finds that."

"I certainly haven't. I suspect you and Frank haven't either."

Annie's laugh filled with irony. "I wish I'd never married him. He's jealous of everyone else in my life. He's afraid my feelings for other people take away from my feelings for him."

"Love immersed in power isn't love, it's control. Specifically, what's he doing to control you?"

"I caught him last week looking through my handbag."

"He can't do that, it's an invasion of privacy."

"I know, but he did. He also tells me, 'Wear this, and don't wear that.' It's maddening. He seems to think I belong to him."

"That's emotional abuse, Annie, plain and simple. I never cared for Frank, but I didn't know he was this bad. Why haven't you told me?"

"I felt stupid telling you." She said, cheeks burning. "How could I have let this happen?" She dropped her chin to her chest, shaking her head.

"The shame you're feeling is not deserved. He's the abuser. Show yourself some grace and leave him. Nobody should have to put up with this crap."

"When I told Daddy I was unhappy, he reminded me that there hadn't been a divorce in the Kingman family in generations."

Caroline sighed. "That sounds like him. It might be the reason I haven't married. Scared that I wouldn't be able to make it last."

"I can't make mine last either."

"And you shouldn't. You don't need to stay in an unhappy marriage, Annie." Caroline leaned in.

"I'm glad to hear you say that, because I've hired a divorce lawyer."

"That's great news." Caroline paused. "Question: Has Frank ever hurt you physically?"

Annie wrung her hands. "He slapped my face and left a mark. And then, he apologized."

"Ok, that's it, you've got to get out now. Let me help you."

"Thanks. But this is something I need to do on my own. He promised not to hit me again. I told him if he doesn't treat me right, I won't support his state election."

"So, he made a deal with you that serves him."

"Yes, I proposed it. He won't abuse me as long as he's running for office."

"What happens after the election is over?"

"I'm gone."

"I hope so but know this: It won't be easy. I've seen abused women in my corporate legal practice, and on average, a woman in an abusive relationship tries to leave seven times before she finally leaves for good."

"Seven times?" Annie was shocked. Why is it so hard to get out and stay out?"

"One of the main reasons is that women believe they can change their men."

"Frank doesn't think he needs to change."

"Why doesn't that surprise me?"

"Why else is it so hard to get out?"

"There's a lot of social pressure to be in the perfect relationship, and social media only makes the perception of perfection worse."

"All those pictures of happy, smiling couples makes it seem like it's that way all the time."

"Yes, and it's not. Women also go back after a breakup, because they feel pressure not to give up on their marriage. Or because they share children. Or because they believe they need to be forgiving."

"Frank always reminds me I'm supposed to forgive him."

"And yet he repeats the same behavior. That's not being sorry. You know how ridiculous that is, right?"

"I do. But it helps to hear you say it aloud. I will get out…and stay out." She flipped her hair back. She didn't disclose the sexual abuse. *I can't let go of the shame.*

"Promise me you'll be careful."

"Like I said, Frank needs me to win his election. Now let's get go back to the ranch and get a nice cup of orange tea." They walked to the car, arm in arm.

The next day, Annie was at home going through Frank's suit pockets getting ready to take his clothes to the cleaners. She hadn't told him about the Will, but she was quite sure he'd be asking soon.

When Annie reached into the pants pocket of the blue suit, she pulled out a crumpled piece of white paper. On the verge of tossing it into the trash, she wondered if he might need it for something. She opened it and read. It was a note signed simply 'K' dated a few days earlier. One of the nights she'd stayed out at the ranch with Caroline. The note thanked him for a fun night at the Menger Hotel.

Annie sank down on the bed, clutching the note. She hadn't considered that he was having sex with another woman. Annie balled her hand into a fist. Who was his paramour? Could it be someone she knew?

And then, the pieces fell in place. *How could I have been so blind? 'K' stands for Kelly. One of my best friends. I've seen the two of them smile and tease back and forth. Her eyes fill with adoration when Frank walks into a room. It must be Kelly. How could they do this to me? Her nostrils flared. How could they do it to Jim? And their children.* Annie stormed around the room in a fit, then picked up the phone and called Frank at the office.

He answered. "What is it? I'm busy here."

"Are you alone?"

"Steve's in here with me."

"Tell him to wait outside."

"Why? What's this all about? I'll be home for supper in half an hour or so. It can wait."

"Afraid not," she shouted. "We need to talk now."

"Don't have a conniption. –Steve, could you leave us alone here for a minute? Thanks. -Okay, he's gone. Now what the devil's gotten into you?"

"It's about the note I found in your pocket, thanking you for a night of fun at the Menger Hotel."

Frank paused a bit too long before saying, "Why were you looking though my pockets?"

"Cleaners."

"Oh."

"Who is she Frank?"

"Okay, okay. She's nobody and means nothing to me."

"If you don't come clean, I'll call the Paradise Press online right now and tell them about their philandering mayor."

"You wouldn't."

"Try me."

"Do that, and you'll ruin us both. This is a small town; I'll lose clients if this gets out. I could lose my position as mayor. Please, Annie."

"How long? How long have you been sleeping with another woman? Or is there more than one? Tell me the truth now!"

"I swear there's only one. About a year."

"A whole YEAR! Where have I been! You're as crooked as a dog's hind leg, Frank Graves, and I hate you!"

"Calm down, Annie."

"Don't you dare tell me to calm down! It's Kelly, isn't it."

His silence spoke volumes.

"You've been having an affair with one of my best friends. How could you? How could she?"

"Darlin, I'm hangin' up the phone now and comin' home. Don't go doing anything stupid, we can work this out."

"Don't bother, because I won't be here," she said, slamming down the receiver. Then she took the chicken she'd been frying for his supper, dumped it in the sink, and poured water over it, watching the steam rise from the pan. She grabbed her car keys from the hook in the kitchen and called Kent's cell. She knew exactly where she was going next.

"Hi, Annie. Is everything all right?"

"I need to see you," she gritted her teeth. "Can you have dinner with me?"

"Sure, it's almost five. I'll leave a little early. Where do you want me to meet you?"

"At Boudro's on the Riverwalk, in about half hour. I'm already in the car."

"I'll leave now and get a table outside."

Let's eat inside where it's cool, please, and order me a Texas Tea, would you? And some of their mesquite grilled quail to start," she said, then ended the call.

A few Texas teas and some blackened prime rib later, Annie was feeling tipsy. She wasn't a drinker. Kent looked puzzled. "Let's get you home."

"I can't drive in this condition, and I can't be seen driving with you. I need to go sleep it off somewhere for a few hours. I'll check into the Marriott on Market, but it's getting dark. Will you walk me, please?"

"Of course." On the short walk to the hotel, Annie linked her arm through his and leaned her head on his shoulder. It was a quiet night, not too hot, as they strolled along the banks of the small man-made river.

When they reached the front desk, she said, "One night, one person." Annie handed the hotel clerk her credit card.

He looked at Kent and said nothing.

"Oh, don't worry about him," she said. "He's only seeing me to my room. Such a gentleman."

"Come on," Kent said, taking the key card. "Let's go upstairs."

"Please come in for a minute," she asked as they stepped off the elevator, not wanting to let go of his hand. I need to talk. It was too noisy in the restaurant."

"We'll do that, then I'll leave, and you can get some sleep."

"I have to go to the bathroom," she said as they walked inside. "I'll only be a minute."

He sat on a black couch and waited.

A few minutes later, she emerged from the darkness and sat next to him. Then she wept.

"Annie, what's wrong? You're not yourself."

"Words can't begin to describe. I'm so upset and angry."

He held her hand again. "Whatever it is, we can figure it out together."

"It's Frank," she said, gulping for air. "He's having an affair with Kelly. It's been going on for more than a year, a whole year! I feel so betrayed.

"I can't believe it. They've betrayed you, Jim, and their kids."

"I know, it's a hot mess."

"How'd you find out?"

"I found a love note in his pocket. When I confronted him, he told me the truth."

"What a scumbag."

"You're telling me."

"Does Jim know?" Kent asked.

"No, he doesn't, and Kelly doesn't know that I know."

"Wow. What's next?"

"I don't know what's next for them, but I'm divorcing Frank," she said wiping tears from her face.

He took a deep breath. "I'm sorry he cheated on you, Annie. His sexual misconduct is despicable. And so is Kelly's."

Annie reached up and kissed him softly. "I love you."

"I love you too, Annie."

"I'll be glad when my divorce is final, and we can be together." Annie reached up, kissed him again, long, and deep. His arms wrapped around her, and her fingers caressed his hair. He kissed her neck over and over. Then a voice in her head told her that going further was not the right decision. She pulled back. and sat up straight. "Two wrongs don't make a right."

"I agree," he said, catching his breath. "If we make love now, we can't ever go back." He stood up from the couch. "Our time will come if we just wait for it."

"We can, and we will." Annie rose from the couch, tottered over to the bed, then dropped on the mattress. "Night." She was out like a light.

Kent pulled a blanket over her, then straightened his tie, and smoothed his hair. He pulled the door closed softly behind him.

Annie got home early the next morning. Frank was waiting.

"Where have you been?" He cussed.

"It doesn't matter."

"Of course, it does. I've been worried."

"Why would you worry about me when you've got Kelly?"

"She means nothing to me, you're my wife."

She glared at him, nostrils flaring. He sounded so casual about the fact that she was his wife. "You broke our marriage vows, Frank. You promised to make love to only me, and you chose adultery instead. Just so you know, I'll be sleeping in the guest room from now on. That is, until the divorce."

"Divorce," he bellowed. "Who said anything about a divorce?"

"I did. I'm getting out. Yes, I'll wait until the election is over, as promised. Then we're done. You're controlling, abusive, and a philanderer to boot."

"Come on, honey. Kelly is—I mean was—an interesting…well, diversion."

"Seriously, Frank? A diversion?"

"I'll stop seeing her. I don't want a divorce. I'll never sleep with her again."

"Just like that?"

"Just like that."

"I don't believe you."

"Annie be sensible, a divorce will ruin me."

"As usual, you're worried about your precious political career. You should know that deception always comes back to haunt you."

"The electorate in Texas cares about family values, and a scandal would destroy everything."

"I can't believe you're talking to me about family values." She shook her head. "You'll be exposed eventually. Hiding what you do leaves you vulnerable to anyone who finds out your secrets."

"I'll make it up to you, Darlin, somehow. Wait…I know. How about those new bathrooms you've been wanting? Done and done, call the contractor, and you can start tomorrow."

"Trying to buy me off again? I'm going to the guest room. That's where I'll be sleeping from now on."

He stood staring at her, mouth gaping open.

She had him dead to rights, and they both knew it. Their relationship had crossed a line into new territory. She'd soon have her own money and didn't need his. Annie walked to the guest room, locked the door, and called Kent. He'd be worried. "Did I wake you?"

"I was asleep, dreaming of you."

Annie smiled. "What a lovely thing to say."

"It's true. Where's Frank this morning?"

"In our room, by himself. I moved into the guest bedroom." A sense of relief filled her voice.

"How'd he take that?"

"You should have seen the look on his face. He was shocked."

"I'll bet. And angry?"

"Angrier when I told him I was going to divorce him."

"Huge step. What'd he say?"

"That he didn't want a divorce and he's through with Kelly."

"Do you believe him?"

"No, and even if I did, I'm done. Our marriage is over."

"Bad for him." He paused. "Good for me."

"Good for us." Annie lowered her voice. "I'd better let you get ready for work."

"Yes, I should be going."

"Bye for now."

She stared at the ceiling. She wanted to go to Kelly and confront her about the affair. *I thought she was one of my best friends. I want to tell that her she has no sexual integrity. "You're no friend of mine," I'll say. Then I'll ask her how she could do this not just to me but to Jim and their kids. They're the innocent parties, and they'll be devastated.* Annie stopped. Jim and the kids. She couldn't risk it. *I can't try to make myself feel better and destroy them in the process. I'll say nothing to her.* Tears ran down her face. *I feel so alone.*

She fell back asleep, dreaming that she and Kent were lying in lush, tall summer grasses, laughing, and pointing at swollen white clouds set against the brilliant blue of a Texas sky. Annie laughed and said, "This one looks like a bear. And that one's a dragon." Kent smiled, tugged her close, then offered her his hand. "Let's got for a drive."

They rode in his car and listened to music on the radio. The song playing was John Denver's 'Annie's Song.' They sang along, 'Come let me love you, let me give my life to you. Let me always be with you.' They were both so happy.

Annie woke with a start, remembering that her mama's favorite song had been 'Annie's Song.' *Mama would have loved Kent. He's not narcissistic, controlling, or self-absorbed. Power and money aren't the only things he cares about. Yes, I made a mistake marrying Frank. But I can learn from it. Kent wouldn't be a mistake. When he and I are with each other, no one else matters. I feel something magic when I'm with him that I've never felt before. Mama would want me to be happy.*

CHAPTER TWENTY-SEVEN

*O*ne morning as Kent was stepping out of the shower, he heard a knock at the door. Who could it be this early? When Kent saw Annie's convertible in the yard, he threw on his sweats and cracked the door open, happy to see her.

"How about spending the day together," she said walking inside. "Frank's out of town."

"There's nothing I'd like better. But I've got a full day at work, and I'm running late." He checked his watch.

"Okay, I understand." She sighed. "I'll go and let you get to it. —But I did book a 2:00 tee time at the Lady Bird Johnson golf course, just in case you had time."

"I didn't know you golfed."

"I've been taking lessons over the past two weeks, wanted to surprise you."

"How did you know I liked golf?"

"I saw the golf bag in your garage, so I took up the sport," she said.

He smiled, pleased.

"I want us to share everything."

"Me too. I'll call the office and tell them I can't make it today. My admin will reschedule everything for me." He paused, then smiled. "I deserve a day off."

"Yes, you do," Annie kissed him on the cheek. "I have another surprise planned for later today, and it'll be worth it, I promise."

He smiled. "Okay, I'm excited. So where is this golf course anyway?"

"Outside Fredericksburg, and you're going to love it, 18-hole, par seventy-one, in a lovely setting. Beautiful live oak trees and manicured lawns, so please get dressed."

"Give me a just a few minutes."

"Take your time, I'm in no hurry."

Twenty minutes later, Kent loaded both sets of clubs in the small trunk of her car and then checked his phone. He found thirty email messages, some that needed his attention. He set his out of office message and shut down the phone. *It's only a day, have some fun.*

Annie seemed to be reading his mind. "You've earned it darling. Would you like to drive?" she asked, dangling her keys in front of him.

"You bet. Hey, I remember reading somewhere that there's a World War II Museum in Fredericksburg, is that true?"

"Yes, it is."

"I've been wanting to see it," he said. "My grandfather served in the Pacific theatre."

"I remember you telling me about that, and he sounds like a great man. Whatever you'd like," she cooed. "It's your day."

"I don't deserve you." He took one hand off the steering wheel and touched her hand.

"No, you don't," she laughed, "and don't forget it."

A few hours later, after a leisurely drive through Hill Country back roads, they reached Fredericksburg. "Very picturesque," he said as they pulled into town. "German architecture, right?" He asked as they passed a sign that read: Founded in 1846.

"Yes, named after King Frederick of Prussia. There are lots of German settlements around here. We can poke around the shops later, if you'd like, and I'll even buy you a souvenir. I have just the thing for the man from California."

"What's that?"

"It's a blue leather-bound book titled, *What Texas Thinks of the Other 49 States.*"

"I'll bet THAT would be interesting," he said.

"Oh, it is. When you open the book, it's filled with nothing but blank, white pages."

He laughed, "That is so Texas."

"True that," Annie said, as they pulled up in front of the stone clubhouse on the golf course. "Let's grab an early lunch at the Red Bird Grill before we head out onto the course. Looks like today's menu is fried catfish, hush puppies, fries, and coleslaw, and it doesn't get any better."

He liked the look of the place, warm and casual, red chairs pulled up to simple wood tables. A rustic stone fireplace with a brown wooden mantle sat at one end of the room, flanked by a set of large windows overlooking the golf course. "I've never had hush puppies before, what are they?" Kent asked.

"You take a little cornmeal, beat in eggs, flour, onion, and a little sugar, roll it into a ball, and then deep fry it. Delicious," she said. "They go great with the fried catfish."

He didn't typically eat much fried food, but the meal turned out to be surprisingly tasty.

And Annie was right about the golf course. Lots of stately old live oaks lining the green grass. He shot an eighty-four, and she shot a ninety-five. "Not bad for a beginner, but you are a natural athlete."

She grinned at him. "Thank you."

"How far to the museum?"

"Not far," she said, but let's take a quick stop by the Runnymede Country Inn first. That's where I hope you and I will spend our honeymoon someday," she said squeezing his hand, and I'd like to get your opinion."

"Speaking of you, me, and our still little threesome, where's Frank today?"

"Houston on business, which is why we have the whole day to ourselves."

"Any progress on the divorce?"

"Frank tries every day to talk me out of it, and he's been so kind since I found out about his affair with Kelly. He's furious that I hired an attorney, who is so good, people pay her not to represent their spouses."

"She sounds tough."

"She is."

"Just what you need."

She smiled. "Let's head over to the museum first."

"Great, I'm looking forward to seeing it."

"The place is huge, six acres with three museums with interactive exhibits."

"Sounds like we'd need a couple of days to see it all."

"That's true, but at least we could get a good start."

Kent checked his watch again. "How about we go another day?"

"If you like. I'm sorry we ran out of time."

"No worries." On the way home, he synchronized his Bluetooth in her car, and she gave him a look. "Just in case I get a call from the office," he said, "I've been off the grid."

A few minutes later the phone rang, but it wasn't the office, it was Karla. He answered without thinking.

"Hi, Kent."

"Hey, Karla, what's up?"

"You sound busy," she said.

"I kind of am." He looked at Annie.

"Are you at work?"

"No. I took the day off to take…to take a …. client golfing." He was surprised at the way that little lie slipped so easily from his lips. He hated keeping secrets from anyone, especially Karla.

"Oh, all right, you didn't sound like you were in the office."

"How about I call you back in a couple of hours?" His voice cracked a little.

"Are you okay?"

"I'll call you tonight."

"No problem, I wanted to go over our plans for the 4th of July."

"Sounds great, talk soon, bye."

"Are you going to California for the 4th?" Annie asked after he hung up.

"That's the plan," he said. "I haven't seen Karla and Carter in almost a year."

"I know you miss them. I hope you have a good time. We're having a big social down at the church, barbecue, and dancing. I'm looking forward to that."

"I hate to miss, and it sounds fun. I should go to California."

"Yes, you should. There's no way I want you to miss seeing your family."

He put his arm around her shoulder. "I'd rather stay and be here with you." Kent pulled up in front of his house and went quiet. *What if she needs me?*

"I think you're upset about not going to California. Please go."

"It's okay, I can go another time."

She leaned over and kissed him, "Your call, and thanks for an awesome day. See you in church Sunday."

He kissed her goodbye, and she waved as she drove off.

Kent closed the door and sat on his couch. It had been a fabulous day, but he knew he had at least fifty work emails waiting for him, and he still needed to call Karla. What was he going to tell her? And what about Carter? Most of all, he never wanted to disappoint the boy.

Kent set aside his thoughts and called her. "Hi, Sis."

"Hi yourself, little brother. Thanks for calling back. Carter and I are so excited about having you come for the fourth, it's been too long since we've seen you."

"I know it has, and I was excited to come."

"Was?" she asked.

"I have disappointing news. I'm not going to be able to make it for the fourth. So how about I come see you both over Labor Day, instead? And Carter will be here in August to go to the lake."

"Something at work?"

"Kind of."

"You have never, ever been good at keeping secrets, Kent Winder. What's going on?"

He paused. "I've met someone."

"That's great, why didn't you say so? Bring her along. You know she's welcome."

"I can't do that yet, it's complicated."

"Why?"

"You're not going to like this, and I don't either. But as I say this, remember it's only temporary. She's married."

"She's MARRIED?"

"Yes, but she's getting a divorce."

"When?"

"Very soon. Her husband is a cheater and he's abusive."

"So, you're having an affair?"

"I am NOT sleeping with her."

"But you're in love."

"Yes.

"Are you saving her from something?"

"Well…. her husband is abusive."

"You could never resist someone who needs rescuing. You were like that as a little boy. Remember that wounded sparrow you nursed back to health? Or the caterpillar you tried to help out of its cocoon? You have a tender heart, and I love that about you. But be careful."

"We are being careful."

"Are you totally immersed in this new love of yours?"

He remained silent.

She continued, more softly this time. "Do you remember your favorite story growing up?"

"Of course. The Trojan War."

"Do you remember the story of Achilles?"

"His father was a King. He killed Hector outside the gates of Troy. What's your point here?"

"Do you remember how he died?"

"Paris shot him in the heel with an arrow. Where are you going with this?"

"You, my brother, are a wonderful man. You're my hero, and Carter's, too. You're strong, dependable, and kind. But like Achilles, you're vulnerable. You have an Achilles heel."

He laughed. "I'll bite. What do you think it is?"

"It's your hubris. In Greek tragedy, hubris was an excess of pride that led to someone's ruin. You think you can fix anyone and anything, and only you can do it. That's your Achilles heel."

"Maybe. But what does this have to do with me being in love with Annie?"

"Is that her name?"

"Yes. That's her name. And she's amazing. She's the one, Sis."

"And she needs you to protect her from her abusive husband. True?"

"She thinks she's got it covered. But I'm still worried."

"You're the only one who can help her, right?"

"Yes, I am, and that's not hubris. It's a fact. Her parents are dead, and her only living sibling is a sister."

"Rescuing others can make us feel good. But it can also make others feel helpless in return. That can turn to anger." She stopped. "Kent, is there a chance you're running to help Annie, to run away from what happened to Sally?"

Kent paused, wondering then said, "I can't answer that right now. But I don't think so."

"Did your new love ask you not to come to California for the 4th."

"No, she said I should come. But she might have been a little relieved I wasn't flying out.

"And you're not going to give up your values for her, right?"

"What do you mean by that?"

"I mean not having an affair with someone else's wife. You've already fallen in love."

"We know what we're doing, and she's getting a divorce. Now, I have lots of work to catch up on. It's getting late. Give Carter a hug and tell him I'll see him in August."

"Given what's going on in your life, maybe it would be better if Carter didn't come in August."

She might be right. "Ok. I'll see you both in September, if Labor Day works. I'll make it up to Carter somehow, I promise."

"You know you're welcome anytime."

"Yes, Thanks. Talk to you next week."

"Bye for now."

When Kent went to bed, he thought about Annie. Waking, or sleeping, she was always in his head. *Yes, I'd like to run away from what happened to Sally. It almost killed me. But I know she'd want me to move on, be happy. I've finally found someone else, and I hope to spend the rest of my life with her. We need that divorce so we can live our lives in the open.*

CHAPTER TWENTY-EIGHT

Annie was excited about today's July 4th social. Frank chose to be in Austin for the festivities, so that made it even better. Her best friends were here, and she was having a really good time laughing and talking with them. The brisket was just right, and the weather was perfect. Kent was sitting with Dustin and Gina, but he didn't look all that happy.

Annie knew the picnic wasn't where he wanted to be. He was supposed to be in California with his family. She was walking in his direction when she saw little Sam go galloping by on Palumbo. He turned to wave at her, just as the horse came to a dead stop next to the tall summer grasses. Sam went flying over Palumbo's head and slammed onto the ground. Gina and Dusty went running. And so did Annie. They all reached Sam about the same time.

Dusty picked him up and brushed him off. "Are you okay, Son?"

Sam was crying, and his shirt was torn.

"His knee got skinned," Gina said, noting the hole in his pants, taking Sam's hand.

"Nothing seems to be broken," Dusty said, checking him over.

By now a crowd was forming. "You all right, Bud?" Kent asked.

"Palumbo threw me off," Sam said shaking.

"That must have been scary," Jim said, reaching over and giving him a hug.

Tears ran down his face as he struggled to his feet, wiping the grass off his pants. "So scary," Mr. Jim.

Annie walked over to Palumbo, took him by the reins, and brought him to Sam. "I'm sorry, Sam," she said. "I bet Palumbo was hungry and the grass distracted him."

"Dumb horse stopped on a dime," Dusty said.

"Daddy, I'm not going to ride Palumbo again, ever."

"Why not?"

"He might throw me off."

"I know you're scared, Sam, and anyone would be. But when you fall off a horse, you have to get back in the saddle."

"Why, Daddy?"

"Because if you wait too long, the fear gets worse."

Sam looked unsure.

"Here's an apple I was saving for later," Dusty said pulling it out of his bag. "Why don't you see if Palumbo wants it."

Sam walked over to his horse, reached up, and tentatively petted him on the nose. Palumbo came closer, whinnied, and gently put his head on Sam's shoulder. Sam fed him the apple and smiled a little, but his face still looked pale.

"How about this," Annie said. "You climb up on Palumbo, wrap both your hands around the saddle horn, and I'll take his reins and walk him around slowly. Then, we'll see how you feel."

"Okay." Annie and Sam walked and talked, while the others stood anxiously waiting and watching.

When they got back, Gina asked, "How'd it go, Sam?"

"A little better, I guess. But I don't want to ride by myself," he said looking down at his boots in the stirrups.

"Why don't I climb on with you?" Annie said, mounting, then sliding onto the horse's rump. She kept Sam in front of her. "How about you hold the reins this time? I'll be right here with you if you need me."

"Okay," he said, and off they cantered.

By the time they got back, Sam was laughing. "I can take it from here, Miss Annie," he said, the confidence back in his voice.

"You got it," she said, slipping off the back of the horse.

"I'm proud of you, Son," Dusty said.

"Thanks, Dad, next time, I'll pay more attention when I'm riding."

"That's the ticket," Gina said, a relieved grin breaking across her face.

Jim smiled up at him, "You're one brave man, buddy," he said patting his leg. "Good job."

Sam nodded, and they all watched him ride off on his own.

"Thank you, Annie," Gina breathed a sigh of relief. "You knew just want to do."

Annie smiled. "If I'm ever lucky enough to have a little boy, I want him to be just like Sam."

"Your time will come," Gina said, squeezing her hand, "I'm sure of it."

"Sam showed real persistence," Kent said.

"One of the things riding horses teaches kids," Jim said. "My boys love to ride."

"How about we all wander over to the dessert table?" Gina suggested. That carrot cake is calling my name."

"Tempting, but I've got some things to catch up on at home," Kent said, "so I'll be going. As always, it's good to see you all."

"I'll walk along with Kent," Annie said. "I need to run home for a bit, so don't wait for me."

When they were out of earshot, she apologized to Kent. "I'm sorry you missed today with your family. I didn't mean to make you feel like you needed to be here for me."

"I'm okay."

"Whenever someone says they're okay, it often means they're not."

He smiled. "I'll be with my family for Labor Day."

She squeezed his hand. "I wish I could kiss you good-bye."

He smiled. "I wish you could too. Then, he looked at her and said, "You were amazing out there today with Sam. He learned a lot from you about regaining his confidence."

"He's a good kid."

"Yes, he is. See you soon?"

"See you soon, Kent, I love you."

"I love you too." He started walking to his car.

"Kent," she called, wait."

He stopped and turned.

"I have an idea," she said, walking up to him. "Have you ever seen the July 4th fireworks in San Antonio."

"No, I haven't."

"Nothing short of spectacular. San Antonians love celebrating our nation's Independence Day, and Woodlawn Lake Park is a prime spot to watch the show around 9 pm. What do you say?"

"I like it," he smiled, "great idea."

"Let's drop your car off at your house, and you can ride with me. But we better get a move on. I know a place we might still get parking in one of the surrounding neighborhoods."

"See you at my house, I'll grab a blanket and a couple of lawn chairs."

Later that night, they watched as thousands of fireworks popped and wheeled across the darkened night sky. "I wonder what the rest of the year has in store for us?" Annie asked Kent, leaning on his shoulder.

"All good things, I hope," he smiled, holding her close.

PART THREE
DISRUPTION

CHAPTER TWENTY-NINE

*A*nnie had been feeling out of sorts for the past few weeks, sick with a bug, she guessed.

She'd thrown up so many times, she'd lost track. Kent had called her cell several times to check on her. Gabriela brought homemade chicken soup, but it was Frank who had been surprisingly attentive. He brought her water and ice chips, kept the guest room dark and quiet, and even stayed home from work to look after her. *Trying to get back on my good side. Too late for that.*

After yet another morning visit to the porcelain goddess, she lay in her bed, staring at the ceiling, and wondering when this would be over. She brought up the calendar on her cell phone. As she scanned it, she noticed the little red dot she put there every 28 days. She tried not to pay too much attention to her periods, except to note them on her calendar, just in case.

She hadn't had a period in almost eight weeks. Annie went into the bathroom and pulled out the in-home pregnancy test she'd stored under the sink and checked the expiration date on the box. Still valid. Then inspected the test to make sure it hadn't deteriorated in the moist air of the bathroom. Looked good. Her hands trembled. *I can't be pregnant, not now. I want to be, and I don't want to be.*

She went to the sink, washed her hands with warm, soapy water, removed the testing device from the foil wrapper, and peed directly onto the stick. Then placed it on a clean towel with the result window facing up. Annie could see the background of the control window get darker, as the urine passed through, and ten minutes later, she saw the word "pregnant."

Is it accurate? She picked up the phone and called her gynecologist's nurse. Connie offered to squeeze her in the next day.

At exactly 10:00 the next morning, Annie sat in Dr. Jeannie's office. There were three pregnant women in the room, leafing through baby magazines and drinking water with a slice of lemon floating on the top. She smiled at them, and they smiled back. *They look so relaxed. I'm a mess.* Thirty minutes later, it was her turn to see the doctor.

She took another urine test, and the doctor did a pelvic exam. Annie removed her feet from the cold stirrups and sat up. "What do you think, Dr. Jeannie? Am I pregnant?

"Yes, you are! Congratulations!"

"I can't believe it." Her eyes widened. "We've tried for years, and now it's finally happened?!"

Dr. Jeannie sat down beside her and gave her a hug. "I know it's been a long time coming."

I can't let Jeannie see that I'm conflicted. She'll have questions. "For years, I've watched my friends get pregnant and have babies. I felt like there was this secret sisterhood where I didn't belong. I was on the outside looking in."

"There's a lot of heartache for women who want to get pregnant and can't. Now, you're one of the lucky ones. I'm sure Frank will be thrilled."

Annie went completely pale. "Of course, he will," she mumbled.

"Are you okay? You don't look good. Connie, will you get her a glass of water, please."

"Yes, ma'am."

"I'll need you back in here every month until the baby is born, and I'm going to put you on a pre-natal vitamin. Make sure you're eating a variety of healthy and calcium-rich foods, drink lots of water, get plenty of rest, and control your stress."

Control my stress? Right. "How long will my morning sickness last?"

"Likely another couple of months."

"What else should I know?"

"I'll send you home with several brochures. You and Frank should sign up for a childbirth education class to help you prepare for the birth of your baby. I imagine he'll want to be involved from the beginning."

"Yes, he will." *How will I ever divorce him now?* When can we know if the baby is a boy or a girl?"

"I recommend waiting until 19-20 weeks to be sure. Does it matter to you?"

"Not to me, but I'm certain Frank will want a boy."

"Well, don't let him blame you if it's not. There's evidence that the father's genes determine the baby's gender, since some of his sperm carry x chromosomes and some carry y."

"Thank you, Dr. Jeannie. I'd be happy with either a girl or a boy. My daddy was hoping for a grandson to someday run the family ranch."

"Sounds like he thought only a man could do that."

"He did."

"If he could see you now, he'd have to change his tune."

"Annie smiled. "You're right."

She left the doctor's office and sat in the car, thinking about her baby. She couldn't keep the news from Frank. *I'll have to call off the divorce. We'll have to reconcile.* Her shoulders drooped. *That's the last thing I want. —Head down and move forward.*

Annie drove out of the parking lot and on to the ranch. When she walked inside, Caroline was sitting at a desk in the den, surrounded by ledger sheets. *Time to tell her the news.*

"Hey, you, how are you feeling?" She asked.

"A little better," Annie said, collapsing into her father's favorite leather chair.

"You look as white as a ghost. How about some tea?"

"Love it, thanks." Annie followed Caroline into the kitchen and asked, "Where's Gabriela?"

"She's taking the day off, but I'm pretty sure I can remember how to make tea." She laughed. "How does orange spice sound?"

"Perfect, have we got any creamer?"

"In the refrigerator, and your usual sweetener is in the pantry."

"Thanks."

"How about a blueberry muffin to go with the tea?"

Her stomach rolled. "None for me, thanks."

"Are you sure you're, okay?" Caroline asked, pouring hot water into their mother's china tea pot.

This should be the happiest day of my life. And it's not. I'm bringing a precious child into a miserable marriage. Annie shook her head. "No, I'm not okay."

"Let's take our tea in the yellow room, and you can tell me about it."

After they sat down, Annie collapsed in Caroline's arms.

Caroline held her and waited.

"The good news is I'm pregnant." she said, pulling back.

"You're pregnant! You're going to be a mother, and me an auntie!" She beamed and started dancing around the room.

Annie couldn't help but laugh. "You're crazy."

"I know, isn't it grand?" Caroline plopped herself down on the couch again.

"My marriage to Frank is the complication."

"Good point. But you could still leave him."

"I don't see how. He'll be so excited, and so will his campaign. My friends at Songbird Community will be over the moon with joy. And then I announce a divorce?"

Caroline steepled her fingers. "From a legal standpoint, if you divorced him, he might try for sole custody once the baby is born."

Annie looked at her. That sounded just like something Frank would do. "I don't want anyone else to know I'm pregnant yet. I have to think this through." Annie's lips and chin trembled.

"You know I'm here for you."

"There's one other thing."

"What?"

"I've fallen in love with someone else."

"Seriously?! Who? Are you sleeping with him?"

"No."

"Thank goodness for that. That would give Frank ammunition. Who is he?"

"Kent Winder."

Caroline's mouth fell open. "The man from California I met at Daddy's funeral?"

"Yes."

"Why didn't you tell me before?"

"I don't know, I am sorry," she whispered.

"Well, one thing's for sure," Caroline said, muscles clenching along her jawline. "As an attorney, I'll do whatever it takes to legally to protect both you and the baby. You're all that matters now."

Annie's chest ached, and her hands felt cold. She couldn't think clearly. What now?

CHAPTER THIRTY

Kent sorted through his office mail, thinking about Annie, hoping she was feeling better.

He slit open a letter from the home office and found correspondence directing him to have a claim investigated. A large insurance check was scheduled to be sent to 556 Autumn Paint Way, Paradise Hills, Texas. Why did that address sound so familiar? Of course, it was Frank and Annie's address.

A check for the claim in the amount of $1 million was scheduled to be made out to Annie, since she and Caroline were slated to split the $2 million policy. But because the amount on the policy had recently been upped from $1 million to $2 million, Pete's death needed to be investigated.

He read on. Pete Kingman's death certificate indicated only a probable cause of death, and there were no toxicology reports. Kent knew he'd have to have an insurance investigator probe the circumstances surrounding his death before the company paid the claim. This wouldn't be good news for Annie or Caroline, and at the very least, he wanted to give them a heads up before putting Lynne on the case.

Kent called Annie's cell. "Hey, how are you? Feeling any better?"

"Not really," she said. "What's up?"

"I'd like to talk with you and Caroline for an hour or so if I could. It's about your father's insurance claim. Where are you now?"

"Out at the ranch, what's the problem?"

"This'll be easier to explain in person. Is this a bad time?"

"Sort of, but it's okay. When do you want to come?"

"I could be there in an hour or so, if that works for you two."

"Sure, come on out."

"See you soon." Kent knew Annie and Caroline were still very tender over their father's death and asking for a toxicology report would reopen wounds that hadn't even begun to heal. But corporate deemed a toxicology report necessary.

He drove out to the ranch, not in any rush. It was a hot, humid day in late August, the kind of day in South Texas where the best strategy was to go from air-conditioned house to car, to office, stepping outside as little as possible. Despite the damp heat, he had his window cracked open, enjoying the fresh smell of country air.

When he reached the ranch, he called from the gate to the main house. Annie answered and beeped him through. Despite the reason for his visit, he was anxious to see her. Caroline, he barely knew. He'd met her only once at her father's funeral several weeks ago, and she struck him as a no-nonsense woman. She liked to take charge of every situation, and could take perfectly good care of herself, thank you very much. Not even a hint of vulnerability that he could see. Not his cup of tea.

Annie was the kind of woman for him. If she could finalize the divorce, they could marry.

He pulled into the side yard, parked his car, and walked through the stone gate. He passed the huge live oaks and walked up to the front door. Kent lifted the heavy brass knocker and knocked twice.

Annie answered. Her eyes were red, and she looked as if she'd been crying. "Come in," she said, taking his hand.

"Are you, all right?" He asked.

"We can't talk now," she said, leading him into the yellow room.

Caroline stood to greet him, stiffly shaking his hand. "Nice to see you again, Kent,"

"You, too."

"Won't you sit down?" She pointed to an overstuffed chair with a flower pattern.

"Yes, Thank you."

The two sisters sat together on the divan staring at him from across the room. He felt awkward. *What's going on here?*

"Annie said you wanted to talk with us."

He cleared his throat. *How best to begin.* "Yes. I work for the insurance company Sound Solutions for Life, and we're the group processing your father's insurance claim."

"Yes," Caroline said, "we know that. Go on."

He unbuttoned his top shirt button. Was it warm in here, or was it only him? "About eighteen months ago, your father upped the amount of his life insurance policy from $1 million to $2 million."

"Is that a problem?" Caroline asked.

"Well, it wouldn't have been, if Sound Solutions for Life were more certain of the cause of death. What we have is a probable cause of death, and as you may know, the results of the autopsy report were inconclusive."

"So how do you think our father died?" Caroline quizzed him.

"Like you, I suspected a heart attack. But the autopsy report sent to our office on request showed no real damage to his heart. Did anyone ask you about ordering a toxicology report?"

"We saw no need for one." Caroline glared at him, eyes hard and flinty. "Are you suggesting our father took his life?!" Her lips curled. "Because he didn't, and no one in town will believe he did."

"Ms. Kingman," he began, "this is a courtesy call, and I don't set the policies of our company, I carry them out. I have no choice but to ask for a toxicology report, since the autopsy found only a probable cause of death. Look, I know this is hard for both of you, and I'm so sorry. I'm even sorrier that I am the one delivering the news," he said, looking at Annie, "but please don't shoot the messenger."

"You're right," Caroline said, voice controlled. "What happens next?"

"I'll assign an investigator to the case. Her name is Lynne Leavitt. She's a friend of mine, the best in the business. She has an office in Texas now as well as Los Angeles, and we've worked together on lots of cases. She'll want to come out to the house, look around, and talk with anyone here the night Pete died."

"The only ones in the house were Gabriela, Frank, and me," Annie said. Then she paused, "and Hy."

Kent made a note. "Lynne will also contact the medical examiner's office and order a forensic toxicology report, then we'll go from there."

"How long will the toxicology report take?" Annie asked.

"Typically, weeks, sometimes months. The tissue and fluid part takes fifteen minutes or so, but then the chemists take it from there. Officials will also need to come to the ranch with Lynne and check out the house and your dad's medicine cabinet."

"And what precisely will they be looking for in the medicine cabinet?" Caroline asked.

"Over-the-counter medicines, prescription drugs, and illicit drugs. They'll also check for any evidence that might indicate that he was getting prescriptions from several doctors."

"I can assure you that our father was NOT a drug addict!?" Caroline insisted, standing up.

"No, ma'am, I'm sure he wasn't."

"Please go on," Annie said.

"The basic toxicology screen looks for drugs in the blood using antibodies that can spot certain classes of drugs. Experts will then decide whether doses of the drugs found in the specimens are therapeutic, toxic, or even lethal. They'll want to determine if the drugs contributed to your father's death, or even caused it. Maybe your father took more of something than he intended, and it contributed to his death, rather than caused it. It may be a simple accident."

"Where will you do the testing?" Caroline asked.

"We'll begin with the Blanco County lab, and if they don't find anything, we'll have to send the samples to the Bexar County lab, which is more specialized. That's why this all takes time. And even after all the testing, 2-5% of the causes of death are still unable to be determined, so we'll see how it goes. Lynne will try and help move things along as best she can. I'll keep you posted every step of the way."

"I suppose we can be grateful for that," Caroline said.

Kent hoped one day Caroline would be his sister-in-law. They'd gotten off to a rough start today.

"I'll walk you out," Annie offered.

He guessed that was his cue. "Good-bye, Caroline," he said standing.

"Mr. Winder," Caroline nodded.

What an ice queen, he thought. Then he noticed that Caroline had collapsed on the couch, head resting in her hands. She looked shaken. Maybe he was wrong about her.

After they left the house, he held Annie's hand. "I've missed you so much."

"I'm sorry Caroline got aggravated, she's worried."

"I understand. I was trying to ease the pain, not cause more."

"I know your heart was in the right place," she said, smiling weakly. "I should get back up to the house. I'm going to stay here with Caroline for a while. There's lots to do around the ranch, and I'm getting more involved."

"Just so you know, I'm leaving for Southern California this weekend to be with Karla and Carter and see my grandpa."

"I'm glad you'll be getting time with your family. Take care of yourself," she said, voice flat. "We'll talk when you get back."

"I love you."

She said nothing in reply, just squeezed his hand, smiled, and walked back into the house.

He drove carelessly down the road, kicking up dust as he went. When he got to the highway, he downshifted and sped up. As he flew along 1604 toward San Antonio, he didn't really care whether he got a speeding ticket. *What's going on? Something isn't right.* There was a heaviness in his chest. He wanted to go home, take a long run, and clear his head. But he was meeting Lynne for dinner.

He arrived at Paesanos early and reserved a small table outside. Twenty minutes later, he looked up and saw Lynne. *I'd recognize those pearl earrings anywhere*, he thought, waving. "Over here, Lynne."

"You must be in the mood for Mediterranean tonight," she said, taking a seat.

"I was, hope that works for you. I took the liberty of ordering dinner for both of us."

"Great, you know what I like, what'd you get me?"

"Lobster ravioli with escargot to start."

"Perfect. Thanks. What about you?"

"The Angus beef, rare, it's really good here."

Lynne got right to the point. "Looks like you got yourself a case close to home."

Closer than you know, Kent thought. "Yes. One of the beneficiaries and her husband are in my congregation, and the other beneficiary is her sister."

"Doesn't exactly make you objective."

"One of the reasons I brought you in."

"Tell me what you know about your fellow congregants."

"Annie and Frank Graves, married, no kids. She comes from landed Texas gentry, he's plain vanilla. My gut tells me he's a dangerous man who will stop at nothing."

"What makes you say that?"

"He's cocky, arrogant, and narcissistic. I had a run in with him at the local gun club."

Lynne looked surprised. "What were you doing there?"

"Target practice."

"You went shooting?"

"In a word, yes."

"Sounds more like something I'd do. You know how I love my guns."

Kent did know that. Lynne had a large gun safe in her new office where she kept weapons of every sort. She shot competitively and even taught gun safety classes. She didn't mess around.

"When you live in places like Texas," Kent said, "you adjust to the local customs."

"I do because I have to. But you surprise me."

About that time, the food came, and Kent dug into his steak. "Just the way I like it. Good and rare, and an excellent cut of meat. How's the lobster ravioli?"

"Tasty. So, tell me about Annie Graves."

Kent wanted to be careful how he phrased his comments. Let Lynne form her own opinions, he told himself, so he took a steadying breath, "She's a church-going woman who cares a lot about her family. A talented singer who loves animals and does equine therapy part time." Kent paused and then laughed. "She can also be competitive."

Lynne smiled. "Rough and tumble Texas woman. I like it."

"She can match a guy in water skiing, but she's vulnerable, empathetic, compassionate."

Lynne said nothing for a minute. And then, she leaned forward, and in a low voice said, "She sounds pretty special."

Kent knew he'd gone too far with the vulnerable bit. *Change the subject. Quick.* "She's nothing like her sister Caroline."

"What's she like?"

"I met her twice. She's a tough lady lawyer from Dallas who runs her own firm and doesn't take crap from anybody. She's living at the family ranch right now, and word on the street is she may be coming back to the Hill Country to help Annie run the ranch."

"What about her legal practice?"

"I understand she'll work remotely here and fly to Dallas for court cases. The flight only takes an hour. She's keeping her home too."

"Interesting, so does the family know I'll be calling?"

"Annie and Caroline do, but Frank doesn't, as far as I know. Get all the information you can on him."

"Will do. Was he in the house at the time of Kingman's death?"

"Yes."

Anyone else?

"Gabriela Hernandez, long-time cook and housekeeper for the family, and Hy Hatch, ranch hand manager."

"What do you think the chances are this is a suicide?"

"I only met Pete Kingman once, but he didn't seem like the type who'd take his own life." Lynne added that to her notes.

"Do you want anything else to eat or drink?" Kent asked.

"Not for me, it's been a long day. I took an early flight out this morning, so do you mind if we call it a night?"

"Nope, long day for me too."

"Okay, I'll keep you informed."

The two shook hands and went their separate ways. *If there is anything amiss about Pete's death, Lynne's the one who can get to the bottom of it.*

CHAPTER THIRTY-ONE

*F*rank sat in the bar of the Menger Hotel. Today would be it for him and Kelly, although she didn't know it yet. He'd told Annie weeks ago he'd broken it off with Kelly, but he hadn't. Today was go time. If he didn't dump Kelly soon, Annie would proceed with the divorce. Hell, she might try and do it anyway. He was not going to let that happen. Frank signaled Auggie and ordered himself a double.

He wanted to have this conversation with Kelly in a public place, so it would be harder for her to make a scene. He didn't want any other bar patrons overhearing their conversation, so he'd carefully chosen 3:00 pm for their meeting. *Well played, the bar is dead.* Frank leaned forward in his leather chair and rubbed his knees, then moved to pick up his drink, which he fumbled, almost knocking it over.

He looked up, and there she was, breathless and beautiful, eyes dancing. Her hair was tied neatly back in a soft lavender ribbon, and a skin-tight dress highlighted every curve. Intimately familiar with each one of those curves, he knew he would miss them. Physically, she was almost perfect, except her chest was beginning to sag a little, and he preferred perky.

Maybe they could sleep together one more time, and then he'd dump her? What would be the harm in that? Neither one of them had known last time that it was over. No, he reminded himself, it's now or never. "Have a seat," he said, standing up.

"Mmmm, so good to see you, handsome hunk," Kelly winked. Sitting down, she reached under the table and touched him. "I'm so happy we're meeting in the bar first today; it's like you finally want to show me off," she grinned.

He grimaced, not sure where to begin, sensing she was not going to make this easy for him. "There's something I need to tell you."

"Honey, you go ahead. Wait, is it about Annie? Are you two getting a divorce? I knew it! I'm ready to leave Jim, as soon as you say the word," she beamed.

Frank groaned inwardly, why did Annie have to find that note in his pocket? He should have been more careful. He and Kelly had so much fun together, and while he didn't love her, he really liked her. He didn't want to end their affair. He'd especially miss their nights at the Menger.

"Fraid that's not it," he said.

"Then, what is it? I'm all ears."

"Annie knows about us."

Kelly went pale. "No. How? When?"

"She found a note from you about six weeks ago."

"She's known for six weeks, and you're only now telling me," she said loudly. "No wonder she's been avoiding me at church. How did she know it was me?"

"Guess your love for me shows."

"Oh," she said, looking at her feet.

He hadn't considered that he might find a way to blame this on her. Perfect.

"I'm sorry, Frank, but look on the bright side. Now's our chance to move away and start over somewhere, just the two of us," she said. "Jim can keep the kids, and they can come visit."

"No can do, Kelly, you know that. A divorce could kill my political career."

"Not everywhere, Frank, only in places like Texas. Let's move to Jersey, my family's still there. Plenty of opportunities for you to make a name for yourself there, and it would be an easy leap to move from Jersey to Washington D.C."

Frank sighed; she still didn't get it. Why was she making this so hard on him? "No, I'm afraid not; for me, once a Texan, always a Texan."

"Then what are we going to do?"

"I don't like this any better than you do, but we've got to stop seein' each other. It breaks my heart, but I must do it. It's the honorable thing to do."

"No… no, not that. I don't want to live without you, I can't live without you," she wailed.

"I care about you so much." *Ha, ha. I'm only in it for the sex.* "I don't have a choice here." It was a good thing there was no one else in the bar. Could he plan his break ups, or what? His muscles relaxed, and his breath came more easily now as he handed her a cocktail napkin. "Dry your eyes, darlin.' You can live without me. Anyone can live without anyone."

She sucked in her upper lip and looked at him, stunned, eyes wide. "You can't mean that."

"Love is nice to have, but it's not essential. Money and power, those are the essentials."

"So, this is you breaking up with me?"

"In a word, yes." *Good grief, where's her spine?* Frank could not abide clingy women. He'd never seen Kelly like this, and he didn't like it.

"No, Frank. No, no, please. I love you, we're so good together."

"I'm sorry, Kelly, but we're through."

"You jerk!" she said, tone changing, nostrils flaring, standing.

There was the old Kelly, there was his firebrand. "Calm down," Frank said, "Auggie is looking our way."

"I don't care what Auggie thinks," she said, face red with anger.

"I do, so, sit down," he hissed under his breath, cracking his knuckles.

She plopped herself down, hard. "What am I going to tell Jim?"

"You're not going to tell him anything. Why would you tell Jim?"

"What if Annie tells him?"

"She wouldn't do that because she doesn't believe in hurting innocent bystanders. That's what Jim is, an innocent bystander."

"Well, then, maybe I'll tell him," Kelly said, jutting out her chin.

He grabbed her wrist and held it. "It would not be advisable for you to tell him, now listen to me. Jim's a good man, and he takes care of you and your boys. It's over between us, Kelly. Go home to your family."

"Jim's boring, my life is boring, and without you, it would be unbearable. I won't let you go."

"Oh yes, you will. There is only one way this ends."

She picked up his drink and threw it in his face. "I hate you, Frank Graves!

"Are you freaking kidding me? This is an expensive suit!"

Kelly stormed out of the bar, as Auggie came over and handed him a cloth napkin. Frank handed him a fifty. Auggie was nothing, if not discreet.

Frank reached for his phone to check messages. There was a message from a woman named Lynne Leavitt. Who the hell's she? Frank listened to the message in disbelief and blanched. She needed an appointment to talk about Pete's death.

CHAPTER THIRTY-TWO

*A*nnie and Caroline sat waiting in Daddy's office. Caroline sat in the high back teal chair behind the seventy-year-old ornately carved desk, an American flag flanking the desk on one side and a Texas flag on the other. Annie stood looking at the framed round picture of Ruby on the wood-paneled wall. "Daddy loved that dog," she said, "and I think Ruby misses him almost as much as we do."

Caroline nodded, tears in her eyes.

Annie sat down in the black leather chair studded with silver nails, her father's favorite. "This is one of those days I'm relieved you're a lawyer," she said.

Caroline smiled. "Yeah, me too. I think."

They both laughed. "When's Lynne Leavitt coming?" Annie asked.

"In about an hour. I imagine she'll want to talk to you first, then Gabriela and Hy. Find out what you each know about the night Daddy died."

"What's there to know? What's she looking for?"

"Evidence of insurance fraud. Two ways that could go. If she determines his death was a suicide, Sound Solutions for Life might deny the additional $1 million, since it's been less than two years since he increased the policy."

"No way he would ever kill himself."

"You and I know that, but Leavitt doesn't. Besides suicide, she'll check for evidence of foul play."

"Foul play? Really?"

"She'll need to rule out murder."

"Murder?!" Annie was shocked at the mention of it. "Who would want to kill him?"

"She'll look at the two of us first, since we're the sole beneficiaries of the policy."

"What? She thinks we might have killed our own father for money?"

"I'm sure that's crossed her mind."

"Sheesh, hadn't thought of that. Guess I'm more of a suspect than you since you weren't even in the house that night."

"Not necessarily. She'll suspect both of us, since life insurance fraud often involves two or more people who committed the crime together. And she'll want to talk to Frank."

"Do we need a lawyer? Besides you, I mean."

"Not yet, I'm just telling you what will be on her mind. Insurance fraud is a big deal in this country to the tune of up to $80 billion a year. People do all kinds of crazy things to collect insurance, including setting their own houses on fire and killing their pregnant wives."

"That's insane."

"I know, my office's insurance fraud expert verified the details." Caroline paused, then continued. "Leavitt will want to search Daddy's rooms too. Has anything been moved or changed since he died?"

"I haven't been in there since that morning. The door's still shut, and I doubt Gabriela has either. Have you?"

"No. Could you get Gabriela? And then, we'll talk with Hy. I want to give them a heads up about what's coming."

Annie found Gabriela in the kitchen. "Would you come into the office for a moment, please? We'd like to talk with you."

"Everything ok? Shall I bring tea?"

"Thank you, but no." Annie hugged Gabriela, who looked relieved.

When they reached the office, Gabriela took a seat. Caroline began speaking. "Gabriela, in an hour or so, a female detective working for a life insurance company is coming out to the ranch. She'll have questions for all of us about the night Daddy died."

Gabriella looked stunned. "I don't know nothing, I only come running when Miss Annie screamed."

"I know, it's okay, just a formality. Be honest, answer all her questions, and tell her what you know."

"*Si*, I will do that." Gabriela looked like a deer caught in the headlights.

Caroline reached across the desk and clasped her hand. "Please don't worry, she said."

Then, Annie asked, "Have you been in Daddy's rooms since he died?"

"Oh, no, Miss Annie, not since that morning when I mopped up the spilled milk and took away the broken glass. It's too soon to go back to his rooms. That would dishonor the dead."

"Thank you, Gabriela."

"Do you have any questions for us?" Caroline asked.

Gabriela stood straighter and smoothed her apron. "Do you want me serve tea and muffins to your guest?"

"That would be lovely," Caroline said, "Thank you. Would you also walk out to the barn and see if you can find Hy, please? I doubt he has his phone on."

"*Si*, Miss Caroline."

Several minutes later, Hy walked into the office and tipped his hat. "Ladies, what can I do for ya?" Hy's legs were a little bow-legged, but he'd spent most of his life on a horse.

"Have a seat, please," Annie said. "We wanted to let you know that a detective working for a life insurance company is coming here shortly, and she'll have questions about the night Daddy died."

"What does she want with me?"

"Information. She needs to make sure there wasn't anything unusual about Daddy's death, before the insurance company will pay the claim."

"What her name?"

"Lynne Leavitt."

"She must have a big hole in her screen door, if she doesn't know Pete died of a heart attack."

"Dad's heart had no evidence of that, so the insurance company wants his death investigated."

"Well, I guess you can't get lard unless you boil the hog. What do you want me to say?"

"Tell her everything you know, and don't hold back."

"Yes ma'am, anything else?"

"Not from me. Caroline?"

"No, you covered it."

"How's the fence mending coming, Hy?" Annie asked.

"Just fine, should be done by nightfall."

"Great, hope we're not working you too hard out there."

"Pete used to worry about that too, and I told him I still have lots of good years left in me. Not sure he believed me." Hy clenched his hand and then relaxed it.

"Of course, you have lots of good years left," Annie said. "Don't know how we'd operate the ranch without you, especially with Daddy gone. So, don't go running off," she smiled.

Hy laughed. "No chance of that."

"Good, we need you."

"I'll call you when the detective gets here," Annie said, and Hy left.

A few minutes later the doorbell rang. "Ready or not, here we go," Caroline said. "I'll answer the door. Why don't you wait here, and I'll send her to you."

"Aren't you coming in with her?"

"No, she'll want to talk with you alone, but I'll be close, waiting my turn in the yellow room."

Annie sat behind the desk and took charge, leaving a chair out front for the detective. She was tapping a pen on the desk when Lynne walked in. She stood. "Ms. Leavitt?"

"Yes, ma'am. Call me Lynne, please, Mrs. Graves."

Annie winced. She'd always hated her husband's last name. As soon as the divorce was over, she'd change her name back to Kingman, something she could be proud of. "I'm Annie." She reached out and offered her hand. "Won't you sit down."

"Thank you," she said, returning her handshake. "What a brilliant office. Especially the teal marble desktop, and so many books on those shelves."

"My mother was an avid reader—except for all the cattle and agriculture books which belonged to my daddy. Why don't we get started?"

"Okay," Lynne said, pulling out her note pad. "What can you tell me about the night your father died?"

"It happened the night of the 'once in a hundred-year flood' you've heard about."

"Yes, I have."

"He went upstairs to the balcony off his bedroom. Said he wanted to keep watch over the ranch and try and gage the damage to our property. Frank and I went to bed, and so did Gabriela. Hy slept in the guest room that night. Daddy didn't want him going back out in the rain, which was growing worse by the minute." She paused. "Any questions so far?"

"Just one. Was Hy up when you went to bed?"

"Yes, as I remember it, he was still watching the news."

"Did either you or your husband leave the room that night?"

"I'm a very sound sleeper, always have been, so I can only speak for myself. I didn't leave the room until early the next morning, but I doubt Frank did either. We were both exhausted."

"I understand you're the one who found your father the next morning."

"I am." Tears spilled across her face.

"I'm sorry for your loss. The two of you must have been close."

"I miss him every day."

Lynne stopped for several seconds. "Where was he when you found him?" she asked softly.

"He was still sitting outside; head resting on his chest. I thought he'd fallen asleep, but he was already dead. I wish I'd look in on him earlier, maybe I could have done something."

"It may be that there's nothing you could have done, in any case. It's hard to second guess these kinds of things. What did you do when you realized he was dead?"

"I shook him and begged him to wake up. Nothing. Then I dropped a glass of cold milk I was holding, shattering it in pieces. I ran to the stairs and screamed for Frank and Gabriella. They came running. I don't remember much after that."

"That's helpful, thanks. I'll want to look at your father's room after I finish my interviews with the ranch hand and housekeeper."

"My sister would like to speak with you next, if you're finished with me?"

"For the time being, thank you."

Five minutes later, Annie walked in with Caroline. "Lynne, this is my sister Caroline."

She didn't offer her hand, and neither did Lynne.

"Good-bye, Lynne," Annie said.

She stood. "Thanks for your time."

Annie pulled aside the floor to ceiling floral drapery that separated the library from the rest of the house and walked out. Once outside the room, she removed her shoes and crept back to where she could hear what was being discussed.

"Do sit down, Ms. Leavitt," Caroline said.

"Please, call me, Lynne."

"Since this is not a social call, I'll address you as Ms. Leavitt, thank you."

"I get that talking to me today might feel uncomfortable."

"My sister and I decided not to have our attorney present, since we have nothing to hide."

"I understand you're an attorney yourself, Ms. Kingman."

"You've done your homework."

"I'll get to the point. As you know, the ME ruled your father's death inconclusive."

"Yes, and while unusual, it's possible that even after all the tests, we may never discover the cause of my father's death."

"That's correct, we might not, but it's my job to rule out the possibilities."

"You may proceed with your questions."

Annie had heard enough. As usual, Caroline was holding her own. Annie picked up her shoes and walked into the yellow room. She curled up with a magazine and waited.

When Caroline and Lynne came into the room, they were both smiling. Annie was surprised given the tone of their initial conversation.

"Would either of you care for tea?" Caroline asked.

"Not for me, thanks," Lynne said."

"This way out, Lynne," Annie said. "Hy's in the barn waiting to speak with you."

*****

Lynne left the house and made her way down the winding road to the show barn. Walking in, she was surprised at the size of the place. It was huge, dirt floors, wooden rafters and dozens of metal pens filled with cows. She'd never been on a working ranch before. Impressive operation, she thought, winding her way past horse stalls.

And then, "You, Lynne Leavitt?" a man asked without turning around. She noticed a pronounced limp.

"That's me."

The man turned, spit on his hand, and offered it to her. "Hy Hatch, Kingman Ranch Hand Manager for more than thirty years."

Lynne took his hand, killer grip. "Nice to meet you. Can we sit?"

"Sure, you okay sittin' on a bale of hay?"

"Works for me."

Hatch's back popped when he threw down two bales. Then, they sat down facing each other, and Lynne could feel straw poking through her pants.

Hatch glared at her. "What's that there notebook for?"

"Helps me remember conversations. The company requires me to take notes."

He grunted. "Go ahead, ask your questions."

269

"All right. What'd you do before you came to the Kingman Ranch?"

"Farm hand for a hay and cattle business out in Navasota, Texas."

"What brought you here?"

"Heard they was looking for a Ranch Hand Manager. Everyone in the state of Texas knows 'bout the Kingman Ranch. Top notch place to work with good pay. After talkin' with Mister Pete, a time or two, he determined I'd make a fine supervisor. Helps that I know most all there is to know 'bout horses and cattle."

"Sounds as if he was lucky to get you."

"Reckon he was."

"I hear you're more like family than an employee."

"Miss Annie tell you that?"

"Yes."

"I've gotten close with both girls 'cross the years, and there ain't nothin' I wouldn't do for 'em." He leaned forward with one hand on his knee and looked hard at Lynne. "Neither one of 'em would hurt a flea."

Lynne nodded. "You friends with Frank Graves too?"

He snorted. "Don't care for him, dodgy politician. You can call a horse a duck, and it still don't change anything."

Lynne remembered that Kent had similar observations about Graves. She changed the subject. "Mind if I ask how old you are?"

"My age ain't no secret, I'm 71."

"Ranch work must be tough. You ever think about retiring?"

"Bless your heart." He scowled. "No, I haven't."

"Did Mr. Kingman ever speak with you about retiring?"

"He might could have a time or two. But I ask you, what would I do instead? Can't dance, never could sing, and it's too wet to plow." His deep laugh filled with sarcasm.

Lynne made a note. 'Kingman talked with Hatch about retiring, and he declined.' "Tell me more about the night your boss died."

"Night of the big flood. I come in the house for dinner and stayed the night in the house."

"Was that unusual?'

"Yep, it was, but it was comin' down in sheets outside. We all turned in early, 'cept Mr. Pete. I didn't know anythin' more until morning when I heard Miss Annie scream." He rubbed the back of his neck. "When I knew for sure, he was dead, I rounded up the boys to carry his body out." His muscles quivered, and his voice shook.

Lynne gave him a minute.

"Worst day of my life." He cleared his throat. "Let's keep movin'."

Lynne continued, "Anything look odd or out of place in Mr. Kingman's room?"

"Not that I could see. A newly opened bottle of Jack Daniel's on the table and one drained shot glass. That was customary. Ever since Miss Susie died, he liked his nightcap. Helped him sleep, I reckon."

"Did he drink a lot?"

"Nope. Once at night, no wine, no beer, only his Jack. Kept a stockpile of the stuff in the cellar, catalogued by year and bottle number. Pretty particular about keeping track of it."

Lynne made a note. "Anything else you can remember about that night?"

"Not really. That's about it in a nutshell."

"Will you be staying on at the ranch with Mr. Kingman gone?"

"Course, them girls really need me." He stood. "Now, if there's nothin' else, I got work to do."

"That's it for now." Lynne stood, they shook hands again, and she made her way to the kitchen to find Gabriela.

When she walked into the kitchen, she could smell muffins, banana nut, a favorite. "You must be Gabriela."

"*Si*, please sit, and I get you some muffins." She seemed nervous.

"They look delicious. Thank you." She smiled hoping to put her at ease.

"You like something to drink?"

"Do you have milk?"

She placed a large, cold glass in front of her, hands shaking. Then, she sat down.

Lynne took a large bite of muffin. "These are amazing."

"*Gracias*." She blushed.

"I understand you practically raised Miss Annie."

"*Sí*, she and I are very close."

"And Miss Caroline?"

"She also very kind."

"Are you close to Mr. Graves, too?"

"No," Gabriela scowled. "I don't like to speak ill of no one, but Mr. Frank don't treat Miss Annie with respect. You have other questions for me?"

"Yes, but first a request. I'd like to see Mr. Pete's cellar. Can you take me down there?"

She looked puzzled but agreed. "I get key from the pantry."

Lynne ate the last of the muffin and drained her glass of milk.

"This way, *por favor*," Gabriela said, leading the way down the dimly lit steps.

When they reached the bottom, she opened the door and turned on the lights. Lynne walked into a well-lit room with a rounded stone roof and a dark brown wooden floor where she saw three large glass cases filled with whiskey. The room had two round tables with six chairs each, and there was also a small leather couch. "Can we sit down?" She asked.

Gabriela shook her head. "No, I don't come in this room. Mr. Pete and ranch hands only, but you can sit, if you want to."

"It's okay, I'll just take a quick look around." Lynne noticed the cases were locked, and a detailed inventory of the bottles was posted on the wall. It seemed that when a new bottle of whiskey was pulled from the cabinet, the date was noted. She looked for the day Kingman died. No bottle was crossed off the list that day, and none since.

"I think I'm through here. I'd like to see Mr. Pete's room, please."

Gabriela nodded and led the way back up two flights of stairs.

When they got to Pete's bedroom, Lynne looked around. Neat, clean, and tidy, clothes still hung in the closet. Then checked the medicine cabinet and found nothing out of the ordinary. There was a prescription for Oxycodone, and the bottle was half empty. She made another note.

Thirty minutes later, she finished, said goodbye to Annie and Caroline and walked down the front steps to her car. Lynne didn't have any answers, but she had a few leads. Next up, Frank Graves.

CHAPTER THIRTY-THREE

*K*ent booked a seat by the window. Typically, he insisted on an aisle seat, but today he was flying to Orange County, and he wanted to see the ocean as the plane neared the airport. The trees of Catalina Island came into view as the plane dipped toward the water. He'd taken the ferry out to the island so many times, he'd lost count. He thought about the little white golf carts, imported buffalo on the interior, and awesome side-walk restaurants. He could almost taste the fresh, sweet crab meat melting in his mouth.

The beaches at Newport coast came into view, close enough now that he could watch foamed white caps mingle with blue-green water as the waves rolled toward shore. Kent couldn't wait to get outside and take a deep breath of salt air.

"Please fasten your seatbelts for our descent into John Wayne Airport," the flight attendant intoned. "Make sure your tray tables are stowed and your seat backs are in their upright and locked position."

He checked his watch, wouldn't be long now.

Minutes later, touchdown, nice and smooth. Kent went downstairs to baggage claim, picked up his bag from the whirling metal carousel, then crossed the street to the rental car lot. He selected a convertible. *Guess it reminds me of Annie.* The sun was warm, and a small breeze blew through the palm trees. He couldn't wait to see his family.

He wound toward the ocean to Pacific Coast Highway, top down as he cruised along the rolling water, inhaling the salt air. Kent passed volleyball teams playing in the sand at Laguna Beach as he continued to San Clemente, a wide grin on his face.

Karla and Carter still lived in the house where Kent and Karla had grown up. The insurance money from his parent's death had paid it off. While he owned half the house, he was more than happy to let them live there rent free after Karla's divorce.

He pulled up the gently sloping driveway to the familiar tan stucco house with the tile roof, dark shutters, and trim. Carter came running to meet him. "Uncle Kent, Uncle, Kent!! You're here!! Finally," he squealed.

"Hey, little man." Kent pulled the boy up into his arms for a hug. "You're getting so big! I think you've grown a foot!"

"I'm this tall now," he said, holding his hand over his head, face beaming.

"Awesome!" He laughed. "Where's your mom?"

"Inside waiting. She made stuffed pork chops with applesauce for dinner."

"Mmmm." His stomach growled. "My favorite."

"Mine too," Carter said, taking Kent's hand and dragging him in the direction of the house. When they went inside, Kent was home. The living room had soaring, vaulted ceilings, and sunlight streaming in through the large bank of windows, bouncing off the green tile fireplace.

He wandered into the kitchen to find Karla and was greeted by all-white kitchen cabinets. She'd also put in a new stainless-steel stove and a refrigerator. He liked the look. He smelled a pot of asparagus cooking on the stove. "Hey, Sis!"

"Hey, little brother, good to see you," she said voice light, wrapping her arms around him. "Dinner's almost ready."

"Uncle Kent is not so little, Mom," Carter corrected.

She laughed, "You're right, honey."

"What can I do to help?" Kent asked.

"We're eating dinner outside on the deck, so if you would please set the table."

"I'm on it."

"I'll get the knives and forks, Uncle Kent."

"Thanks, buddy," he said, tousling Carter's red hair. They walked out into the back yard that ran the length of the back of the house. The birds of Paradise, the palm trees, the hibiscus. Even a hot tub. Only a few miles from the beach, they enjoyed a peek-a-boo view of the ocean. Kent stood and stared at the water, hands in the pocket of his jeans.

After dinner, Kent walked Carter up the open stairwell to take him to bed. He could see Karla down below, stretched out on the couch, curled up with a book. She loved to read.

"Look at my new rug, Uncle Kent." The rug was a bright teal color that matched a flock of seagulls flying over a splotch of ocean.

"Nice!"

"And in the corner, I still have the big giraffe you bought me when I was five."

"I'm glad you kept it." Kent sat in the gray recliner and put the yellow pillow behind his back. Carter sat in front of him on the ottoman. Story time. "How about reading 'Where the Sidewalk Ends,' Uncle Kent?"

"One of my favorites." Kent read, "And there the grass grows soft and white, and there the sun burns crimson bright."

When he finished, Carter asked for a tuck. Kent pulled the blue blanket with the sailboats around him and turned out the light. "Sleep tight, and don't let the bedbugs bite."

"I don't have bedbugs."

"I know," Kent smiled. "That's what Grandpa used to tell me when he tucked me in at night."

"Did you have bedbugs?"

"No, it's just an expression."

"What's an expression?"

"Something you say when you can't think of anything original." He grinned.

"Oh, okay, love you."

"Love you, too, buddy. Good night." Kent walked downstairs and sat next to Karla on the couch. "It's so good to be home." He leaned back.

"We love having you here. —May I ask how things are going with Annie?"

"You don't waste any time, do you."

"Nope."

"She still hasn't left her husband yet, but she will." He raised his eyebrows.

"I hope so."

Kent paused. "I loved Sally, and I miss her. But I've stopped running."

"I'm glad about that. I really am. There's one other thing I wanted to say. I'm worried about you keeping a secret about your new friend. Being honest means not only telling the truth but living the truth."

"Uncle Kent," Carter called down from the landing above, his voice cracking. "Why aren't you being honest with my mom?"

Kent looked up, horrified. "Come down here, buddy, please," he said in a low tone.

Carter walked slowly down the stairs, then Kent got up and gave him a bear hug. "Come sit next to us."

As he sat, Kent looked at the floor. "Your mom's right. People make mistakes when they keep secrets or don't tell the whole truth."

"I made a mistake once, Uncle Kent. I took some candy samples from our neighbors' mailboxes. Mom made me put them all back and tell the neighbors what happened. They hugged me and forgave me."

Kent smiled. "Thanks, for sharing that story," he said, chest tightening, thoughts fragmented.

"Let's get you back to bed, Son" Karla said softly.

The next day, Kent took Carter to visit Grandpa in the care center. He was elated when they walked in. As he placed his arms around them both, Kent could feel those arms growing frailer. "Great to see you, Kent. How are you?"

"I'm okay, and how are you?"

"Not bad for an old man, not bad. How are you today, Carter?"

"I'm happy, Grandpa, now that Uncle Kent's here."

Grandpa patted Carter on the head and smiled, "He's your go to guy, Carter."

"So are you, Grandpa."

"I know, and I like that. But I'm getting old."

"Are you going to die, Grandpa?" Carter asked.

"One of these days. But remember, besides your mom, you'll always have this stand-up man in your life," he said pointing in Kent's direction.

Kent didn't feel much like a stand-up guy. He'd have to deal with those feelings later. He wasn't going to ruin his trip home with family. "I love you, Grandpa."

The next morning, the San Clemente sun kissed Kent's bare back as clouds dimpled across a deep blue sky, and a soft breeze waved from the ocean. He took a deep breath. *There's nothing as clear and clean as ocean air.* He stood a minute watching the waves roll rhythmically in and out, then turned to Carter. "Time to build our sandcastle, buddy."

"Yay, Uncle Kent! He jumped, fist in the air. Then he looked at his mom lying asleep on her towel several feet away and lowered his tone, "She can sleep while we build."

"Good plan," Kent said, smiling. "We'll surprise her with what we've created."

They picked up some sticks over by the trees and built a castle. An hour later, Carter went to get his mom. "What do you think?" Carter asked her.

"Best sandcastle I've ever seen."

"Yes!" He threw his hand in the air. "I'm getting hungry."

"Me too," Kent laughed.

"All right, all right, Karla smiled. "Let's go home and cook some steaks."

Kent did the grilling for a late lunch. He waved a puff of white smoke out of his eyes, then said to Karla. "Steaks are almost done."

"They smell good. I'll see how the baked beans are doing."

"While you're in there, would you please bring me the tray of veggies? I'm almost ready."

"You got it."

He flipped the filets over one more time and turned the flame down a bit. Medium rare, just right. It was great weather for an outdoor picnic. Kent felt centered and content. It was a perfect afternoon with the family Kent loved, and the three of them enjoyed a delicious meal.

"Best steak ever," Carter said when he finished. "Gotta go now. Doug's mom is picking me up for soccer practice. Big game next Friday."

"Soccer's my favorite, just like you," Kent said. I'll come back this season and watch you play."

"Wow! Awesome." Carter grinned. "Bye, Mom."

"Bye, love you, Son." She looked at Kent. "It's so great having you here."

"Thanks. Just what I needed too."

Karla smiled. "When you get back to Texas, please do something just for you."

He squeezed her hand.

That night before bed, Kent sat alone and closed his eyes. *Is Annie getting a divorce or not? What if she doesn't? Okay, here's the thing. I can't in good conscience keep 'us' a secret anymore. So, we take a break until the papers are filed? Yeah, right. And just how are you going to tell her that? It might end your relationship.*

CHAPTER THIRTY-FOUR

*F*rank's face was pinched, arms crossed against his chest as he waited for Lynne Leavitt. *She has nothing on you*, he reminded himself. *The experts might never come up with a definitive cause of death.* Frank didn't want to appear nervous, so he walked out onto the balcony to get some air, taking several deep breaths.

When he saw her walk across the parking lot, Frank sized her up. Tall, good-looking gal, red hair and penetrating eyes. Frank had done a little research on her career and found that she was an expert in white collar crime, including uncovering insurance fraud. *Pete is dead and buried, you're in the clear.* Frank walked inside and sat behind his desk.

Moments later, his admin rapped on the door. "Ms. Leavitt is here."

"Show her in." When she came through the door, Frank stood, and the two shook hands.

"Nice office," she said looking around. "Impressive law library. My dad was a lawyer, mind if I have a look around?"

"Help yourself."

"Are you in practice with anyone else?" she asked, scanning the long rows of books.

"No, just me, always been just me."

Lynne picked up a small elementary school math book with a bent corner that she found on the end of one of the rows of books. "What happened to this one?"

Frank froze. He'd thrown that book at his mother one day when she questioned him about his math homework. Hit her head so hard, it had drawn blood and left a dent in the book. Frank liked having a reminder of what he'd done to her, so he kept the book around. But what to tell Leavitt? Frank's confidence ebbed, and the vein in his forehead pulsed. Then, it came to him.

"A bully at school took it out of my backpack and threw it at me. Hit my head so hard, the cover bent, and I had to go in for stitches."

"What a little heathen."

Frank scowled at the use of the word 'heathen.'

"How old was he?"

"Twelve. Sixth grade. I was in fifth."

"Did they punish the kid?"

"Eventually, yes."

"What'd they do to him?"

"Suspended him for a week."

"That's it?"

"That's it." Frank looked Lynne right in the eye.

"Why do you keep the book around?"

Frank clenched his feet under the desk. What was with this nosy sidewinder? "It's a reminder not to take crap from anyone." *That should do it.*

"Makes sense to me."

Frank relaxed again. "Care for a bottle of water?"

"Yes, thanks." Lynne sat down.

Frank took two cold bottles from his fridge and handed one to her. "I'm on a tight schedule today, so why don't we get started?" He took a long swig.

She opened her briefcase and took out a notebook then leaned in to ask the first question. "I understand you and your wife were at the ranch the night Pete Kingman died."

"That's right. Annie had driven to the ranch earlier that day to help give birth to a cow. When the storm started, I drove out to make sure she and Pete were okay. I knew they had a long night ahead."

"Did you take anything with you?"

"Like what?" Frank bit the inside of his lip.

"I don't know. You tell me."

"A rain slick and my briefcase. That's it. I keep a change of clothes out at the ranch. "Why do you ask?" His hands felt clammy.

"No reason. Hy Hatch told me everyone turned in early that night."

"You met with Hatch already?"

"Yes."

"There's a guy with a beef."

"What do you mean?"

"Pete told me he'd tried to retire him a few times. Wouldn't hear of it. Told Pete he needed to take a stronger stance with him."

"Did he?"

"Don't know. But if I were you, I'd keep Hatch in my sights."

"Why? You think he might have killed Kingman?"

"Course not," Frank sneered. "Just makin' conversation. Pete died of a heart attack, plain and simple. Irrespective of what the autopsy report says, he was an old man with a-fib. His daddy died of a heart attack. It all fits."

"What about suicide? Do you think Kingman could take his own life?"

"Hadn't thought of that. Guess it's possible. He never did get over his wife's death, and he was always feeling poorly."

"I'm sending tissue samples to the Bexar County lab. We may know more in the next few weeks."

Frank's tone deepened. "The experts might never come up with a definitive cause of death."

"That may be, but I've gotta dot all the I's and cross all the T's. You know how it is."

"Sure do. Back in a minute. Need to take a whiz, too much water." Frank left the room and went down the hall to the bathroom to splash cold water on his face and hands. Then, he dried them with a towel and took a few deep breaths.

When he returned, Lynne went on. "I know you're short on time, so I'll get right to it. Where were you when Mr. Kingman died?"

"I believe the coroner said he died around midnight." Frank leaned back in his chair.

Lynne rechecked her notes. "That's what it says here."

"I was in bed. I'm always in bed by ten."

"Was anyone with you?'

"My wife."

"Were you asleep at the time?"

Frank winked. "Probably. We'd just had ourselves a little roll in the sack, and I was spent. If you know what I mean."

Lynne returned a blank stare and said nothing. Frank wished he could throw a quick punch at that face.

"Did either of you leave the room for any reason?"

"Not that I recall."

"I believe your wife was the one who found him dead the next morning?"

"That's right. She left the room early to go check on him."

"Did she wake you?"

"Not until I heard her scream. Then I came runnin.' Couldn't imagine what the problem was. Thought she'd hurt herself. When I got to Pete's rooms, I could see he was already dead. His eyes were wide open, and his tongue was lollin' out." Frank swatted at a fly that had landed on his desk.

"What'd you do?"

"By that time, Hatch was there. I told him to get the boys and take Pete's body out. That's about it. Anything else?"

"Not for now."

Frank stood. "If there's any way I can be of further assistance, let me know."

"Thanks, I'll do that."

Frank ushered her out the door and collapsed in a chair. *Does she suspect something? What if the lab report shows traces of aconite? Of course, if it does, it would come from Pete's favorite brand of whiskey. Suicide, that's it! Leavitt suspects it herself. Pete committed suicide.* Frank stretched his legs out under the desk and began humming.

CHAPTER THIRTY-FIVE

*A*nnie sat in an ice cream parlor on the Riverwalk, waiting for Kent. She'd arrived early and ordered a double scoop of salted caramel ice cream; lately, she couldn't get enough of the stuff. She was having a hard time sitting still as she scanned the crowd and waited for him, muscles jumping under her skin. *Everything's falling apart. I don't want to lose him. I love him more than I've ever loved anyone.* She wiped away tears.

And then there he was, walking toward her. Annie wanted him to hold her in the worst way. *What will happen to me now?*

"Hi there," he said, taking a seat in one of the black wicker chairs. His eyes were dull as he leaned over and pecked her on the cheek. He wasn't even looking at her. Annie felt lightheaded. *Remember, the baby comes first.* "I have something to tell you." She looked down at her hands, dark circles under her eyes, gritting her teeth.

"Is it good news?" He brightened. "Have you filed the papers?"

"No, I'm afraid not." She looked away, depressed.

He cleared his throat. "Well, then I have a question for you."

"What is it?" *Anything to delay the bad news I'm about to share.*

He took a deep breath. "How about we take a break until you file for divorce?" He gazed down at his hands. "We've both been lying about us to the people we love. Please, consider it."

"Oh, Kent," she groaned. "I'm so sorry to tell you this, but I can't get a divorce." Her voice broke as she twisted her ring.

"Why not?" Kent looked horrified.

"I'm pregnant." She clutched the napkin tighter in her lap.

Kent's mouth gaped as he sat speechless. Then he said, "I'm happy for you about the baby. —That doesn't mean you have to stay with Frank. Don't go back to him Annie, please. He's abusive and controlling. Get your divorce. Don't do it for me, do it for you."

"If I left, Frank would fight me tooth and nail for custody of the baby. He's powerful and he might win. I'd risk everything to keep my baby. Including my life."

Kent slumped as the server stopped at their table. "Can I get you anything?" She chirped at him."

"No thanks," he said in a flat monotone staring off into the distance. He was about to lose another woman he loved, but this time she was choosing to leave him. He covered his face with his hands.

"How about you, ma'am? Another ice cream? Yours has melted."

Annie glanced at her dish. She'd completely lost her appetite. "Nothing for me, thanks," she said, shaking as the server walked away. "I'm so sorry."

Kent looked at Annie. "I'm sad about us."

"Me too. Leaving you is breaking my heart," she sniffled, the muscles in her back stiff.

"I know the feeling."

Her gaze was unfocused. She stood up, knocking her spoon off the table. "I need to go."

"Annie don't leave like this," he said, touching her back. "We can still be friends."

"I wish we could. This must be it for us, Kent. A clean break is the best break." She shrugged out from under the touch she once loved most. Then turned and walked out of the ice cream parlor, threading her way through a crowd of people who all seemed to be staring at her.

Kent threw a twenty on the table, raced to her side, and walked with her. They passed a mariachi band dressed all in white and singing, *Celito Lindo*. Someone was getting married, and the couple looked so happy.

"I thought we'd never say goodbye." Kent said.

"I know. This is killing me too. But it's the right thing to do." She bit her lip.

He paused. "I hope Frank will be everything you want him to be. I really do." He stopped, and she rushed on, leaving him standing on the sidewalk staring after her. *He looks so dejected, watching me walk away from him. Makes me so sad. —You have to go back to Frank. It's his baby too.* Her eyes blurred. *Maybe he'll change when he finds out we're having a child together?*

When she got home, she was still trembling. She wandered through the house, looking for Frank, her mouth as dry as cotton. He was sitting at the desk going over bills. He brightened when she walked in, stuffed the bills back in the drawer, then closed it.

"Hi, darlin, been waiting for you. Would you do me the honor of havin' dinner with me tonight," he said standing. He looked boyish with a big expectant grin on his face. Then she heard him mutter, "Please," under his breath.

Unlike him to even use that word with me. Might as well say yes since I'm not leaving him. Her hands felt cold. "Dinner sounds…nice."

"It's been too long," he nodded. "My little fling with Kelly is over, Annie. It's really over this time. It's just you and me now."

"Do you promise?"

"I swear it's true."

She sat on the love seat in the office and said, "Come sit here by me, please." Her belly fluttered.

Frank crossed the room and sat next to her.

"I have some good news," her voice trembled.

"What is it? I'm all ears."

"It's not just you and me anymore, Frank." She touched her belly. "Baby makes three."

"Are you saying what I think you're saying?"

"Yes. You're going to be a daddy." Her breath bottled up in her chest.

A smile broke across his face, then he fell to his knees, and took her hand in his. "I can't believe it, I can't believe it," he repeated over and over. Then he thrust both arms into the air. "Yes!!! I was afraid this day might never come."

"I have another doctor's appointment tomorrow with Dr. Jeannie. Will you come with me?"

"Wild horses couldn't keep me away." He said in a loud voice.

Annie reached over and kissed him on the cheek. "Thank you for being so happy." She could breathe again.

"Are you kidding me?! Of course, I am." He grabbed a footstool, "You should put your feet up. What can I get you? Are you thirsty? Do you want some water? Are you okay?"

She laughed, "I'm fine, Thank you."

He whooped again and grinned. "How far along are we?"

She liked his use of the word, 'we.' "Ten weeks."

"Ten weeks! Why didn't you tell me, before?"

"I was scared."

"Scared? Scared of what?" And then he paused. "You and I have had our problems. But it's nothin' we can't fix, especially now."

Is he being kind for a reason? Does he want something? Or is he just happy about the baby?

He grinned. "I bet it's a boy."

"I'd be happy with either a boy or a girl, Frank."

"A girl can't carry on the Graves name, you know that."

Annie winced, wishing she could go hide somewhere, unable to sit still.

"When will we know the gender of our baby?"

"We could try an ultrasound in another few weeks. Dr. Jeannie said that at 19-20 weeks, it's accurate."

"Let's go out and celebrate tonight, anywhere you'd like. I know, let's go down to the Riverwalk. How about 'Biga on the Banks?'"

She felt nauseous when she heard him say, 'Riverwalk.' Her eyes narrowed, and she stuttered, "Not the Riverwalk, Frank. Not tonight." She could feel her body heat rising. Would she ever go to the Riverwalk again, or would she forever hold the vision of Kent standing there as she walked away from him? "Would you be okay if we went downtown to Bohanan's instead?"

"Is my little mama feelin' like a steak?" he asked, hugging her.

"Yes, that's it, a steak, a big, juicy filet. I've been ravenous ever since I found out I was pregnant."

"Well, you are eatin' for two now," he said, grinning again, looking proud of himself. And then, he turned and looked directly at her. "Of course, we need to remember that I always come first. Even ahead of the baby."

Annie's blood ran cold, and she avoided eye contact. *Such a selfish thing to say.* Then she stuffed her disappointment and fear. *My baby is all that matters.*

CHAPTER THIRTY-SIX

Kent hadn't eaten much in days, and he hadn't been to church in weeks. He didn't want to run into Annie. He rubbed the back of his neck, sweating. *You have a meeting in a few minutes with Lynne to discuss her findings on the circumstances surrounding Pete's death. Get hold of yourself.*

"Ms. Leavitt is here," Darlene said, poking her head through Kent's office door.

He walked out to greet her. "Hey, Lynne, come on in," he said, trying to sound cheerful.

"Thanks. It's been an interesting couple of weeks."

"I'll bet. Grab a seat over there at my table, and I'll be right with you."

"Will do."

He put his computer in sleep mode, looked at the clock on the wall, and joined Lynne.

"You in a hurry today?" Lynne asked? She looked at him.

"I've got an appointment this afternoon that I can't miss. We should be good, though, what have you got?"

"Lots of data and a few suspicions. I'm expecting the lab report any time now."

"Let's take a look at your findings." He tried to be all business.

"First, I'd like to give you my impression of each person connected with the case, based on my interviews. I'll begin with a few people I think we can rule out as suspects."

Kent agreed. Lynne typically had good instincts about people.

"I'll start with Annie Kingman."

Kent was relieved to begin with Annie since that meant Lynne had tentatively ruled her out. He listened intently.

"Annie strikes me as being consistently inconsistent."

"What do you mean by that?"

"On one hand, she is a strong Texas woman. On the other hand, she also seems unsure. That's what I mean by inconsistent. It makes me wonder if she's suffered some kind of trauma."

Kent blinked and said nothing. Annie's abuse at the hands of her husband was not his story to tell. He wasn't even supposed to know about it.

"She has a kind heart and loved her father. With or without her father dead, she's financially secure."

"Makes sense."

"Next, her sister Caroline. There's a feisty one. Strong, no nonsense, highly educated, direct and opinionated."

"Sounds a lot like someone else I know." Kent smiled.

Lynne laughed. "Point taken. We began our conversation as adversaries and ended it as friends."

"Only you could pull that off." *Lynne can put anyone at ease—when she chooses to. Otherwise, she can make them sweat.*

"Caroline has a good sense of humor and a vulnerable side, if you know where to look. At any rate, once again, she's never lacked for money. Besides her father's money, she's a partner in a successful law practice in Dallas."

"So, you're ruling money out as a motive?"

"Not entirely."

"I'm not following. Kingman had two heirs, and you just told me you don't suspect either one."

"What about Frank Graves?" Lynne raised her eyebrows.

"Hmmm. I thought he was a thriving attorney. And he's got real estate investments."

"Turns out he's a poor money manager. I've been snooping into public records. The IRS had a $20,000 lien against him, which was only recently satisfied. My guess is they seized money from one of his accounts. They like to do that."

"The IRS doesn't mess around."

"Nope. Graves does have a trust fund his father left him when he died five years ago."

"How'd you find that out?"

"It's been long enough since he died that his Will is a matter of public record. Frank's father had money, and

Frank was his only heir. He gets annual distributions from the trust fund, rather than getting it in one lump sum.”

“Sounds like his father might have been aware of his spending habits.”

“That’s my guess. However, the trust fund is all but drained. Here’s my concern. After Texas Mutual pays the insurance claim, Graves may want Annie’s money, and the Kingman Ranch operation. He’s got motive in my book.”

“Chilling thought. He was in the house at the time too.”

“Right. So, he had access.”

“ If Frank killed him, any idea how he might have done it?”

“I checked Kingman’s rooms. Nothing seems to have been changed or moved since he died, apart from cleaning up some broken glass, according to the housekeeper. There’s still an open bottle of Jack Daniels on his table. His favorite, night cap every night, I hear. I got permission from the family to remove it and have it dusted for prints. I’m still waiting for the results.”

“Why the interest in the bottle? Wasn’t a night cap his normal pattern?”

“Yes, but the bottle didn’t come from Kingman’s private stock. He keeps meticulous records in the cellar, which I checked.”

“So, you think it may have been brought in from outside?”

"Likely, although it could be difficult to trace."

"Anyone else in the household who might be a person of interest, besides Frank?"

"One other potential suspect, Hy Hatch."

"The ranch manager? Why him?"

"Kingman had been asking him to retire. There was no way Hatch was going to do that. With Kingman gone, the girls need him to help run the ranch. It's weak but worth checking. But my intuition tells me that Hy Hatch is a stand-up guy."

"I think you're right about that. He has the family's best interests."

"Something else. I found oxycodone in Kingman's medicine cabinet. The bottle was almost empty. We need to leave suicide on the table, at least for now."

"He didn't seem like the type," Kent said.

"That's what everyone else I spoke with said. Except Graves. I want to go back to him, there's more to discuss. First, have a look at his father's obituary." Lynne passed it across the table to Kent, who read it aloud:

"Lloyd Graves of Seguin passed away on May 15, after problems with his heart. A memorial service will be held Saturday, May 19, at the Life Church in Seguin, with Pastor Curtis Dunscomb officiating, followed by second service May 20 at the Payne funeral home in Paradise Hills. Private interment will be at the San Geronimo Cemetery. Lloyd is survived by his son Frank Graves of Paradise Hills."

"Anything jump out at you?" Lynne asked.

"Not really, no."

"I went to the Bureau of Vital Records and checked Lloyd Grave's death record. It reads 'assumed heart attack,' which once again means the cause of his apparent heart attack couldn't be determined."

Kent was stunned. "Could be a coincidence."

"Maybe, maybe not."

He stopped. "So, Frank may have killed two men?"

"Maybe. It would be a stretch to go back now and investigate his father's death. And it wouldn't be in our wheelhouse, of course."

"No. But we could share your suspicions with the police, if it comes to that."

"Once we know more, yes. Something else about Graves. When I met with him, I spotted a schoolbook in his library with a banged-up corner. When I asked about it, he told me some story about a kid at school hitting him over the head with the book, leaving a hole in little Frank's head. Sounded bogus to me, and it turned out I was right."

"How do you think the book got dented?"

"A few of my friends on the force granted me access to some old hospital records in Seguin. I looked for records around the time Graves was eleven, which is when he claimed the school bully hit him over the head. Graves was never in the emergency room that year, but his mother was. She'd been struck in the head and required stitches. Story was she'd run into a door."

"Sounds like a lame excuse."

"I'm with you. My money is on Graves. He was a little hellion as a child."

"If you're right, and he kept the book he used to hit her with…?"

"Makes him a real sicko."

Kent swallowed hard. It was time to tell Lynne about Annie. "He also abuses his wife."

She paused for several seconds, looking quizzically at her friend. "How would you know that? Is the word all over town?"

"Hardly." Kent looked down at the desk and then back up at Lynne. "I've been emotionally involved with her for some time. Emotionally, but not physically."

"I don't have to tell you she's married."

"No, you don't. I fell and hard. But it's over now."

Lynne leaned over and said, "Sounds rough."

"It was," After a few minutes of silence, he continued. "The more I know about Frank, the more I'm afraid Annie might be in even more serious danger than I thought."

"Let's think about this for a minute. Graves doesn't want a divorce for financial reasons. I'm pretty sure Texas law permits tracing and partitioning of assets from inheritance gifts to be the property of the recipient, and not community property, in the event of a divorce. If she leaves him, he won't have access to her money. So, he won't hurt her right now, only because it wouldn't be in his best interest."

"He's a dangerous man, and she thinks she can handle him."

"No one can handle that guy, except maybe the law. I'll let you know when I have more information." She collected her things and left.

Kent needed to call Annie right now and tell her to be careful. He picked up the phone, tugging at his tie, feeling sick. Her voice mail kicked in. 'You've reached Annie Graves, and I can't come to the phone right now. Please leave a message.'

"Annie, it's me. Please, we must talk. Call me."

He tried her cell several more times after he got home. He left messages, but she wasn't returning his calls. Finally, he gave up waiting for her call and went to bed. He didn't sleep, tossing and turning. He stared at the ceiling in the dark.

The next morning, he tried her again, and this time she answered. "Kent," she breathed quietly. "Please stop calling me."

"Annie! We need to talk."

"No…no, we don't."

"This is serious. It's about Frank."

"It's too late for us, Kent." Her voice cracked. "Frank's so happy about the baby, he's busting a button. You and I are through. Frank and I have reconciled."

"I get that, but he's still a dangerous man. What if he hits you or worse?

"He won't. Like I told you, I'm teaching him how to treat me."

Kent swallowed hard. *There's absolutely no way anyone can teach Frank anything.*

"Do you think he knew we were in love?"

"I'm guessing he had his suspicions. Kent, please, if there's a chance for Frank and me to be a family with our baby, I must take it. And how would it look to this small town if I left him and then married you?"

Kent sat in quiet silence, then said, "I wish you the best. Please be careful, Annie. Bye."

An hour later the phone rang again. He jumped for his phone. "Hello!"

"Hey, Kent, it's Lynne."

Back to business.

"You there?" She asked.

"What's up?"

"Got news from the lab about Pete Kingman's death."

"What'd they find?" Kent held his breath.

"Traces of aconite root mixed in a Jack Daniels whiskey cocktail."

"Poison?"

"Right."

"Sounds more like murder than suicide."

"Well, it wasn't a heart attack. The lab found Kingman's fingerprints on the glass, and no one else's. We don't know where the bottle of Jack came from. I'm still working on that."

"Murder or not, the company will pay since you've cleared both legal heirs. And it's been almost two years since Kingman took out the policy. Keep me posted on the bottle of Jack." Kent hung up, climbed into the shower, and let the water run.

CHAPTER THIRTY-SEVEN

*F*rank was working in his office when someone pounded the front door. "What the…" he said aloud. He stood and opened the door, his breath catching in his throat. Putting on his best smile, he said. "Good morning, detectives, what can I do for you. They handed him a piece of paper. He read it. "This warrant is bull crap."

"It's enough for us to search your house, Graves."

"Whatever you think you're looking for, you won't find it. But, hey, you're the ones with the warrant."

"That's right. So, let's take a drive to your house. We'll meet you there."

Frank climbed into his car, palms sweating. Driving home was usually a breeze, taking only nine minutes. Longest nine minutes he'd ever experienced.

When he pulled up in front of the house the detectives were there waiting. They walked inside with him, and Frank found his house full of law enforcement, searching. *Annie's out at the ranch. Good thing she's not here to see this.* He asked the sheriff, a friend of his, "What exactly are you looking for?"

"You've got the warrant. Frank. The district attorney has determined that you're the prime suspect in Pete Kingman's murder. You know what that means. The DA has sufficient probable cause to issue a search warrant."

"Yes," Frank said, "but the warrant must be based on the totality of the circumstances."

"That's right, and here it is in a nutshell, Frank. First, you have the motive, your wife's money. Second, you had the opportunity, you were in the house where it happened. Now we're searching for the means to commit the crime: poison."

"What kind of poison."

"Aconite root."

Frank laughed. "Oh, you'll find that all right. I combine aconite with licorice root for my asthma. There's no smoking gun here."

"I hope you're right. And you know that's up to a jury to decide."

After they found the aconite, the sheriff took him to the lockup. Frank called his attorney, Charles Terry, who promised to get there as soon as he could.

When they reached the Wise County Courthouse, Frank walked inside flanked by deputies. Even though he was a well-known attorney, mayor of a small town, and running for the Texas legislature, he was treated just like everyone else. He lingered for hours at the jail waiting for his fingerprints and mug shot to be taken. "I'm not some common criminal," he hissed under his breath. "They'll be sorry when this is over and I'm out."

They handed him a blue shirt with the white words 'county jail' printed on the back, ordering him to put it on, just before they put him behind bars in the courthouse jail as a temporary detainee. He couldn't believe he was sitting in the county lockup. At least they had the decency to put him in his own cell. He paced up and down, mumbling, "Where's Terry?"

An hour later, Charles Terry arrived, a man in his early seventies who'd known Frank a long time. He wore his signature black suit, bolo tie, and a tan Stetson cowboy hat. Black cowboy boots adorned his feet. The jailers took Frank out to meet him in a small room.

"How'd you get me out here so fast?" Frank asked.

"I went to the bailiff and promised candy for Christmas if you know what I mean. Told him to call and have you brought down asap." He winked at Frank. "Now let's talk. The District Attorney is going to ask for no bail."

"That's crap. The evidence against me isn't that strong."

"I've read the arrest report. You tell me what happened that night."

"I was out at the ranch during the flood. Annie and I were in bed, and I slept next to her the whole night. She admitted she didn't see me leave her side because I didn't."

"Is she a sound sleeper?"

"Yes."

"What about the aconite found at your house?

"I use it for my allergies."

"Who do you think put it in the whiskey and killed Pete?"

"Well, if he didn't kill himself, my bet is Hy Hatch, the ranch hand manager. He was afraid Pete would retire him and get someone else."

"I think we can create enough doubt to get you out on bail before a trial. You know as well as I do that murder suspects can be granted bail if the evidence against them isn't strong enough. I'm guessing bail will be set at anywhere from 200,000 to 400,000. How will you cover the cost?"

"I'll use money in our bank account to put 10% toward it, then work with our local bail company, Bails & Bonds."

"That works. I can't prevent you from spending the night, Frank."

Frank blanched, clinching his hands, dreading his claustrophobia. It would be murder to spend the whole night in jail.

Terry continued, "I can get you a bail hearing with the judge tomorrow afternoon. If we can get you bail, you'll go home tomorrow."

They shook hands, and a deputy escorted Frank back to his cell. He spent the night in a cramped, small cell and didn't sleep a wink. Sweat drenched his shirt. He stood all night at the cell door looking out through the small bars. Tears ran down his face. He felt like a baby, knowing the chances were good that he could be prosecuted and sent to prison. *I won't let that happen. I know just what to do. But I must get out on bail tomorrow.*

The next morning's *Paradise Hills Tribune* headline read: "Mayor Frank Graves booked at Wise County Jail in suspected murder case."

CHAPTER THIRTY-EIGHT

*A*nnie was at the ranch when she heard a loud rap on the door, followed by the sound of an immediate, ding dong, ding, dong. *Someone's impatient.* "Gabriela, could you see who that is please?" She called from the parlor.

"On my way," Gabriela said. She hustled past the parlor door saying, "Caroline on work call in office. Good she can't hear bell."

Annie was surprised when Gabriela brought Cindy to the parlor. *Something must be really wrong.* "Is everything all right, Cindy? Are you okay?"

Cindy swallowed hard. "I'm so sorry to be the bearer of bad news." She handed over the newspaper, hands shaking. They both sat down as Annie read the headline in absolute shock. "What?! Are you k-k-kidding me? She stuttered. My husband's been arrested for killing my daddy? It can't be! I never took him for a murderer!!"

Cindy held her hand. "I know this is a lot to take in."

Annie blathered on without thinking, "Frank's abusive, yes. But a killer? Are they sure?"

"He's been arrested but not convicted," Cindy said. "Abuse, you say? Tell me about that."

Annie described the control, the manipulation, and the hitting, while Cindy sat horrified. Then she asked, "Is there more you're not telling me?" Annie looked down at her feet. Cindy leaned in. "Has he ever abused you sexually?"

"Over and over," Annie whispered, tears running.

"That makes me angry and sad. I'm so sorry I didn't see how much pain you were in."

Annie hung her head. "I was too ashamed to tell you."

"The shame isn't yours, Annie. Frank's despicable behavior isn't your fault in any way. I'm not ashamed of or disappointed in you in any way. And neither is God. You are precious in his sight."

Annie broke down, letting her bottled-up feelings flow. Then curled her shoulders over her chest. "I want to let the shame go. I really do." She took a deep breath.

"Those awful things that were done to you do not get to define who you are." Cindy said.

Nausea rolled in Annie's stomach. "But Cindy, what if I'd called the police about the abuse? Frank might have gone to jail. Then Daddy could be alive today."

"Or Frank might have killed you instead."

Annie's face blanched, and she looked at her, mind racing. She looked up, then paused. Her shame and guilt began to melt away, turning to anger over what Frank had done to her. "I won't let him make me a victim anymore." Her nostrils flared.

Cindy hugged her.

"You are a blessing. You turned my life around today." Tears ran down her cheeks.

Cindy held her hand and said, "You, God, and your angel mama turned your life around today. I was simply a catalyst."

"I love you, Cindy."

"I love you more than all the stars in the sky," she smiled. Then left the house.

Caroline walked into the parlor a few minutes later. "Lynne called. Frank's bail hearing is set for later today."

"And I'm going."

"Then I'll go with you, and I'm driving."

Two hours later, Annie and Caroline were on their way to the Wise County Courthouse in Decatur. Caroline had always loved the Romanesque Revival structure, named after Virginia congressperson Henry A. Wise. "He was the one who supported the annexation of Texas by the United States," she said, hoping to distract Annie.

"I remember," Annie said looking out the window. They drove past Frank's office on Walnut Street. "Do you think Frank did it? Did he kill Daddy?"

"He's the prime suspect, so we'll see. Innocent until proven guilty. But if he did, I hope he rots in jail for the rest of his life."

Annie growled. "If he did it, watch out buster!"

She and Caroline took their seats in the courthouse a few minutes before Frank went before the judge. The DA presented her case, and then it was Terry's turn. He explained why the Sheriff found aconite in Frank's garage. "It's not because he dropped aconite in Pete Kingman's whiskey, "he said, glaring at the DA. "It's because he has severe asthma. The evidence in this case is not strong. He pleads not guilty."

"Your honor," the DA stood. "We ask that the defendant not be granted bail. This man has resources. There's always a flight risk."

"Your honor, Terry countered, "The defendant's wife is expecting their first child. Frank Graves is an honorable man, the mayor of Paradise Hills. He is not a flight risk. I urge you to grant bail."

"Will the defendant please rise," the judge said. "You are hereby released on $300,000 bail, pending further court proceedings. You are warned to stick to your bail conditions." he pounded his gavel.

Frank turned and shook Terry's hand, then called to Annie, "I did not kill your daddy, my love. This is nonsense. You'll see."

Annie left the courtroom and headed for the ladies' room, where she threw up, over and over. She stayed for twenty minutes, hoping to avoid the reporters out front. When she and Caroline finally made their exit, they marched down the steps of the courthouse and into the waiting mob outside. Caroline put up her hand and said, "My sister has no comment. Please step aside."

As they drove home, Annie asked Caroline, "How does bail work?"

"The bonding/bail agency, acting for Frank, will arrange with the court to have him released from jail in exchange for collateral. He'll be out tomorrow. I spoke with Charles Terry while you were in the restroom and told him to make sure Frank uses his office as collateral and not the house the two of you own in house Paradise Hills. If Frank skips bail, the agency will have the right to claim his office to pay the bond, not the house. How much do you know about your finances, Annie?"

"Not enough, I'm afraid. But that changes right here, right now."

"Here's what else could happen if Frank skips bail. The bail agency is responsible for ensuring that Frank shows up in court on the day of his trial. If he doesn't show, they could send a bounty hunter after him. The U.S. is one of the only countries in the world that still allows bounty hunting. The only thing they're not allowed to do is go across international borders into another country."

Annie paused. "So, if Frank crosses the border from Texas into Mexico, he's home free."

"In essence, yes."

"I want to hire a Private Investigator to follow Frank. If he tries to leave the country, I want to know when and where. Let's go see Lynne."

"An excellent idea. Frank won't be released until tomorrow, so we have time. Her firm is licensed in both Texas and California, and I found the one in California. It's called, 'She Spies.' She started her career as an investigative journalist.

"Interesting. I'll call ahead to see if she's in." Turned out she was. They drove directly to her vintage office, then sat in the leather chairs, waiting. When Lynne walked through the door, she had her hair swept up in a bun behind her head.

Annie explained what she wanted.

"I'm all over it," Lynne said, peppering Annie with questions: "Tell me more about Frank's normal daily routine. What time does he leave the house in the morning? Where's his office? Where does he like to go for dinner? When does he go to sleep?" Her final question was about their house phone. "Do you have a landline?"

Annie nodded.

"Does Frank use it?"

"He prefers it."

"If you can get me in there today, I'll put a tap on the phone."

"I'll make it happen," Annie said.

"I'll also set up a surveillance team with a confidential assignment and have the house and office watched. They'll work round the clock. When he leaves, he'll be followed."

"And I'll be joining the team," Annie said. "I'm going to go back home today to stay, until he goes to trial."

"Are you sure about that?" Lynne asked.

"Absolutely. I'll tell him I believe he's innocent. I'll pretend I'm happy when he gets home tomorrow. Then I'll watch him like a hawk."

That evening when Annie walked into the Paradise Hills house, the place was a total wreck. Papers from the search were strewn everywhere. *I'll deal with that in the morning. Right now, I need some time to sit and think.* She shifted debris from the couch to the dining room table, then curled up under her favorite blanket, head rolled back. *How could I have been so stupid to think I could teach a man like Frank how to treat me? How could I have ever believed that a child would be safe in a home with him?* Tears filled her eyes. *And how could I have let go of the love of my life? Kent will never want me back. I've broken his heart.*

CHAPTER THIRTY-NINE

A week after getting out on bail, Frank slipped out of bed in the middle of the night. Dressed in black pants and turtleneck, he stole out of the house. Then manually opened the garage door, slipped his car into neutral, and rolled it down the driveway. The night was cold and cloudy, with no stars. He shivered in the cold shadows underneath the live oak tree framing the street and looked at his watch, just after midnight. The trunk of his car was packed and ready. Time to skip town.

His best chance of avoiding trial and being sent back to jail was to disappear in Mexico. He'd drive to a cousin's house in El Paso and trade cars before crossing the border. Frank knew he'd be happy to exchange his old range rover for Frank's Jaguar. He looked up at the bedroom window where Annie slept soundly and patted the fake passport in his back pocket. It helped to have connections.

He had only one thing left to do on his way out of town: Kill Kent Winder. Frank knew there was something between Kent and Annie. It was tough enough to leave his wife and unborn baby behind. There was no way he was going to let Winder have them.

Frank thought about taking another life. Pete's cause of death had been ruled inconclusive, but Frank couldn't poison Winder. Too close to Pete's death. Winder's death needed to be a suicide. Shot by his own gun, dumb sucker.

When he reached Winder's place, the lights were still on. He dropped the gun to his side, walked up to the front door and knocked, stepping away from the peep hole.

Kent opened the door, Frank shoved him inside, and pressed a black barreled handgun against his chest.

Kent looked shocked, and Frank laughed. "What's the matter? Scared of a little ole pistol?"

"What are you doing here Graves?"

"Are you freaking kidding me? Isn't it obvious? Now turn around, put your hands on your head, and move into the living room. Over there, next to the fireplace. Where do you keep your Colt?"

Kent didn't respond.

"Answer me, or I'll shoot you right here and now," Frank barked, waving his gun.

"Okay, okay. Take it easy. It's in the bedroom, top shelf of the closet."

They walked into the bedroom. Frank ordered Kent to take his Colt down from the shelf and hand it to him, butt first. Frank then held a gun in each gloved hand. "Now go back down the hall and into your living room."

When they got to the living room, Kent flinched at the fire popping and licking against the large oak log in his stone fireplace.

Frank laughed. "Nervous, are we?"

"What do you want from me?"

"Well, that's an easy one. I want you dead."

"If you're here to kill me for falling in love with your wife, it's over."

"Whatever. She thinks she loved you, and I suspect you're tryin to talk her into leavin' me. Here's how this is going down. You're going to shoot yourself in the head with your own gun, California boy."

"I won't do that. You can shoot me, but you can't make me shoot myself."

"You won't have to. I'll do it for you. It only needs to look like you did it."

"No one will believe that."

"Yes, they will." He pointed the pistol at Kent's head. "After they read the suicide note I typed up here for you. Still depressed over your wife and baby's death, you couldn't take it anymore." Then, he said, "This is your fault, Winder. I hate killin.'

"You hate killing people?"

"Let's just say this ain't my first rodeo, boy."

Kent paused for a split second. "Pete Kingman, the Jack Daniel's Whiskey.

"Yeah, I bought that bottle. You might be a dumb ass, Winder, but you're not as dumb as I thought. Anything else you'd like to say before you blow a hole in your own head?"

"Drop the gun, Frank," a voice ordered behind him. It was Annie.

He was surprised but didn't budge. "Sorry, Darlin'," he said. "No can do. I'm gonna' keep my gun trained on Winder, and if you try to shoot me, I will kill him." Hearing a gun cock inches from the back of his head, Frank said, "Put the gun down, Annie. A killer you ain't."

"You killed my daddy! How could you!? I'm going to shoot you in the head right here and now if you don't drop the gun."

"Whoa, whoa, there, little girl," he said. "I'm our baby's daddy. Think about it, you don't want to be the one to tell him someday that you killed his own daddy. Why, he'd never forgive you." Frank heard the hammer on Annie's gun relax a click. Taking advantage of her hesitation, he spun around and ducked. She fired, and a bullet whizzed past Kent's head, grazing his right ear. He touched his ear.

Frank grabbed Annie's gun. "Git over there next to your sorry ole lover, girl," he ordered, putting her gun on the table.

"Leave her alone, Graves!" Kent growled, blood dripping from his ear.

"Well, aren't you two the lovely lookin' couple? Why'd you do it, Annie? Why'd you hook up with this sidewinder?"

"First, I never slept with him. Second, he didn't kill my daddy! That makes you the sidewinder."

"I'm sorry about Pete, Darlin, but our money was running out. We needed your inheritance."

"You killed him for money?"

"Why else?" he asked, surprised.

"And now what are you going to do? Kill your wife and our child?" She shouted.

"Why'd you have to come out here? I had everything all planned out." Frank said.

"I followed you using Gina's car. And I had our phone tapped."

"What?!"

"It's over, Graves," Kent said. "Put the gun down."

"This party ain't over, loser, it's barely gettin' started. I'll shoot her with your gun, and then you'll kill yourself. Double suicide, very Romeo and Juliet like. The star-crossed lovers."

"Even if anyone believed that which they won't, there's still the little problem of the lab report. I'm not the only one with a copy, and I guarantee you'll be the prime suspect. Best case is you spend the rest of your life behind bars at Huntsville prison. I hear they call it the 'walls unit.' Very small and dark. Worst case, they execute you."

Frank broke out in a cold sweat. Kent had the best and worst cases confused. *I can't be confined in small, dark spaces for years. Two nights in the county jail about destroyed me.*

"I'll be long gone by then, Winder."

"What you don't know is that there's a silent button with no lights, in my closet, next to my gun. I pushed it when I reached for my gun. The police will be here soon, and you'll spend the rest of your life behind bars in solitary confinement. You can run Graves, but you can't hide."

"The detectives I hired are also on their way," Annie said. "You're finally going to get what's coming to you."

Frank stood stock still, seconds passed, and no one moved. *Legal judgement is coming for me. I can't believe that sap Winder got the best of me. And my own wife too. Then he heard the sirens. My life is over, reputation destroyed.* He mumbled, "I can't spend my days alone in a cage, and my nights trembling in the dark. I'd never survive."

Frank cocked his gun, raised it to his own head, and fired one shot. The bullet traveled through skin and muscle and smashed into the bones in his cranium, the smoke and powder burning a circular hole in his flesh. In the blink of an eye, Frank Graves was no more.

Annie fell to her knees, blood staining her hands and clothes.

Kent slumped down the wall, muscles slack. He pulled his shirt up and covered his ear. Then looked at Annie, who sat on the floor. "Can I help you in any way?"

"I feel like a huge wave of water just threw me under the river." She looked up at him with tears running down her face and shook her head. "Frank almost killed us both."

"But he didn't. Because together we were too smart for him. We'll get through this."

She wiped tears and a weak smile broke across her face. "You know something? You're right about that. We do make a good team."

"Yes, we do." Kent sat down next to her and took her hand in his. "I never stopped loving you, Annie."

"Even after I pushed you away. Can you ever forgive me?"

"Yes. Breaking up with me didn't change how I feel about you."

"I hope so, because the idea of not having you in my life still hurts me."

"I'm here for you, Annie. Whatever you need."

"Could we really put this mess behind us?"

"We can have a new life together and give your baby a home."

"Are you okay that my baby isn't yours, Kent."

"Doesn't matter. We could marry, and I'd adopt the baby."

She stared at him. "You'd do that?"

"Yes, Annie. I want a baby as much as you do."

"This is a lot to process right now," she said staring at Frank's dead body.

"Take as much time as you need. I'm not going anywhere." Then they heard the sirens screaming. "Law enforcement must be pulling up outside." Kent stood up and went to the door, hands trembling.

When Sheriff Mac and his men pushed their way into the room, Annie was still sitting on the floor. "What happened here?" Sheriff Mac asked her.

"Frank sh…sh…shot himself in the head," she gulped.

Mac touched Frank's arm. "It's still warm," he said. Then he turned to his deputy. "Ring the coroner. I don't want anyone coming near Frank's body until the coroner gives us permission." Then, he looked at the clock and noted the time. 1:00 am.

Mac looked at Kent's ear but said nothing. He directed his attention to Annie. "Let's get you over to the couch."

She took his outstretched hand, stood, and moved to the couch. Mac turned to Kent and demanded, "What happened, Winder?"

He reminded himself that he was clearly the outsider in Paradise Hills, and a man lay dead in his living room. "Graves came out here to shoot me."

"Go on," Mac ordered.

"Annie followed him and found him threatening me with a gun. She tried to get his gun and ended up accidentally shooting me in the ear. Frank took her gun away, and he used my gun to blow a hole in his own head."

"So, it was your gun that killed him?"

"Yes."

"Why would he want to kill you, Winder?"

"He knew I was on to him for killing Pete Kingman."

"So, Frank really did kill Pete?" Mac's eyes widened. "I still thought he died of a heart attack."

"That's what Graves wanted us to believe. He used aconite, mixed in with whiskey to kill him. Frank confessed to Pete's murder right before he shot himself."

Mac looked at Annie for corroboration.

She nodded, tears dotting her face.

"Is that why you were following Frank? Did you have your own suspicions?"

"Yes. I was afraid he'd break his bail and skip the country. That was his plan. Check the trunk of his car, it's filled with luggage. I was surprised when he turned in to Kent's place."

Mac turned to Kent. "This is an unnatural death, and a man was shot with your gun. Still requires some investigation. The Medical Examiner will have to corroborate that Frank's wounds are consistent with killing himself. I'll need you to come in and answer a few questions Monday, so don't even think about going anywhere."

Kent nodded. "I understand, Sheriff."

Putting his hand on Annie's shaking shoulder, Mac said, "The ambulance is on its way. The paramedics will take his body to the morgue. I'll take you to the morgue in my car, and you can call Caroline on the way."

Annie turned to Kent. "I'm sorry you got mixed up in all this."

He knew she meant it.

Mac said, "After the evidence team does its work, we'll get someone out here to clean up the place. You better have someone look at that ear, Winder, so get yourself to the ER tonight. Have the doctor or nurse photograph the wound and get a copy of the image."

"Will do."

And then, everyone was gone.

Kent sat alone in the middle of his living room. Frank's blood and brains still stained the carpet, and blood spatter colored the nearby walls. A man had committed suicide in the house where he lived. Kent had almost been killed too because he'd fallen in love with the dead man's wife. His thoughts were going in circles. He needed to calm down. He went to his bedroom and tore off his bloody shirt.

One thing was for sure: He couldn't sleep with bits of Frank's brain embedded in the carpet in the next room. The coroner had arrived with the deputy, and they were examining Frank's body. Kent pulled an overnight bag out of his closet and started to pack. He'd stay in a hotel near the ER.

CHAPTER FORTY

*A*nnie sat in Caroline's car, watching a full moon cast its eerie shadows across open fields. As they drove back to the ranch from the morgue, neither said much. Annie's nerves prickled up and down her skin, then she leaned her head back against the seat and closed her eyes. As soon as her eyes closed, the picture of Frank putting a gun to his head and firing it played across her mind. She sat up with a start.

Caroline looked across at her. Do you want to talk about it?"

"No." she said. "Not yet. I can't."

Caroline didn't reply, but Annie didn't miss the worried look on her face.

Annie's life had changed in a split second. Her husband was dead, and she was a pregnant widow. She felt a kick against the hand resting over her belly. *You have your child to live for. And maybe Kent too.* She looked at Caroline and managed a half smile, "If my baby is a boy, his name will be Peter Kingman the third, after our grandpa and our dad. He'll be the best darn cowboy in these parts."

Caroline's eyes filled, "I love that. I know it doesn't seem like it right now, but we'll be fine. We're Kingmans, and we'll get through this."

Annie hoped she and her baby would survive those pitying small-town tongues, wagging about Frank killing her father and then killing himself. People were going to say whatever they wanted. She couldn't stop that. But she didn't have to let it get to her. *My goal is not to please others anymore. It's to do what's right for me and the baby.*

"Are you sure you're okay?" Caroline asked, keeping one hand on the wheel, and touching Annie's shoulder with the other.

"Not yet," she said. "But I will be."

"I'm going to be a supportive sister and auntie. I promise you that."

Annie forced a small smile and knew she would. Nausea tore through her body. *I wish I were sorry Frank killed himself, but I'm not. I feel so safe with him gone. He was an evil man, an abuser, and a killer.* She quivered. *And he almost killed me and the baby. Kent too.* She gritted her teeth. *I will never be someone's victim again, ever.*

"We're home, Annie," Caroline soon said.

Gabriella stood at the window waiting. "Come in, come in, my little ones," she clucked, as they walked through the door. "I have hot tea waiting."

On her way to bed, Annie walked by the family portraits in the hall, stopping in front of the one of her Grandmother Kingman. Her image stood ram rod straight and proud. Her grandma was a bright, strong woman, whose husband died when she was in her early fifties. Annie began talking aloud to the picture. "I wish I'd known you longer. I know you sang, just like me." She sank to the stairs. "I hope we're alike in other ways too." In her mind, she heard the portrait whisper, "Each small step forward is a win." A ray of hope.

Carrying the Kingman legacy was hard. But now I realize what else it really means to be a Kingman. It means coming from a long line of strong people. Men and women who cleared the land, built ranches, and bought and sold cattle. Women who delivered precious babies, then lost them to disease. But no matter what happened, they picked themselves up and kept going. Annie got up from the stairs and stood straight. *Yes, I hate Frank. But I refuse to let that hate destroy my soul. Yes, it will take time for me to heal, I know that. But I'll get there in the end. I don't want to live in the past. And I refuse to let my feelings for Frank ruin my future.*

CHAPTER FORTY-ONE

*K*ent parked his car next to the Blanco County Law Enforcement Center. He walked past several Dodge Ram trucks sitting in the lot, with the Hill Country logo stamped on the side. Sheriff Mac was standing outside, gun holstered, brown Stetson on his head, yelling at a guy in cuffs. "Head on in," he called to Kent. "I'll be along directly."

When he walked through the double doors, one of the deputies waved him into the waiting room. On the wall, big as life, stood a picture of Mac accepting an award from the Sons of the American Revolution. The picture was book ended by an American flag on one side and a Texas flag on the other.

Kent sat in the room for thirty minutes, drumming his fingers on the table, waiting. He'd never been on this side of the equation before, and he didn't like it.

Finally, Sheriff Mac came in and sat across from him, putting his hat down on the table. "There are a few things I need to clear up," he said.

"Okay."

"First off, remind me how long you've been living in our little community."

"Going on twenty months."

"Not long. Most of our residents have lived in the Hill Country their whole lives. Take the Kingman family, for example. They've lived here for generations." He paused. "You come from California, right?"

"Yes, San Clemente."

"Tell me again why Graves was out at your house the night he got himself killed."

"He said he came to kill me."

"Because he thought you were on to him about Pete, right?"

"When Graves first threatened to shoot me, I suspected we were getting close to finding out he was the killer. I wasn't positive he'd killed Kingman, until I heard him brag about it."

About that time, Lynne walked through the door. "Lynne Leavitt," she said introducing herself to the sheriff.

"And what might you be doing here?"

"Insurance fraud detective, working for Mr. Winder on behalf of the insurance company Sound Solutions for Life."

"Insurance fraud, you say?"

"Yes. I've been investigating the claim that the Kingman family filed after Pete Kingman died. I've brought information with me applicable to Frank Graves' suicide."

"Hasn't officially been ruled a suicide yet."

"It will be."

"You sound pretty sure of yourself."

"I am," Lynne said, leaning forward, pulling out a large folder. "You do have two witnesses who saw Graves shoot himself in the head, right?"

"Don't be a smartie," Mac said. "Winder's gun was the weapon, and I need to get confirmation that Graves' wounds are consistent with suicide. One of my deputies should be walking that report in here shortly."

Lynne didn't miss a beat. "I've corroborated Frank Graves' admission to Mr. Winder that he killed Pete Kingman."

"I heard about the lab report and the traces of aconite. But what proof positive do you have that it was Graves who done it?"

"Hacked into his computer and found several searches for aconite root that went back years. One recent search described how to crush it into a powder and dissolve it in liquid."

This was news even to Kent.

"If that ain't a fact," Mac said, interested.

"I found the bottle of whiskey Graves used for the aconite powder still sitting untouched on the table in Pete's room, the day I went out to investigate," Lynne said. "There were no prints, but the bottle didn't come from Pete's cellar. I eventually traced it to a market in Wilderness Oak. It was sold the morning Pete was killed. Graves used a credit card to make the purchase that same morning. The whiskey was on the store receipt."

Mac didn't look that surprised. "Feller was on a first name basis with the bottom of the deck," he said disgusted.

Even though Graves' motive was self-serving, he did us all a favor by killing himself.

Mac went to the door and called one of his deputies. "Got that report, yet?" He paused for a response. "Okay, bring it on in here."

"Here ya' go, Boss."

Mac opened it and read carefully, then he looked up. "Looks like you're free to go, Winder. Wounds were consistent with suicide."

Kent exhaled. "Thanks."

"You can have your gun back too."

"I never want to see it again." His body tensed. "You keep it."

"Up to you."

Kent stood, "If there's nothing else…"

"Nope. You plannin' on stayin' in these parts?"

"My job is here, and I have friends here, so yes."

Lynne stood without speaking, and she and Kent shook Mac's hand before walking out the door. When they got to the parking lot, Kent bear hugged her. "I don't know what I'd have done without you. I mean it."

"All in a day's work," she grinned. "What about you and Annie?"

"I'm thinking of asking her to marry me."

"A word of advice from a friend?"

"Sure."

"Annie doesn't need protecting."

"You're right. I need to remember that when I talk to her. —If she says yes, I hope you'll come to the wedding."

"I'd be happy to, and I wish you luck. You're a good man."

"Better now." Kent said.

PART FOUR
HEALING

CHAPTER FORTY-TWO

*A*nnie drove to the parsonage to meet with Cindy and Mark. *I need to talk with both of them.* When she walked through the door, they embraced her, tears gathering in their eyes. Cindy took her hand and said, "I can't imagine your pain right now."

"It's a lot to take in," Annie mumbled.

Mark said. "Please come sit with us in the living room, and let's talk."

"Can I get you anything?" Cindy asked.

"No thanks. I'm okay. I wanted to talk about Frank and what happens next."

Mark said, "We love you, Annie." Then he paused. "If you agree, I suggest there be no celebration of his life at Songbird Community church."

"I agree." Annie said. "No one I know wants to celebrate him. He has no siblings and he's been estranged from his mother for years." Her eyes darted to the side." Besides killing my daddy, he may have killed his own."

"What?!" Mark asked. "What makes you think that?"

"Lynne has her suspicions."

"Wow! I'm so sorry that in trying to offer Frank a measure of God's grace, I didn't clearly see the evil man he really was."

Annie said. "You know, Pastor, I'd like to believe that everyone can be redeemed, like Scrooge was. But some people can't."

"Those who really want to change must first acknowledge what they've done wrong. The next step is to ask forgiveness for those they've hurt."

"Frank never believed he was in the wrong about anything," Annie said. "He defended every action he took, regardless of the facts or who he hurt."

"That's so sick," Cindy said. "Frank was a charming but manipulative man who lied easily. He had no guilt, no remorse, and no empathy for others."

"Your description fits him to a tee. I wish I'd known then what I can see now,"

"We all wish we could have," Cindy said.

"I can't believe I thought I could change him."

"Please don't beat yourself up, Annie," Cindy said. "It's common for women to think they can change their men. But we can never, ever change others. Only they can do that."

Annie took a deep breath. "I'm going to remember that." Then clutching her purse, she turned to Cindy. "I've decided to share my abuse story with others. Maybe it can help someone." She rubbed her arms. Annie wanted to move on. But she still sometimes flashed back to the shattering experiences she'd had at Frank's hands. *It will take time and therapy to let that go. I think being open about what happened to me will help.*

"That's brave and very generous." Cindy said. "I'm proud of you."

"Thanks for saying that. I'm going to need your support."

"You've got it. Always." She smiled. "Is there anything else we can do?"

"Let's talk out loud for a minute about Frank's remains."

"Please, go ahead," Mark said.

"I want to have his body cremated, then send his ashes to Seguin where he was born. I'll ask the funeral home there to simply scatter his ashes somewhere in the cemetery. I have no plans for a marker."

"Under the circumstances, I understand," Mark said.

Cindy laid her hand on Annie's. "If you need me anytime of the day or night, I'm a phone call or text away. Your friends will want to be here for you too. Please let them. They may not know what to say. But it doesn't mean they don't care."

"I hope you're right," Annie said. "Paradise Hills is still a small town where everyone knows everyone else's business. I'm pretty sure everyone's talking about me now. And I'd like to get ahead of that as much as possible."

"I understand," Cindy said. "The more they know, the less likely they'll be to gossip."

Annie paused. "Something else I've realized. People are going do what they're going to do. But the way I react to their behavior is up to me. It's not up to them."

"You're right about that, Annie, and so smart," Mark said.

"Most people have no idea that how they react is their choice." Cindy agreed.

Annie nodded. "Took me a long time to get there."

"But you did," Cindy said. "And your friends do have good hearts. I think they'll want to help you heal."

"There's something else." Annie stared out the window, and they waited. "I've been less than honest with you about Kent. I fell in love with him while still married to Frank. We never slept together," she rushed on, "but that didn't change how we felt. I broke it off with him when I found out I was pregnant." She looked down at her hands.

"Thank you for being honest," Cindy said. "Honesty is at the heart of spirituality."

"I understand your need for love and support in the middle of abuse," Mark said. "But you were married."

"Yes, and I wasn't true to my vows."

"Not completely, no. —But you never committed adultery. So, please park your guilt right here with me, right now, and let's move on."

Annie looked up. "Thank you, Pastor."

Cindy asked. "What about you and Kent? He seems like a very good guy."

"Yes, he is. I'm not sure yet about us. I'll let you know."

A few days later, Annie sat alone in the yellow room waiting for Kent. Gabriela was off, and Caroline was out shopping. Annie went to the door as she heard the bell. When she saw Kent, her hand went to her heart. "Come in, please," she said, opening the door.

"Would you be okay with a hug?"

She reached out for him. When he held her, she almost melted. *Yes, we still love each other.*

He breathed into her hair, "I want to be with you, together with no secrets."

"And I want to be with you. But it must be right for both of us,"

"I agree."

"Please come in."

They walked hand in hand and sat next to each other on the loveseat. She touched him lightly on the arm. When he looked into her eyes, she pulled him in for a long and satisfying kiss. She could see the warmth in his eyes, and she knew she trusted him.

"We're good together, Annie."

She drew her finger across his lips. "You showed me what real love could be, Kent."

Annie stood, walked to the window, and looked outside. "Let's take a walk."

Kent went down the three front steps and then held his hand out to Annie. That she liked. They wandered down the long brick path, passing the pond. There wasn't a cloud in the sky, and the morning air was cool. "If you'll give me the chance, I promise to take good care of you," he said.

She stopped walking. "I need to be cared for, Kent, just like you do. —But I never want to be taken care of again. I want your support, not your protection."

"I get that. Karla's told me more than once that I need to stop being a rescuer."

"She's right, and I'm no longer a victim. I'm a survivor and capable of taking care of myself."

"You certainly are. Being a rescuer isn't good for me either. I burn out on what I think other people need and ignore what I want."

"What you want is as important as what I want."

"Thanks. We'll do this together. You lean on me, and I'll lean on you."

"Exactly. With Frank, it was always about him. With you it's about us." She turned and stared back at the house. *I'll never leave the ranch again. I can breathe here. It's my heaven on earth.*

"What are you thinking?"

"How much I love my childhood home."

"I know the ranch means everything to you."

"It's my world. I hated living in town when I was with Frank."

"I support your vision for running the ranch. I know it's your passion."

"She paused. "Kent… if we ever married, do you think you could live here? On the ranch?"

His face went blank for a minute, and then he said, "I could, yes. The commute isn't bad from here to San Antonio. Whenever you live with someone, there's always give and take."

"We can grow as a couple and as individuals too."

"My grandpa used to say, 'Go into marriage with your eyes wide open. After that, keep one eye closed." He smiled.

"You know, I like that. So, that means we'll be patient with each other's imperfections. I never want to try and be 'perfect Annie' again."

"I promise you'll never have to do that. And there's never been a 'perfect Kent,' so no worries."

She laughed, then said, "I'm happy to hear that."

He grinned. "Just one question. If I move to the ranch, will I have to pay rent?"

They both laughed. "Of course not," she hugged him.

"Joking aside, I will pay rent. We both have our own money, and we'll divide expenses evenly. I have no interest in your family's wealth."

"I didn't think for a split second you did."

"We want our relationship to last, so we'll live life in the open."

"No more secrets; no more guilt. I know how important open and honest communication is. I talked with Pastor Mark and Cindy about us."

"Glad they know."

"You're a good person, Kent. I do love you."

"I love you too. We belong together." He turned and took both her hands. "Annie Kingman, if you'll let me, I'll spend the rest of my life focused on our happiness together." He pulled out a sparkly diamond ring, then dropped to one knee. "Will you marry me?"

A smile broke across her face. "You're the love-at-first sight, man of my life, Kent. I can trust you to be who you say you are. So yes." They kissed and she said, "This means you're stuck with me forever you know."

"Forever," He stroked her hair.

"Forever and ever." They kissed again.

"You're the one I was meant to find when I moved here. If you're willing, I'd like to adopt your child. Become the official father."

"The child will be ours. Last name Kingman, though."

"I'm fine with that."

She touched his face. "How do you feel about writing our own wedding vows?"

"I already know what I want to say."

"So do I," Annie said, kissing him again. "I'd like to keep our engagement between us, please, just for the next few days. Gina is having our friends over to her house for brunch. Now besides talking about the bad stuff with them, I'll have something wonderful to share."

"We're getting married, and we're starting a family." Kent hugged her close.

CHAPTER FORTY-THREE

Annie drove her car up Gina's driveway, the last to arrive. She saw four other cars parked on the street. Dustin answered the door when she knocked, and Annie went inside, a little nervous. Her friends were seated in the dining room. Gina had set out an assortment of hors-d'oeuvres, paired with fruit. Annie added a charcuterie board to the table, then sat down.

Gina turned to the others and said, "Thank you for coming today to support Annie. As we all know, Paradise Hills sometimes thinks anyone's business is their business. That's obviously not true, and she could use your help."

Annie said, "I appreciate your friendship. I do realize I'm the talk of the town, and I'm here to be completely open with you. I've learned when I hide nothing, I have nothing to fear."

Gina nodded. "I like that. And we all have baggage." She looked around the table.

"I'm about to dump mine, so get ready," Annie said.

They sat still, listening.

"You all know that Frank murdered my daddy, then killed himself. You also know I'm pregnant." She took a huge breath and stopped. "What you don't know is that my husband abused me. Both emotionally and physically."

They froze in place, saying nothing.

"It's still hard for me to say the word abuse aloud. And please don't look at me like you feel sorry for me. I'm no longer a victim. I'm a survivor."

Annie told them her story in detail. When she finished, Gina said, "You've been honest and courageous with us, your friends. Group hug." They all stood, came from behind the table, and wrapped their arms other each other.

"I'm asking for help from our closely knit group," Annie said.

"You're our friend," Gina said, "and we want to see you happy.

"What can we do?" Teresa asked.

"You know my story now, so please share it when someone asks about me. I'm hoping it might help someone else who's being abused."

"You think there might be more abuse happening here?" Becky asked.

"Sexual abuse happens far more often than we think. I've done some research. Did you know that one out of every six women in our country has been the victim of an attempted or completed rape?"

Her friends buzzed with the news. "One in six? Are you serious? I had no idea it was so bad."

Gina said, "There are probably more women right here in Paradise Hill who have been or are being victimized. We just don't know who they are."

Stunned silence, as Annie continued, "No one is expected to have to endure abusive behavior. Ever. It's illegal, but it still happens all the time."

"We have to do what we can to help," Teresa said. "If we tell your story, others might come forward too." They all agreed.

"Thank you. This won't fully erase my trauma, but it will help."

Gina squeezed her hand.

"So now that you know the worst of my past." Annie smiled, pulling a small box out of her pocket. "I have good news to share. Kent Winder surprised me with this." She put the engagement ring back on her finger. "He and I have been close since he moved here. And no, we were not having an affair."

"The ring's beautiful! Congratulations!" They all echoed. "Do you have a date?"

"Not yet, but soon. And, get this, he wants to adopt my baby."

"I love that! Gina said. "He'll be there for you, and so will we. That's a promise." They all agreed.

*****

A month later, Annie walked onto the upstairs porch at the ranch where she could see for miles and miles. The sun was up, announcing the light of a new day. The hills were again littered with spring bluebonnets, and a gentle breeze blew off the Pedernales. It was a picture-perfect day for a wedding. Annie glanced at the clock on the wall. —*Time to get dressed.*

After putting the finishing touches on her makeup, she looked outside to make sure everything looked just right. White tables and chairs had been set on the expansive lawn facing the river, and the afternoon sun gleamed shimmery pink over the top of a large white tent. Gabriela had outdone herself with a three-tiered chandelier cake, white and blue frosting with a small spray of bluebonnets on top. The guests were beginning to take their seats.

Annie smiled when she saw the entourage of red golf carts approaching up the lane. Caroline and Karla were in the front car, beaming. Caroline held a large spray of flowers in her hands, hair pulled back in a chignon, revealing their mother's white pearl earrings.

Dustin, the best man, drove another car, dapper in a black tuxedo and boutonniere. Gina sat by his side. The rest of the bridesmaids and groomsmen followed behind, as Annie counted at least five golf carts. The guests loved it and clapped. Caroline would act as the maid of honor, and Gina and Karla would be standing up as Annie's bridesmaids.

After alighting from the golf carts, the wedding party took their places and waited for Annie's entrance. Carter stood tall in a blue suit complimenting his red hair. He walked down the aisle first, carrying the wedding rings nestled in a white silk pillow. Annie came next, escorted by Pastor Mark. The guests stood as a string quartet played the wedding march. Annie glowed as she walked, acknowledging her guests with a nod and smile.

Dustin gave her a kiss on the cheek, then shook hands with Kent. Annie stepped to the side and lit two memorial candles, one for her mama and one for her daddy. They'd been married on this same lawn. Tears of both joy and sadness glistened in her eyes.

Pastor Mark thanked everyone for coming to share in the celebration, then said, "Today, Annie and Kent have decided to create a new chapter in their lives, together." He smiled at the couple. "We're all honored to be here to witness the love and commitment they have for each other."

Then he read the same sonnet his own father had read at Pete and Susie's wedding, 'How do I love thee, by Elizabeth Barrett Browning.' He concluded with the words, 'I love thee with the breath, smiles, tears, of all my life; and, if God choose, I shall but love thee better after death.'

The line 'smiles and tears' captured Annie's attention. *Life's not a fairy tale for anyone, and sometimes the endings can be devastating. I'm fortunate Frank's gone, and Kent is here by my side.*

Pastor Mark continued, "Rings, please." He paused while Carter stepped up, then said, "Annie and Kent, these rings are a symbol of eternal and everlasting love. Please say your vows."

As Annie gazed into Kent's eyes, he began to read: "Annie, you are my heaven on earth. I will be your best friend forever, and I promise never to go to bed angry. I'm a better man with you than without you. I vow to always keep you close to my heart. I can't imagine growing old without you by my side."

Annie's eyes watered. Her turn. "Kent, you're the right man for me because I can be my best self with you. I take you as my partner and will walk hand in hand with you, wherever our path leads us, living, learning, and loving together, forever. I can't wait to begin the rest of our lives together."

Mark smiled, then asked, "Kent, do you take Annie to be your lawfully wedded wife?"

"I do." He said, choking back a happy tear.

"Annie, do you take Kent to be your lawfully wedded husband?"

"Oh, yes, I do." She grinned. They exchanged rings.

"Annie Kingman and Kent Winder, I now pronounce you husband and wife" They kissed, and everyone clapped again.

Annie smiled. "Thank you. Being together with you, our family, and friends, is what makes our day so special."

The guests moved inside the show barn for dinner, the scent of tantalizing barbecue with Tex-Mex cuisine thrown in for good measure pierced the air. After they filled their plates, Mark offered the first toast, "To the happy couple," he said. "We love you." He and Cindy looked so proud of the new couple, and Annie was happy, knowing they'd be loving grandparents to her baby.

When everyone had eaten their fill, Annie and Kent stood and cut the cake, stuffing huge pieces into the other's mouths, leaving blue frosting smeared on both faces. Everyone laughed as Annie wiped crumbs and frosting from Kent's face, and he returned the favor.

Then, the dancing began. The wedding couple took the first one, gliding across the wooden slats to the sounds of the song, 'All of me, why not take all of me.'

After they finished, Lynne said to Annie. "You're an amazing woman."

"How so?" She asked, looking at her.

"You really don't know, do you? You're a woman capable of running her own ranch, and you're a loving wife and soon to be mother. I'd say that's an incredible combination."

"Thank you, Lynne." They hugged.

About that time Kent reached out his hand and took Annie in his arms again. They twirled around the floor again, while everyone else danced and sang along to "Ob-La-Di, Ob-La-Da, Life goes on."

That night Annie and Kent slept together for the first time. He was cautious and careful. He asked and didn't push. He waited. She was hesitant and a little scared. They soon kissed all over, touched, then came together in the best way. *So, this is what making love can be. He's shown me what a good man is.*

"How are you feeling?" He asked when they finished.

"Safe and happy." She cuddled up next to him.

The following morning, Annie, Kent, and Caroline ate breakfast together, beginning with a big skillet of Gabriela's tasty chilaquiles. Best breakfast nachos ever.

"I don't think I heard where you're going on your honeymoon tomorrow," Caroline said mouth full of warm tortillas.

"Italy," Annie said. "First Venice and then Lake Como; we love the Renaissance architecture there."

"Take lots of pictures. Italy is on my bucket list," she said smiling. "How long will you be gone?"

"Only two weeks. The baby's due in about four months, or we'd stay longer. "We're so excited," Annie said, joy filling her voice, looking across the table at her new husband. *Hope is what's most important, and I have it again. I'm going to make the life I've always wanted.*

CHAPTER FORTY-FOUR

*K*ent paced up and down inside his office with the door closed. *The baby's past due. Dr. Jeannie has decided it's time to induce labor. Tomorrow.* He chewed the inside of his cheek, then grabbed his cell to call Karla. *What if it happens again? What if I lose Annie and the baby?*

"Hi," she answered. "Everything okay?"

He got right to it. "The doc told Annie she wants to induce labor. Something's wrong."

"I know you're worried, and I understand why. But inducing labor isn't usually too risky."

"What if her uterus ruptures?" he asked, voice strained.

"That could happen, but only rarely."

"What if she has a postpartum hemorrhage?"

"I see you've been doing your homework. Did you talk with the doctor"?

"I googled it."

"So, you went straight to Doctor Google, instead of Doctor Jeannie?"

"Docs don't always tell me what I need to know. I'm scared of losing another wife and baby. I know it makes no sense."

"What you're feeling is completely normal. Just remember you can't always be in control."

"Touché. This shouldn't be about me, anyway. I've got to stay positive. For Annie's sake."

"I get that. But it's easier to stay positive if you process the negative first."

He stopped. "You're so smart. That's why I called you."

"I've told you that before."

"I know, I know." They both laughed.

"I'll pray for both you and Annie."

"Thanks. Love you, Sis."

"Love you too, little brother. Keep me posted."

"Will do, bye."

Annie woke up early the next morning, and her hands trembled as she tugged clothes over her very large belly. She passed by the mirror and swore she could see her heart pounding in her chest. She stopped and offered a silent prayer for the health of the baby.

"Annie," Kent called up the stairs. "Are you ready?"

"On my way."

"Plenty of time, so take it easy," Kent said, putting his arm around her shoulders. He picked up the overnight bag that sat waiting by the front door and loaded it into the car.

Fifteen minutes later, they arrived at the hospital. Kent let Annie out at the emergency entrance and then went to park the car. It was a cold and frosty morning.

Annie walked carefully across the sidewalk then went inside to check in. "Mrs. Annie," the receptionist welcomed her warmly. "Please have a seat for just a minute."

Annie sat down and waited, clearing her throat a couple of times. Someone she didn't know took a paper cup by the water cooler, filled it, and handed it to her. *Such kind people here.*

After Kent walked in, one of the hospital volunteers took them down the hospital corridor to the delivery rooms.

"I didn't imagine it would look like this," Annie said, surprised.

"Me neither, I was expecting something a lot more sterile," Kent said.

"I'm glad it's not. It looks, well, homey." A large picture of a rolling field of spring bluebonnets hung on the wall. In the middle of the room stood a bed made with white, freshly washed sheets, covered with fluffy blankets that were warm to the touch. There was a small bouquet of dried yellow and orange flowers on the table.

Annie went into the bathroom to put on the hospital gown, fumbling with the ties in the back. Then she climbed into bed to wait for Doctor Jeannie, feeling lightheaded.

Someone knocked at the door. "Just me," said Cindy, opening the door a crack.

"Come in," Annie said, her voice sounding small. She'd asked Cindy to be with her and Kent today. She was relieved to have her here, and she relaxed just a little.

Cindy gave Kent a hug and then moved to Annie's bedside. "How are you doing, love?"

"I'll be better when this is all over. Truthfully, I'm kind of scared," she said, eyes widening.

"You couldn't have a better doctor than Jeannie. It's going to be fine; I promise."

Annie smiled.

Kent said, "Thanks for being here for us, Cindy."

"Wait. I'm feeling something," Annie said. "The contractions are starting. They're starting! Jeannie won't need to induce labor!"

"Prayers answered," Cindy smiled.

Kent took Annie's hand in his, relief and gratitude sweeping his gut.

Then Annie felt pain like she'd never experienced before. She was having a hard time catching her breath.

Kent opened the door and called the nurse. "Come quick! We need help here."

She came in and administered an epidural. Kent and Cindy sat on either side of the bed and held Annie's hands as she screamed through her labor pains. An hour later, the nurse came into the room to check on Annie. "The baby's head is starting to crown," she said.

"I'll get Dr. Jeannie." Kent said, running.

Moments later, Jeannie rushed into the room, pulled up a three-legged metal stool, and wheeled herself under the baby, just in time. She looked at Annie. "With the next contraction, big push. Here we go. You got this. Last one, now, deep breath. He's almost out."

Annie pushed while the others encouraged her. Jeannie announced, "Here he comes!" Annie panted. Then paused. No sound. Kent's eyes got bigger, and his palms filled with sweat. Then a beautiful baby boy slid his way into the world, took a breath, and started crying.

Jeannie looked at Annie and said, "You did great."

"Is he healthy? Annie asked.

"He's just right."

The baby cooed.

Cindy said. "Just look at him. He's amazing."

"He's perfect," Kent grinned.

Jeannie smiled, cutting the umbilical cord. The nurse reached over, placed a drop in each of his eyes, and then put him on the scale. He weighed 8.5 pounds and measured twenty-four inches long. "A big, healthy, baby," she said, tucking him gently into Annie's arms.

"Hi baby," she said cuddling him. "This is where life begins, little man." Tears of joy ran down her face. She fell immediately in love with her son Pete. Then watched sleepily as Cindy gushed over the baby.

When Annie looked completely exhausted, Kent reached for Pete, cradled him carefully in his arms, and cuddled him down the corridor to the nursery. He handed their son to the nurse on duty, who placed him in a plexiglass crib. Several howling babies surrounded him. Then he called Karla to give her the good news.

The next day, Kent pulled the car around the front of the hospital to pick up his wife and baby. One of the nurses was pushing a wheelchair with Annie and the baby in it. He reached over and kissed her as she got into the car.

When they reached the ranch, Gabriela, Hy, and all the ranch hands were gathered, waiting. Caroline was anxious to meet her nephew. The air filled with excited buzzing sounds as Annie carried little Pete into the yellow room and placed him in a bassinet that had once belonged to her. There were lots of gifts for her new baby scattered around the room.

"*Por favor*, can I hold him?" Gabriela asked.

"Of course," Annie said, picking him up and placing him in Gabriela's arms.

"He looks just like his grandpa," she said.

"Yes, he does," she smiled. They all looked at little Pete and agreed.

Before Annie put him to bed that night, Gabriela took out a large towel and laid it on the table so Annie could give her baby a sponge bath. Then, she handed her cotton balls and a little pan of warm water. Gabriela showed Annie how to wash her baby so the cord wouldn't get wet. After she finished bathing him, Gabriela wrapped him in a towel and handed him to Caroline. She rubbed oil gently into the little folds of his skin.

It was Kent who put on his pajamas, rocking the baby back and forth, smiling. Annie loved how involved he was already. *There's a definite effect on a child who has a connected father. Our son will live in a house full of love.* Annie laid him gently in the cradle. *I know every day will pass too fast with you, little Pete.* She kissed his cheek. *I never knew how much Mama loved me until I had you.*

EPILOGUE

*A*nnie and Kent took the baby to church for the first time. Most people rallied around little Pete and welcomed him as one of their own. What the others thought simply didn't matter anymore.

Gina's boys came up to say hello and meet little Pete. "Is that your new baby?" They asked, excited.

"Yes, what do you think?" Annie turned Pete around so they could see him.

"He's awfully little," Sam said.

"And he doesn't have much hair," the other offered.

Annie laughed. "You're right, but he'll get there."

"He's handsome," Dustin said. "Has a lot of his Grandpa Pete in him."

Annie's face glowed. She peered into her baby's eyes and found that same determined look her daddy had.

Dustin shook Kent's hand. "You're a lucky man to have these two."

Kent smiled at Annie and the baby. "Don't I know it."

Annie looked around the room at her friends and neighbors. *I don't know what lies ahead for any of us. There are no guarantees. We have both good days and bad days ahead. But we'll move forward with faith together, surrounded by people who love us.* She smiled. *We're all still a work in progress, and that's okay.*

ACKNOWLEDGEMENTS

I want to thank all those helped make this book a reality.

To Soni Rice, a wonderful editor and friend who helped my characters when they got stuck.

To professional readers: Lori Wynne, Marcia Nielson, and Joe Coykendall.

To Brenda Sevcik, my writing critique partner, and other members of the Roswell Writer's group.

To beta readers, Diana Dahlin, Karen Paavola, Dodie Truman Stallcup, Ursula Thomas, and Dana Witherspoon.

To my daughter, Alicia Swann, who helped make things better. That's what she does.

Susan N Swann is the published author of a memoir, and two historical fiction novels. Her most recent, *Angels in the Fog*, was a number one new release on Amazon in its category. *Walls of Silence* is Susan's first foray into romantic thrillers and the mind of a killer. She graduated with a degree in English and taught high school literature and writing before earning a master's degree in clinical psychology. Susan lives outside Atlanta.

9 798218 973452